DRIVEN

LEGATUM - BOOK 2

LULU M SYLVIAN

GRIFFYN INK

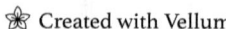 Created with Vellum

A special shout out to Alana, Dana, and Lea for sciencing for me.
Thank you to William Shakespeare for making Roman more
eloquent than I ever could on my own.
Thank you to my editor Lea (a completely different Lea) for
cleaning up my words so I'm not too terribly embarrassed to place
them next to Shakespeare's.
And a very special thank you to the Opryland Hotel for being
beautiful, surprising, and having indoor balconies.

PROLOGUE

Roman pushed through the doors to his father's office. The walls were dark, lined with bookshelves laden with leather-clad tomes. A single small window and low lighting gave an overwhelming sense of weight and oppression. When he was small, Roman had thought this was a room of power. Now he found it to be nothing more than a living tomb.

The older man behind the oversize desk looked withered, tired. He sneered at Roman's crumpled suit.

"What brings you here Roman? I thought you were still in Frisco."

Roman threw the report he had carried all night at his father. The paper had clearly been crumpled, then smoothed out again. The report indicated that the man Roman had thought his cousin was in fact his half brother.

"How many bastards do you have?" He growled his words.

Blackston swept the papers away in a dismissive motion. They lay discarded on the edge of the heavy wood desk.

"You can't ignore this, Father. How many?"

"Is that all you found out from your little DNA project? That I have other children?"

Roman stared at his father, he pierced the man with his glare, his lips pressed tight, his nostrils flaring. What he had been working on was not *some little project*, but the discovery that wolf-shifter DNA showed up as identifiable gene markers in human DNA tests.

"Of course I have other children. I don't know, maybe four, maybe five." Blackston's tone was as dismissive as his hand wave.

"Does Mother know?" Roman's voice was quiet.

Blackston blanched. His wife, his mate, Roman's mother was gravely ill. He had dropped everything to be by her side during her extensive cancer treatments. "You will not tell her anything." His words were clipped and measured.

"What, about all your philandering and resulting offspring? I'm sure Mother is aware on some level that you are an asshole. Or more specifically should I not tell her about Dallas?"

"That would kill her."

"It's not my place to tell her that you sired a son on her sister. You're right, this will kill her, as sure as the knife in her back put there by Aunt Bev. You're disgusting, you know that?" Roman paced back toward the double doors that separated his father's domain from the rest of the house.

"Beverly loved me; it's what she wanted."

Roman spun, facing his father. "You're her alpha; you took advantage of her. Anything beyond that is a paltry excuse explaining away your bad behavior and poor decision-making skills."

Roman turned to push his way back through the heavy wood doors.

"Where do you think you're going?" Blackston barked.

Roman heard the creak of leather as his father sat forward in his chair, leaning toward his son. He could picture the old man's hands gripping the arms of the chair until his knuckles turned white.

"I'm going to visit Mother. I may have spent all night on a plane to hear your answer in person, but I am not about to waste the trip and not visit her before I fly back and take care of the business you effectively abandoned." Roman sneered at his father. "Then again, that's probably how you dealt with all your bastard offspring, just abandoned them, didn't you?" Roman stepped back into the office.

"I didn't abandon my children," Blackston protested.

"Then tell me, how many of us are there?"

His father fell back into the chair, seeming to collapse under his own guilt. "Just you and Dallas."

Roman scoffed. "What happened to four or five? Have you ever been honest about anything?" He had looked up to his father once, a long time ago. That was before he realized his father lied to get ahead, lied to maintain control. When he was younger, Roman never understood Blackston's behavior as some power gambit to maintain control of the family. He had willfully overlooked his father's bad behavior, brushed it aside as old-school wolf when he finally understood. He took over running the company when it was clear ignoring the old man's bad habits would cost them dearly. But this... this Roman would never forgive.

"There was a girl, bu..."

Roman cut him off. "Girls count. Any more?"

Blackston sighed heavily. "Lost one to a miscarriage. The stupid girl drank too much."

"You're a real bastard, aren't you? What's the surviving girl's name? Who is she?"

Blackston shook his head. "It was Ashley." He sounded defeated.

Roman breathed heavily out his nose. Ashley had been a friend; she had died young. Taken her own life. He looked at his father one last time before pushing out of the office.

1

Julia slipped her feet back into her red pumps. The figure on the bed groaned. She looked down at him. A muscular arm with a tribal tattoo wrapped around a well-defined bicep reached out into the empty space she'd recently abandoned. A single eye peered up at her from beneath a disheveled mess of dark blond hair. *Why are they always blond these days?*

"You leavin'?" a deep male voice, gravelly with sleep, asked.

"Yeah," she said, pulling on her jacket. "I have to get ready for work."

"Mmm, okay." The man rolled over. "You need a ride?"

"No, I have a car coming. I had fun, thanks."

He had been fun. She'd let him take her home from the bar last night. It wasn't something she had planned, but he had been charming, and he took care of a need without any complications. Julia found that one-night stands usually satisfied her physical and emotional requirements. She didn't need or want a relationship. She liked the carnal actions and the subsequent release. But more and more her body wanted something, someone else. No, she didn't want the complication of having to deal with another person's fragile ego or emotions. This guy with his surfer good looks and a name she'd already forgotten was all the relationship she was interested in. He had been a pleasurable distraction. At least that was what she kept telling herself.

A gentle snore indicated the man had already fallen back to sleep.

Julia checked her phone one last time before letting herself out of his apartment and heading down to the sidewalk in the predawn light to wait for her car.

She watched as a man in a crumpled business suit slid out of a cab. He made some comment about the morning walk of shame and how she should be more careful outside, alone in the dark. Julia shook her head. He was clearly participating in the same morning walk, only he felt the need to attempt to shame her for her night's activities and try to make her nervous. Julia had no shame, nor fear of the night; she was more frightening when she got angry than most things out here.

He said something else she didn't pay attention to. When he called her a bitch, she laughed. "You have no idea."

~

Julia headed toward her office. Tall double doors provided the entrance to her elaborate CEO office of Truria, the Palatine's family umbrella corporation. Her assistant, Kathleen, intersected her path, stopping her a few feet shy of the entrance.

"Roman Aventine."

"What about him?" Julia snapped. She had felt relaxed after last night's dalliance. Thoughts of Roman Aventine put her immediately on edge. Their families were now cooperating, on both a personal, and a professional level. Unfortunately the latter put Roman in her presence entirely too often.

"He's in your office." Julia glared at Kathleen. "He walked right in and sat down."

"I guess you really couldn't call security on him."

Kathleen shook her head. "Not while you two are working together. He said he has information to share that should be delivered in person."

Julia sighed and entered her office. In person? That either meant this could have been delivered effectively in an e-mail or it was bad news.

Roman sat in one of the overstuffed leather chairs that made up the informal seating arrangement in the center of her large office, flipping mindlessly through a magazine. His demeanor and posture did not hint at anything negative. Julia strode past him to her desk, pretending not to notice. That took more of her concentration than she cared to admit. She wished he had e-mailed her. Roman assaulted her senses. Senses that rebelled against her inclination to ignore him completely. Senses that wanted nothing more than to focus on him solely. Her body parts seemed to take on independent thought and action, as if they were no longer attached. His clean sandalwood and musky scent made her nose twitch. She shut down the signals invading her brain from her nose. Her nose wanted to bury itself in the crook of his neck and inhale him deeply. Her fingers rejected the papers in her hands as she dropped the stack she had been holding onto her desk. Paper was not what they wanted to be touching.

"Don't get comfortable. I have a meeting starting in ten minutes." She purposefully did not look up at him.

"Good morning, Julia," Roman said in a cool, crisp tone.

When he spoke, she wanted to cover her ears and cry for him to leave her alone. Her ears wanted nothing more than to hear him say her name again. Her brain was losing the battle against her body when it came to Roman Aventine. She had to forcefully brace herself against the sensual onslaught of his presence.

"What brings you to Truria so early, Aventine?" Julia clipped her words. She only used his last name when he particularly annoyed her. Today she fought an uphill battle. Her resistance must be down after a night of sexual play. It wasn't that she was more drawn to Roman than usual. No, it was her body still enjoying the endorphins and lustful hormones. He was a man, and her body was simply reacting to him on that level. She really should pay more attention to her cycle; she was probably ovulating or about to, so her body had ramped up her sexual desires. That was it. Hormones.

"A desire to see you first thing when I wake up brings me to your door." Roman stood. His tall, lean frame was dressed this morning in a cool gray suit. The cut of the suit—and how it hinted at the wide shoulders and firm chest under-neath—looked as if it had been made exclusively for Roman. Then again, the way he wore suits, clearly they were custom-tailored. A fit like that was not found on a sales rack. The crisp white shirt and cobalt tie set off his clean-cut, fair good looks and his bright blue eyes. Eyes that seemed to contain a wicked gleam just for her.

Julia shook her head to clear her mind. She hated that he seemed to glow when she looked at him, as if he should be surrounded by a heavenly host singing his praises.

"Stupid hormones," she growled under her breath. That didn't explain why she seemed to be fighting this battle within herself more and more. Last time they had a meeting, she had found herself not listening to any of the words he said. She had been focused on his lips and the way they shaped words, and the tone of his voice. Surely her response to him couldn't be blamed on the same hormonal surges from a few weeks ago?

Julia smiled at his sarcastic flirting. She knew he held just as much animosity for her as she did for him. The contempt between them was palpable and obvious to all.

"I thought you moved back to Boston?" she asked, joining him at the center table.

"Mother and Father moved back home after her treatments were complete. I was merely visiting."

Kathleen entered with a tray of hot coffee.

Roman thanked her as he took one. She handed one to Julia. "Need me for notes?" she asked.

Julia glanced over to Roman. "No, not that kind of meeting. Please show Ms. del Fuego in when she arrives." Julia's gaze returned to Roman. "I thought you and Aventine Industries's interests would move back to HQ with your father."

Roman's mother had received treatments for her cancer at a prestigious Northern California university renowned for its advancements in cancer research. That family's presence in an area the Palatines held had led to a much needed truce. Blackston Aventine, Roman's father, did not have the focus to deal with the petty squabbles or much bigger brawls that would come from one family invading another's territory. Especially two families that had considered themselves rivals and enemies for so many centuries. At his wife's insistence, the Aventine primary alpha allowed Roman to reach out and begin peacemaking overtures that had resulted in the current atmosphere of tolerated animosity. At least that was how Julia thought of it.

The atmosphere of peace had led Roman to share an important discovery with the Palatines. Not only were they now working together to further their combined knowledge, but they were in partnership on expanding their businesses into a new market. Roman seemed to take advantage of this new business alliance and make the most of any opportunity he could to pester Julia.

"Oh, the home office doesn't need me in person. I can handle practically everything remotely, and if not, Boston is a red-eye away. I wanted to be here for Mother. She's doing so well now, but I've decided to stay." Roman's gaze pierced her. "I much prefer the scenery in San Francisco."

Julia glanced away. She felt as if a blush spread across her cheeks. *Don't be stupid; you don't blush.*

Roman continued. "I found a symposium of genetics I think we need to attend. From the rundown of talks, it looks like we will both learn quite a bit. Also—" He leaned forward, showing Julia the screen of his tablet. The displayed web page showed a list of presentations and breakout sessions regarding the sequencing of the human genome and how certain test results will be utilized for drug testing applications. "I think this would be a place to start locating some resources for our little project of cornering the market on a certain piece of genetic data."

Julia picked up the tablet and began scrolling through.

Several months earlier, a local geneticist related to the

Aventines discovered that wolf-shifter DNA was showing up as an unknown ethnicity marker on genealogical genetic tests. As a wolf herself, the geneticist was able to confirm her suspicions through a small sample of controlled tests she ran at the lab. To the best of her knowledge, no one else had noticed. She hoped anyone who ran into that bit of genetic coding would see it as junk DNA—extra bits of DNA without biological function. Until a secured lab facility could be accessed, further research was on hold. They didn't yet know where else within the genetics that wolf-shifter markers would show up, or why it was showing up as it had.

In a move of good faith, supporting the newly formed alliance between the Aventine and Palatine families, Roman had shared this discovery with Julia and Morgan, her brother and her family's primary alpha. Julia, the newly appointed CEO of the Palatine family business, spear-headed the move to acquire a genetics laboratory in partner-ship with Aventine Industries. Her goal, to find a way to prevent the genetic data from falling into the wrong hands in order to preserve the wolves' privacy and secrecy.

Wolf shifters are a very private species. Families tend to keep to themselves. Even her family in California, who traced their historic roots back to the Etruscans before the founding of Rome, did not maintain connections with extended family that had stayed in Italy. This genetic discovery was forcing them to reach out and find other fami-lies. A delicate balance of research, spying, and direct ques-tioning was required to identify other wolf shifters. There was no magical way to identify each other. The genetics information needed to be contained. Education was para-mount. Identifying family members who may have left the fold was now integral to survival and secrecy.

The pressure on Julia to become enough of a genetics

expert to be able to know what she needed kept her up late at night reading thousands of pages of research. She still needed to understand more before she could pursue proprietary rights to the genetic associations that indicated shifter. That was, if locking down their genetic code behind a wall of patents and other legal ownership was even a plausibility.

The conference looked promising.

"It's next week," she sneered.

"Then you had better book your ticket today." Roman chuckled.

"How long have you known about this?" She wouldn't put it past Roman to have withheld this information for weeks, just to be a pain.

"I haven't been hording this; I found it last night. This is important to both our families. I'm not that big of an asshole, Julia." Roman lifted one perfect blond eyebrow.

"But you do admit you are an asshole."

Roman laughed.

Julia's hormones took over her brain again for a moment, and she delighted in the way his face lit up with mirth.

Her assistant's voice brought Julia back to business. "Ms. del Fuego," Kathleen announced.

Cyan del Fuego never seemed to walk; she glided. She slid into a room in a way that drew everyone's attention. Tall, sultry, and exotic with sleek black hair cut into a severe bob, Cyan was as wickedly charming as she looked.

Roman approached her. "What an enchanting surprise to see you this morning, Cyan." He bowed over her hand.

Julia's stomach clenched as she watched him brush his lips across the backs of Cyan's knuckles. His lips were on another woman, and she felt her eyes flair. With what? Emotion over Roman? No, Julia would not allow herself to even consider that situation. So what if she remembered those lips on hers. She shook her head. No. No emotions toward Roman. She needed to get her focus back on the business at hand.

Cyan del Fuego was not only a respected business-woman who contracted Julia's family for large-scale construction work on her growing boutique hotel chain, she was the representative of the Del Fuego coven, the leading vampirical governing body on the West Coast.

Today's meeting was over the mundane needs of the Cyan Group, who was contracting Truria's subsidiary, Seven Hills Construction. Julia was filling in for her brother, Morgan, on the negotiations while he was still away with his bride on an extended honeymoon.

"This is fortuitous to run into you here this morning. I have no new information to share with you, and am pleased to be able to tell you directly," Cyan said in her lilting accent, her gaze on Roman's chiseled face. "Have you heard anything from your father about this unfortunate situation?"

"My father hasn't bothered to let me know if there are any active threats against him. The man I have watching his back confirms there has not been any activity of concern," Roman said.

"What of you?" To Julia it sounded as if Cyan purred.

Roman shook his head. "If Palatine hadn't told me there was a threat, I would never have known. There hasn't been anything. But do keep me posted if you hear of anything. I look forward to meeting with you again."

"Hopefully our next meeting will be more social, less business." Cyan chuckled.

Roman's comments to Cyan indicated that there had been meetings between the two of them that dealt with the issues of being vampires and wolf shifters cooperating in an ever-changing world.

Roman's attention returned to Julia. "I look forward to our trip." He left the two women.

Julia felt a loss she did not want to acknowledge.

2

"You're leaving me for a week?" Mel huffed. "So that means you won't be in town for the Fernando show. Damn. I don't want to go alone."

Julia sat across from Melinda at their favorite taqueria, where the portions were excessively large and the food always delicious. Mel constantly reminded Julia there was more to life than work. She wore her heart on her sleeve. And it was a very compassionate, loving heart, with room for everyone, especially the suave, slick guitarist from Argentina.

"What about one of your friends from work?" Julia eyed her burrito, planning a strategy of attack. Had their burritos gotten bigger? She couldn't remember them being the size of her head before.

"I'd prefer to be with someone more like us. I don't know what kind of audience it's going to be." Melinda leaned forward and tapped her exposed canine tooth at Julia. "I don't want to supply the snack food."

"If I said something like that, you'd be calling me out for

racial profiling and pinching at the skin on your arm." Julia pointed at Mel's darker skin.

They'd become best friends when Melinda's family sent her to live at the school the Palatines ran on their estate in Sonoma. Melinda had hit puberty late. Her mother had thought the wolf-shifter ability had ended in her family line. Melinda's father was fully human, and her mother couldn't shift. She hadn't told Melinda's father or Melinda about that particular aspect of her family history. So when Melinda started shifting, it was a total surprise. The girl had been terrified, having had no clue or preparation for what was happening. The revelation destroyed her parents' marriage.

When Melinda first arrived at the school, shaking like a scared rabbit, the other kids relegated her to omega status. They harassed her relentlessly. With a guiding nudge from her mother, Julia reluctantly befriended the nervous Melinda. Julia quickly learned her new friend was insanely smart, had a wicked sense of humor, and liked the same music. They quickly bonded over boy bands and Sour Patch Candy. Melinda became the beta to Julia's alpha.

"Yeah, well black men don't suck all the blood out of your body."

"I've met one or two who have tried." Julia snickered. "I'm sorry we'll miss Fernando. I'm sure he'll do more shows."

"Sure he will, in Argentina." Mel pouted. "You had better have a good excuse for abandoning me."

"Genetics conference in Nashville. Aventine found a good one, so we're heading out in the morning."

Mel dropped her taco and leaned in. "You're leaving with Tall, Hot, and Blond for a weeklong getaway?"

"I'm not going away with him. It's a business trip, and we

both happen to be going." Julia bit deep into the large burrito in her grasp. Melinda's insistence that there was anything going on between her and Roman was rapidly approaching the point of annoyance.

"Fine, live in denial. You had better bring me back a souvenir." Mel's taco disintegrated as she picked it up. "Uhg, why do you do this to me every time?" she asked the taco.

"They always do that," Julia mumbled around the food in her mouth. "Why do you expect something different? It's never going to happen."

"I should know better, but their tacos are the best. Besides, the universe sometimes surprises you."

"So what do you want me to bring you? I'll already be on the lookout for a snow globe for Caro's collection. You want tacky magnets, a touristy T-shirt? What?" Julia asked, looking at her best friend, knowing the request would not be as simple as expanding Caro's extensive collection. Melinda would want the impossible. And as always Julia would do her best to deliver.

Melinda wiped her hands on a series of small paper napkins. "How about a hot country boy? You know, big muscles, a tan, and a sexy Southern drawl."

Julia laughed—impossible as expected. Of course if Melinda was with her, she could capture her own country boy with her big golden eyes and sparkling grin. "You want me to ship him back or drag him home unconscious in my luggage?"

"Either works for me. As long as he is over eighteen and has washboard abs. A boy with core strength can do amazing things," Mel mused. "I bet Mr. Suit Porn is ripped under all that designer wear."

"You need to cool down." Julia eyed Mel; she was

heading into dangerous territory. Mr. Suit Porn was Mel's nickname for Roman since he always wore a suit whenever she met him, and she thought he looked particularly good in them. Mel had a point; he made pin stripes sexy. To Julia, admitting that out loud would somehow be admitting defeat to the battle inside her. And that could be very dangerous to her mental fortitude.

"What I need is to go wash taco off my hands." Mel held her sticky fingers away from her body as she stood.

Julia continued to attack her burrito after Mel left. Mel was right. Roman was well-defined underneath those layers of tailoring. Julia may have only gotten a hint at his physique when she had run her fingers over his shirt, but she could still feel the memory on her fingertips from that afternoon at her adopted sister JoJo's wedding. His shirt had been smooth, cool silk, the man underneath hard and firm. And she was going away with him. Maybe… No no no no no. No, not maybe. Just no. This was a business trip. Work, not fun.

"Whatcha thinking?" Mel asked as she sat back down.

"Oh, just planning the wardrobe for the trip."

"You're taking sexy underwear in case you bone him."

"I'm not packing sexy underwear, Mel, as I have no intention of doing anything with that man," Julia protested, "except go to a conference and do business and be boring. Blah, blah, blah, blah, blah." She waved her hand back and forth, indicating all the assorted work required with attending a conference.

"Julia, at least think about it."

That was Julia's problem. She did think about it. She thought about Roman entirely too often, and not in a business context. Not unless it was thinking about him bending her over her desk, pushing her skirt up, and taking her from behind. Her brain flooded with images of business-place erotica starring her and him. Roman in that pale blue Tom Ford, the one that brought out the flash in his eyes. The two of them doing it on the conference room table. Going down on him in the elevator without hitting the stop button to park it between floors. Julia coughed, temporarily forgetting how to breathe. "What I need to be thinking about is how much of this genetics terminology I can learn in the next twenty-four hours."

Roman ran through the city. His feet pounded the pavement in time to the throbbing music in his earphones. Dawn's thin gray light started to brighten the darkest corners as he past buildings. Roman ran; he didn't jog. His speed was that of a sprinter as he tackled the hills. Instead of running down inclines, he hurdled them; instead of rounding corners to bypass obstacles, he climbed them, vaulting over cars and up and over panel trucks. The city was just coming awake, the streets were relatively empty, and except for a few service vehicles, morning deliveries had yet to begin. This time of morning Roman could dart through construction sites, over vehicles, up the sides of buildings practicing his parkour skills without much interference.

Without breaking stride, he landed one foot against a brick wall, the other foot hit the opposite wall as he ran up a corner. Four steps and he leaped to catch the lower edge of a fire escape. He swung himself up and onto the landing before climbing to the next landing. From there he jumped the relatively narrow gap to the building across the alley. Roman continued to climb several stories to the roof. He ran across the rooftop, jumping down onto the top floor of a parking garage. He dropped and rolled, letting the impact transfer throughout his body. He was back on his feet, continuing his run.

Parkour was as close as he could get to the freedom he felt when running in wolf form, something he couldn't do while living in a city, especially a city located so far from open spaces and wolf populations. Running cleared his head; with the upcoming travel schedule he didn't know if he would get a chance to get out for at least another week. With parkour he had to focus on his movements; he couldn't think about anything other than foot placements and jumps. It was remarkably refreshing to not be preoccupied with thoughts of his impending day or worry about family members, or be distracted with thoughts of Julia Palatine.

No, he didn't need thoughts of her warm hazel eyes that flashed gold, or her flowing chestnut hair that coiled into ringlets at the nape of her neck when she wore her hair twisted into a knot. He didn't need to remember her warm, full lips against his or how the slope of her waist to hips had felt under his hands.

Roman misstepped and landed with a flip onto his back. He laughed as he stared up into the violet blush of the dawn-lit sky. This was ridiculous. Julia was entirely too distracting. It was time to effectively begin wooing her. He closed his eyes to assess the damages he'd sustained in his fall. Nothing. Julia's visage drifted past his closed eyelids. Distracting and beautiful, and he needed to prepare for his trip with her. He wanted to be at the airport early to make sure the seating arrangements were to his liking. Roman got to his feet and jogged back to his apartment.

Jogging gave Roman time to think. He puzzled out the death threat against him that Morgan had warned him of. So far nothing but rumors had come of it. Cyan del Fuego had indicated her people had found out nothing more, and they were actively pursuing the man who had issued the threat. Yet it nagged at him in the back of his mind; how could it not? Someone out there wanted him dead, and he had no idea why.

3

Julia jostled her way along the center aisle of the airplane. Her assistant had booked her a direct flight to Nashville. The security check had delayed her. She'd boarded late. She was irritated. Flying itself didn't bother Julia much; it was the hassle surrounding air travel that bothered her. Thank goodness she was in business class; she didn't have to fight her way too far into the plane.

Julia scanned the overhead compartment for a place to store her bag. Nothing near her seat.

"Julia."

The familiar masculine voice with a slight New England accent caused her to roll her eyes before she turned around.

"You planned this. I don't know how you did it, but you planned it." She sneered at Roman, already seated by the window on the row next to her seat. He closed the laptop in front of him.

"Purely fortuitous, I promise."

Julia slammed her carry-on into the overhead compartment across the aisle. She turned around and dropped into the seat next to Roman, then glared at him. The light from

the window refracted around him, giving him the appear-
ance of having a slight halo. She was going to have to get her
eyes checked. The way light bounced around in her vision
concerned her. Of course she couldn't really think of any
other time it happened, just around Roman. It had to be
stress induced and not anything else she was willing to
accept. She tucked the briefcase that doubled as her purse
into the space by her feet.

"Fortuitous, huh?"

"Of course. We can now spend several hours together,
and you can discover just how charming I really am."

Julia cocked an eyebrow at his arrogant declaration.

"Good. We should develop a strategy on how we want to
approach this conference. I think we need to learn as much
as possible, which means we take a divide-and-conquer
approach." Roman opened his laptop. A few clicks and he
turned the monitor to face Julia. "I've been reading up on
the presentations. I think we both should attend these two
presentations, but we should make sure to attend separate
breakout sessions."

Julia nodded; she had to agree, his approach was logical.
Roman pointed out several other presentations he felt
would be beneficial for them to attend.

"We can regroup in the evenings and compare notes. I
think meeting in my room would be most convenient. Of
course, we could always meet in your room." Roman gave
Julia a slow wink.

She rolled her eyes at him in response. "You're out of
luck." She smirked. "I have a roommate."

"How did you get so lucky?"

"I've been in communication with the Meyers family in
Canada. Toronto area. They are sending one of their best
and brightest to help us figure out this genetic connection.

Dr. Cynthia Kimbro, a chemist. She has a heavy scientific background naturally, and I've been told she is interested in genetics as it impacts her work in pharmaceuticals. I figure she is going to be more than a few steps ahead of us when it comes to translating all this DNA jargon into English.

"The hotel is booked solid. They couldn't get her a room, so she's in with me. I just hope she doesn't snore. We will also be meeting up with Sholto van Haas."

"Dutch?"

Julia shook her head. "An alpha from South Africa. He was already planning on flying in to meet over all this DNA stuff. He agreed to change his travel plans and should be joining us tomorrow or the day after. I'm slowly making more connections, but..."

"We hide well."

Julia agreed. "We hide well. Let's just hope we can continue to hide in this new and improved information age."

Roman nodded.

"Can I confess something to you?"

"You are finally falling for my charms?" Roman asked; a smile played on his perfect lips.

Julia caught herself looking at his smile and becoming distracted. She shook her head and shot a glare at him. "Roman, play nice. I'm serious."

He cocked an eyebrow at her, an expression that she interpreted as a silent smart-assed reply along the lines of *I am too.*

"This genomics thing is... well, it feels just out of my reach." She bit her lip. "I have a grasp on our priority to acquire some labs, but who are the scientists we're going to be able to work with? Are they going to be trustworthy? Can we find scientists in the families we already know who are willing to start focusing on gene studies? I've had such tunnel vision on this problem lately, and the solution feels like it's over there." Julia gestured with her hand as if she pointed over a hill. "I can't see it; I can't figure it out."

"It's a completely different direction than either of us have spent our professional lives working toward. You know what your company has been doing for years. You know construction, clean energy, wine. You know property management; you know investments. Aventine Industries has its own diversified portfolio and holdings, and I know how to chase after your business to make you nervous. This science stuff is new for us both. But—and I'm not being cheeky here—I have confidence, and the ego to support that confidence, that the two of us working together will be able to conquer this. We will do this. We will learn and understand. Julia..." Roman quietly looked into her eyes, pausing for a moment. "I'm not blowing smoke up your ass when I say this: you are a very smart businesswoman, smarter than me, and I'm damned good at what I do. I brought you in when I learned about the DNA evidence for that very reason." He picked up her hand. "I'm following you here, and I have no doubts to the direction you lead."

An electrical charge raced up Julia's arm from Roman's touch. Her eyes widened.

"You think that I'm smarter than you? And all this time I thought you were just an ass."

"I will deny that outside of this conversation." Roman twitched his lips into a half smile.

Julia chuckled, and then sighed, removing her hand from his before she allowed his touch to become any more of a distraction than it already was.

She didn't like the feeling of a concept being beyond her grasp. She did like to know that she had Roman's support, especially now that he knew her struggle. Somehow confiding that vulnerability to Roman eased her mind, as if a weight had lifted from her shoulders. She no longer bore the burden on her own. Roman was there to help carry the weight.

Julia riffled through the case at her feet and pulled out a stack of printed pages held together with a binder clip. Armed with a pen and a highlighter, she began reading.

Roman was physically uncomfortable in his seat. Fitting into airline seats outside of first class was never exactly comfortable. Folding his long legs into the confined space always proved to be an issue, especially if the person in front of him chose to recline their chair. However, currently his discomfort had nothing to do with his business-class seat on the plane. Roman was entirely too aware of the woman in the seat next to him. He had been pleasantly surprised when she boarded the plane in black yoga pants that hugged her ass and a long tunic. Of course the tunic had pulled up when she placed her bag into the overhead compartment, giving him an unobscured view of her well-formed backside. That view had sparked his arousal. An arousal that had waxed and waned in intensity during the flight. Currently he was painfully hard, yet he had no intention of moving.

He glanced down at Julia. Her face was perfect and at peace. She had been right; he had bribed the attendant at check-in to place him next to her. It was only pure luck that the attendant was a romantic, and he had convinced her that he was going to surprise his girlfriend, and that he had plans on proposing during this trip. A strand of hair curled along the side of Julia's face. At some point while reading she had fallen asleep and slumped against his shoulder. Roman was content to have her resting against him. She belonged there; she fit.

She had the faint shimmering of the glowing mate aura. It subsided as his brain recognized it for what it was. He knew why she fought him so much. She didn't want to give up her position or power. Neither of which he wanted from her. If ever there was a woman who was fiercely independent and deserved support, it was her. He hoped that she would allow him to accompany her as her consort. It was rare that Roman ever met an alpha with more personal governing strength than himself; even his father no longer had that level of fortitude. Roman recognized it and was drawn to that power in Julia. Julia was the only female alpha he had ever known, and he wanted her.

Roman shifted carefully, so not to wake Julia, as he adjusted himself to find comfort. His arousal throbbed against his trousers. His balls were going to be tight, sore, and neon blue by the time they reached the hotel. He contemplated moving so he could wrap an arm around her and hold her for the rest of the flight. That would be a bad idea; she wasn't comfortable around him yet. She would not be pleased to wake up and find herself in his embrace, at least not yet.

Roman chuckled slightly. She hadn't let herself relax around him since her adopted sister's wedding. She had been so tantalizing that day. Beautiful. The dark hair that she typically wore in a bun or a sleek braid had cascaded loose around her shoulders, its natural curl giving her an air of wild abandonment. Her gown had emphasized her curves, curves she typically hid under pantsuits. The dress had shown off a small waist and ample hips. Its amethyst hue brought out the green tones of her hazel eyes. She blamed the wine, but Roman knew she used that as an excuse. Julia had been slightly tipsy—not so much to lose all reservations, but enough to let her act on her emotions. Roman reveled in the memory of her boldness. They had been dancing, and he had been asinine and flirtatious. Originally doing so to goad her, since she never let her barriers down around him. Then she'd responded; she moved closer into his embrace, pressing into him. The feel of her perfect breasts against his chest burned into his memory. Not one to disregard the offered gift of her returned attentions, Roman had leaned down to nuzzle the side of her face with his own. She had smelled like flowers, like night-blooming jasmine.

She had pulled away, then led him off to a secluded covered walkway. She had been aggressive with her attentions. Her eyes had sparked with gold when she pushed him back against a wall before pressing into him and covering his mouth with her own. Julia had made it clear that she wanted Roman, and he'd willingly obliged. Her lips had been soft, her tongue sweet with sugar and wine. He tried to not dwell on the lost opportunity. Julia's brother, Morgan, had interrupted their making out, and Julia, embarrassed, had run off.

Roman reached across and brushed the stray hair from her brow, remembering how it felt to bury his hands in the mass of her hair. He longed to kiss and hold her again. Did she not realize they were ideal mates? Did she not see the glow? She didn't need to be embarrassed for how he made her feel. He wanted to shout how she made him feel from rooftops.

Roman had been trying to get Julia to attend a conference with him for several weeks now. He enjoyed their verbal sparring but had reached his limit. She had wanted him once; he would have her want him again. He needed to be with her for more than a few hours at a time for her to realize what they were to each other. Hopefully this week together would give him an opportunity to successfully seduce her. If nothing else, he would declare his intentions of wooing her.

The plane jostled and jumped as they encountered turbulence. Julia woke with a start. She looked up into Roman's eyes.

"I'm sorry; I didn't mean to invade your space." She wiped at her mouth as if to make sure she hadn't accidentally drooled in her sleep.

"You're fine. I didn't mind in the least. You must have been exhausted. You've been asleep most of the flight."

"I've been up reading papers every night trying to get a grasp on the science around gene data." She scoffed. "I feel like I'm crashing for an exam. I wasn't on you for too long, was I?"

"About three hours," Roman answered evenly.

"You should have moved me or woken me up," Julia declared apologetically.

Roman's voice lowered. "You can rest on me anytime."

"Ass," she hissed.

Roman smirked, typical Julia covering her unease in anger. "Asses are made to bare, and so am I."

"Are you quoting Shakespeare?" Julia let out an involuntary gasp as the plane bounced with a jerking motion. Reaching for the armrest, she missed, and her fingers bit into Roman's thigh in her momentary panic.

"I' faith you are too angry," Roman replied, raising his eyebrows.

"Oh, I know this." Julia closed her eyes; she appeared to be trying to recall something. Hopefully she would welcome the opportunity to concentrate on something other than the bouncing airplane.

"Something about a wasp." She held up her finger in a small triumphant gesture.

Roman smiled. "Come come, you wasp. I' faith you are too angry."

"Ah... If I be waspish, best beware my sting. Hey, wait a minute, are you calling me a shrew? Or are you distracting me?" The plane jumped again; luggage moved in the overhead compartments. Julia blanched.

"Has the flight been this bad?" she asked.

Roman shook his head. "We flew over a storm about an hour ago; you missed the worst of it. Are you a nervous flier?"

"Not typically, but..." She trailed off as the plane dipped and shimmied.

"But this isn't any fun," he confirmed. "If you need distracting, we could always make out."

Julia rolled her eyes at him. "I think trading Shakespearean barbs fits the bill right now."

"Thou speak'st aright. I am that merry wanderer of the night." Roman cocked a single eyebrow at Julia to see if she recognized the line. After a pregnant pause with no response, he continued. "I jest to Oberon and make him smile when I a fat and bean-fed horse beguile."

She snapped and pointed at him in recognition. "Puck, *Midsummer Night's Dream*. I don't know anything from that one. Fair is foul and foul is fair?"

"That's *Macbeth*."

"How come you know so much Shakespeare?" she asked.

"Studied classics?" Roman's tone was more questioning than a statement.

Julia shook her head, not satisfied with the answer that clearly wasn't forthcoming.

"Drama geek in high school. Big-time drama geek in college, worked the local summer Shakespeare festival my first few years of college."

"You were a theater major?" Julia asked incredulously.

"Minor. That and I discovered girls swoon when you quote the bard."

Julia laughed and began softly singing. "Brush up your Shakespeare, and the women you will wow."

It was Roman's turn to look at her with an expression of disbelief. "Musical theater?"

"Howard Keel in tights, and Cole Porter. *Kiss Me Kate* was one of my mom's favorites. She really liked 1950s movie musicals. That and *Taming of the Shrew* with Elizabeth Taylor and Richard Burton. I think that was her favorite of Shakespeare's plays."

"And you?"

Julia paused. "Hey, we're descending. Must be getting close."

"How can you tell?" Roman asked.

"Can't you feel that? The pressure changed in my stomach. We are starting to sink."

"I can't tell." He chuckled. Any change in pressure Roman felt in his abdominal area was caused by Julia's smile.

The clerk leaned across the counter and circled a room located on a colorful floor map. "You have a room that looks out over our Cascades Atrium." She handed Julia a small envelope with a card key.

Julia glanced down at the map in front of her. "And the conference?"

"You're with the"—the clerk paused and referenced her monitor—"Gene Tech conference." She returned her attention back to the map. She circled a hallway located through the second large atrium area.

Julia nodded.

"Thank you. Could you check to see if you have any more rooms available for the duration of the conference?"

The clerk bit her lip and began typing on her computer. Her nod turned into a shake. "I'm sorry; we don't have anything available for that block of time. We are pretty well booked up right now."

"For one conference?"

"Oh no, ma'am, we have lots going on. Um, let's see; this week we have two weeklong conferences going on, plus several single-day meetings, at least two weddings, and of course there's a big game on Saturday. People start arriving for that on Thursday, or earlier."

"Well, thank you for checking. I would like to leave some messages." Julia pulled out her planner to review information. "The first message is for Cynthia Kimbro. She should be checking in tomorrow. She's rooming with me; please let her know I am here, and this is my cell phone number." Julia dictated the number before continuing with her message. "'Please call or text if I'm not in the room.'"

The clerk nodded as she took down Julia's message.

"Has Sholto van Haas checked in yet?"

More clicks on the computer. The clerk paused. "Would you like to leave a message for him as well?"

Julia left another message for Van Haas, expecting that she would hear from him at some point in the late morning.

Julia turned to see Roman leaning on the back of a sofa

waiting for her, the jacket to his travel-worn suit draped over his arm. He stood when she made eye contact. She grabbed the handle of her rolling luggage, and closed the distance between them.

"Where are your bags?"

"I had them sent to my room; I thought I would walk you to your door."

Julia raised her eyebrows at him. "It will make it easier to find your room later."

She narrowed her eyes at him.

"You are quite expressive—and entirely too suspicious. We are here for almost a full week; I am sure we will be in and out of each other's places for impromptu meetings when we need to discuss issues of a more sensitive nature," Roman explained.

Julia let her face relax.

"So where are we going?" Roman asked, taking the map from her. He studied the paper for a moment before pointing the way to a bank of elevators.

For all the fuss and maps of the hotel, Julia wasn't overly impressed. The hallway they walked down was slightly wider than most, but all in all it was merely a hotel hallway. The lobby had been lovely. There had been a bar and a large skylight and an overabundance of plants and trees. Most hotels had an impressive lobby, but the rest of the building was always the same meeting rooms and the same hotel rooms. The newness and style of finishings varied, but only slightly in Julia's experience.

They stopped in front of her door.

"I will pick you up for dinner in, say, an hour?" Roman asked.

"I can just meet you—"

"No," Roman insisted. "Too many places to get missed in

this place. Besides, it's not like they have only one restaurant. I'll pick you up. We can bypass that awkward waiting for each other to be seated, or getting seated early while the other one is waiting."

"Fine." Julia huffed as she pushed open her door.

"Good; decide on where you want to eat, and I'll see you in an hour." Roman began to walk away.

"Make it an hour and a half; I'm feeling the need to freshen up after traveling."

Roman nodded, then turned and continued walking.

Julia pulled her bag into her room.

Typical hotel room. She looked around; the room was slightly larger than others, two beds, nice bathroom. She turned her attention to the balcony. The clerk had said her room looked out over one of the atriums. Julia thought that meant the pool area or a bar. She opened the doors and stepped out onto her small balcony.

She laughed in amazement as she gazed over the immense space. A wrought-iron railing separated her from an indoor rainforest. She had not expected this; the lobby hadn't even come close to this level of grandeur.

A glass domed ceiling high above let in daylight; below, thousands of plants and trees grew. The trickle of a waterfall could be heard from somewhere nearby. People strolled through the lush garden on a raised walkway, not quite a full floor below her room. She looked down; farther below, on the ground floor, there was another path.

She retreated back into her room, grabbed the map, then returned to perch on one of the small chairs on the balcony. She studied the map, this time not just looking at how far apart her room was from the conference, but at all the other areas inside the hotel.

And to think, she had scoffed when she learned they

would be at the Opryland Hotel, it sounded like some kind of amusement park; she laughed out loud when she saw there was a boat ride in the next large atrium over. While reading over the list of amenities she noticed Roman had written his room number in the upper right corner.

According to the map it was up two floors, on the opposite side of the hotel, and in the next section over. Good. She didn't need Roman to feel the urge to be friendly neighbors. It was bad enough to put up with his flirting while she convinced herself she didn't want him.

That thought stung; she was convincing herself. Yes, Roman was good-looking. Tall, well over the six foot mark, slender with wide shoulders. Julia sighed, remembering the feel of his firm chest, the bulging of his muscular arms, and the softness of his lips. She closed her eyes; his bright blue eyes stared back at her. She clenched her lids tight and shook her head, clearing it of visions of Roman Aventine.

She could not let her mind take her there. Roman was business only. No matter what Melinda said, she didn't need to mix business with pleasure. She didn't need the complication of getting involved with someone, then having to work with them. One-night stands took care of getting involved; she wasn't about to have a one-night stand with someone she worked with. No no no no no.

Genes; she needed to focus on genes. She stepped back into the room and searched through her briefcase looking for the study she had attempted to read on the plane. Her mind began to wander again. Genes. She thought Roman would look good in jeans. The tuxedo he wore to her sister's wedding had set off his figure nicely. Did Roman even wear jeans? She had only ever seen him in a suit. Of course he looked better than any model with his chiseled features, pale blond hair, and sharp blue eyes. And he always wore the right tones to show off his coloring. Denim, faded from years of wear to that worn indigo color would set his eyes on fire. *Wrong kind of genes, Julia. Focus!*

Julia sat staring at the wall, the unread stack of reports on her lap. A loud knock brought her back to the moment. She stared at the door, waiting for another knock.

"Julia," Roman's familiar voice called to her.

She padded across the room and opened the door.

"I thought you were planning on taking a shower or something," Roman asked, raking his gaze over her figure.

"Well, it turned out to be or something." Julia stepped back into her room. "Let me get my shoes on."

A moment later she joined Roman in hall.

"Have you seen this place?" she asked. "There is a boat ride in the next atrium over. And it looks like they have a full-scale replica of an antebellum mansion."

Roman chuckled. "I haven't seen the inside area yet."

"Doesn't your room have a view overlooking the inside?"

"No, all I can see from my room is a parking lot," he explained.

"Too bad. I have a little balcony that overlooks a rainforest; it's really quite beautiful. Completely unexpected."

Also completely unexpected, Roman had not flirted with her all evening. Julia hadn't realized her guard had been up until he left her at her door after dinner. Actually he hadn't flirted with her since she woke up while on the airplane. The Shakespeare had been a welcome distraction but not his standard flirtation. Maybe her resistance to him had paid off, and he had finally given up. That realization left Julia just a little empty.

She flopped down on the bed, burying her face into a pillow. She sank into the softness. She had the room to herself for the night; after tomorrow she would have a roommate. The thought brought her head up, and she looked at the room phone to see if the message light was on. It was.

With a groan she plodded over to the phone and picked up the receiver. She pushed the button that automatically dialed the voice-mail system for hotel guests, and followed the prompts to retrieve her message. A raspy breathing sound emanated from the receiver.

"Hello? Hello?" she asked before remembering this was a voice-mail system. She played the message again, listening closely; maybe the message was messed up, and the breathing was wind or noise over the actual message. No, definitely breathing.

She hung up the receiver, staring at the phone for a full minute before she picked it up and dialed the operator.

"Hello, yes, can you tell me who I can speak to about the voice-mail system for my room?" Julia waited while she was connected.

"Hi, yes, I have a question about a voice mail I received. Is there any way you can access the messages left for my room? I received one that was rather disturbing." She paused, listening to the manager on the other end. "Some heavy breathing. Can you track if it originated from inside the hotel?" She listened again. "Well, thank you. I understand."

Nothing. The hotel could access and listen, but they wouldn't be able to track down the origin of the call.

She picked up her cell phone and punched in Roman's number.

"Aventine," his smooth tenor announced.

"Roman, you didn't try to prank call me in my room, did you?" Julia asked in an accusatory tone.

"Julia, if I am going to flirt with you, I do so openly and in your presence. Prank calls are not my style. Why? What happened?"

"I just had an odd message, sounded like heavy breathing."

"Did you see if the hotel can trace it for you?"

"I did; they can't. I thought I would confirm that it was or wasn't you behaving inappropriately."

"I never behave inappropriately." Roman sounded offended.

"Oh really?" Julia chuckled.

"I always behave with propriety and decorum, Miss Palatine. However, the words I say at times may hold a double entendre or three. I cannot be held accountable if you select to pick up on the more lascivious meanings." She could hear the smirk in Roman's tone.

"I've noticed." Julia scoffed. So much for thinking he had stopped flirting with her.

"Do you need protection this evening? I have an extra-large bed. I'm happy to share."

"There went that double entendre."

"Sorry, it slipped. I do have an extra-large bed, I also have a sofa and, I believe, a sofa bed. You could have your own room with a closable door," Roman explained.

"Oh, you got a suite?" Julia asked.

"All the regular rooms were sold out. We can use it for meetings—tables, chairs, the whole bit, no inappropriate commentary intended."

"I'm fine. If I need a security detail, I'll call in my own dogs, thank you."

"Are you sure you're okay?" His tone dropped.

"Yeah, it was probably some kids pushing in numbers at random. I'll meet you at the conference check in in the morning. Good night, Roman."

"Good night, Julia." It sounded to her as if he lingered on her name a bit longer than usual.

4

Julia couldn't sleep. Bad dreams left her feeling suffocated. The empty quiet hotel room didn't help that confining feeling. She needed air; she needed to get outside. If she could shift and go for a run, that would be best. But that wasn't an option here. She threw a jacket on over her T-shirt and slipped her feet into Birkenstocks.

She wasn't concerned with wandering the hotel in her pajamas in the early morning hours. Anyone up this early would either be an employee of the hotel or too busy with their own situation to be worried about seeing her in her sleepwear.

She strolled through the ground floor paths of the Cascades Atrium; it really did feel as if she were outdoors. It had that sense of nature, which was good since she wouldn't have time to go outside during the duration of the conference. It was eerily quiet and dark.

She wandered into the next atrium over, past closed shops that were set up in a shopping district that was designed to look like the old French Quarter in New Orleans. It reminded her of the Main Street walk in an amusement park. Julia picked up a folded paper brochure from a display. She flipped the panels open and began reading about the history of the hotel; the hotel had been built next to an amusement park. She nodded to herself. Okay, that made sense. Destination location, encompassing the entire experience: park and theme hotel.

Julia continued to wander through the empty "streets" of this section of the hotel. The inside river snaked around next to the path she followed. She could see the rails underwater that guided the boats. As initially silly as she'd thought it was, she wanted to make sure she took the boat ride at some point.

Movement caught her eye. She looked up and, for a moment, thought she saw a brown wolf skulking through the underbrush across the water from her. She stared into the large room. The dim light and tiredness impeded her ability to focus clearly. Nothing. Must have been one of the large fish in the river causing a ripple to catch light.

Julia attempted to wander to that side of the atrium; the design of the space prevented her from getting any closer—the river widened, creating a buffer between the public area and the planted area.

Even if she had seen a wolf, who could it be? Roman's wolf was large and pale. An almost pure white timber wolf with gray markings. She had seen him at her family's estate, Mission Run. Morgan had invited the entire Aventine group that was in California over for a relaxing weekend, a gesture of friendship amid treaty negotiations. His father hadn't come but Roman had, and he'd taken advantage of the ability to run as a wolf through the vineyards. As far as Julia knew, she and Roman were the only wolves here. Cynthia Kimbro, the woman from Canada, hadn't arrived yet, and neither had Van Haas.

Julia stared for a longer time into the planted area. Her vision started fading. She began nodding off. *I'm seeing things, I'm so tired.* There wasn't a wolf, just the dancing of shadows.

Julia turned around and began making her way back toward her room. She still had time to sleep for a few more hours before she needed to be up and functional for the conference.

Julia furiously scribbled notes. The keynote address sounded as if it was delivered in a foreign language. A quick glance around the meeting hall let Julia know she wasn't the only one taking notes. It was like she was back in college, frantically trying to write down every word the professor said, hoping to be able to translate her notes later into intelligent pieces of information. Her ears were only able to absorb so much before it all became a bunch of mumbled syllables.

She knew she only needed a base level of comprehension, enough to grasp what she was learning on the fly. But that paradigm shift ah-ha moment of clarity and understanding had yet to happen for her.

She glanced over to Roman. His expression of intense concentration made her think she might not be alone in this sea of genomic jargon.

It infuriated her that he didn't take notes. She always attended business meetings with a pad of yellow legal paper like the one she scribbled on now. Roman only ever took notes when it came to phone numbers or financial figures. His memory was impeccable. That annoyed her no end. She was more capable of big-picture strategy, yet she had to take notes. Process the words. Comprehension came through her fingers writing longhand.

She flipped another page and continued transcribing the presentation. Quickly, she scribbled a thumbnail of the presentation slide in the margins of the notepad.

She leaned over. "You're getting all of this if I miss something, right?" she whispered.

"Relax, Julia. It's all going to be online by the end of the day. And yes, I am getting it," Roman whispered back.

Julia's phone vibrated against her leg. She looked down. A text. She picked up the phone, relieved to read basic English that she could comprehend, no scientific buzzwords. She expected to receive messages from either Dr. Kimbro, or Van Haas. The text appeared to be from Van Haas.

Palatine- arrived. Meet me in room 536 ASAP.

Julia sighed. Definitely the alpha. She quickly keyed in a reply.

Mr. van Haas? The keynote presentation will be over in approx 15 min. Can we meet at coffee shop in atrium?

Room 536 20 minutes.

Yep, alpha playing bullshit alpha games. She nudged Roman and showed him the message on her phone.

"He has no idea what he's up against," Roman whispered in her ear.

Julia smirked; Roman was right. She had grown up around a lot alphas, all of them male. She knew how to negotiate their standard bull. Especially when a new one tried to establish dominance in undeclared territory. If she metaphorically had to pee all over this hotel and conference to make her position known, she would. She appreciated that about Roman. He may infuriate her on a personal level, but he never played those bullshit alpha games.

Remembering back to the alliance negotiations, Roman was clearly the stronger alpha physically and mentally, though his father was still the head of the Aventine family. Her brother, Morgan, and Roman's father, Blackston Aventine, had played those game. Games, to her, that wasted time, were infuriating, and nothing more than ridiculous posturing dominance. Julia knew Morgan hadn't enjoyed the process, but Blackston seemed to enjoy the foolish anti-quated ritual that only established him as the leader of his family. Something everyone in the meetings was already well aware of.

Morgan and Julia had been raised with a very different mind-set. They had not been raised to rely on games for dominance. Alphas came to their strength through personal fortitude and skill. Leadership was a natural consequence of achieving one's rank. Alphas didn't need posturing to prove themselves. Their track record and position within the enterprise took care of that. Games were left to kids, not adults.

It did not mean that when meeting a new alpha, games didn't happen, just that with some alphas, they were so confident with themselves they didn't need the posturing. For Julia, as a woman, she found herself having to play the games entirely too often; it left her with a jaded view of the entire process. She didn't play anymore. She lay waste to the playing field and got the entire issue solved in one large sweeping move.

Julia continued to take notes. She scribbled some words and circled them, reminding herself to get Roman to fill in the missing information.

Everyone filed out of the meeting, scientists and other attendees dividing up into smaller groups. Julia paused to check her phone for the room number information again.

"Shall we meet for lunch after the next session?" Roman asked while checking the schedule.

"Sounds good. I don't know if I'm going to get to my session on deep sequencing. A lot depends on Van Haas and how much posturing crap I have to deal with." Julia snorted. "You know the average businessman can be a pain in the ass; adding dominant wolf into the mix is..." She shook her head, not completing the thought.

"I'm a perfectly charming businessman," Roman defended.

"And a complete ass," Julia added.

The hotel was large, and Van Haas's room was about as far from the conference as a room could be.

If Julia tracked steps, she knew she would be meeting her goal and then some. She didn't need it. She was naturally inclined to being physically fit, one of the traits that came with the wolf heritage. However, she frequently would participate in the office walking step count competitions. It helped office morale, made her more approachable as a good boss. She did have personal body issues most women seemed to struggle with, but with her perfect hourglass figure, Julia's complaints were that as physically capable as she was, she didn't have an athletic build; she didn't have that elusive abdominal muscle definition. Her breasts were a tad too large to be considered professional, and her hair, when left alone, seemed to have a mind of its own, long, thick, and with just enough curl. She typically wore it pulled up into a sleek coil on the back of her head or in a thick braid.

She knew she approached Van Haas's room when she saw a tall man in an all-black suit standing outside a room door. Either Van Haas was a powerful alpha and had minions, or he had ego issues and hired henchmen.

She approached the door and stopped. Julia raked the guard with her glare and waited while he knocked, then opened the door. Julia did not step in; she glared at the guard and cleared her throat in expectation.

"Mr. van Haas, Ms. Palatine is here," the guard announced. Bullshit alpha games, Julia thought as she passed the man as if he were now invisible. *Yeah, I can play that.* She smirked to herself.

Van Haas had a large suite; she stepped into the sitting room area, then stopped. She scanned the furnishings, then picked a chair and sat, crossing her legs, without invitation.

"Ms. Palatine." A burly man with a cleanly trimmed, full beard and head full of wavy dark ginger hair approached.

Julia held out her hand to him.

He clasped her hand between two meaty paws "It's a pleasure to finally meet you in person."

"I left a message for you yesterday; clearly you have been here for a bit."

"Forgive me." His accent had sharp edges and long ahs. "I was rather tired and recovering from jet lag. I felt it would be best to meet after I had a chance at a bit of recovery."

"Understandable. You will want to attend a session or two after lunch. We will meet; there are four of us." Julia did not acknowledge Van Haas's henchmen. "We plan on comparing notes and discussing our situation after dinner."

Julia stood, indicating she was done with this nonsense. "You have my number; let me know if you have intentions of joining me for lunch before attending the afternoon session. I am late for a panel on deep sequencing." She turned without giving Van Haas the opportunity to contribute to the discussion.

Her audience with him was over.

Van Haas asked, "Will we be meeting in your rooms?"

"Undecided." She turned back toward the door, sneered at the guard, who rushed to open the door; then she stepped through into the hall.

Her posture slumped as soon the elevator doors slid closed. Being the all-high bitch was too easy somedays. She preferred to treat people like people and not furniture. She had been raised to treat those who work for you with kindness, respect, and autonomy, and they will respond by rising above and beyond expectations and prove more loyal than money can buy.

Van Haas's men were clearly just hired guard dogs. She wouldn't want to face one in a dark alley, they were still large and formidable, but she could tell a big enough paycheck and they would expose their necks to another leader.

Julia stared at the closed elevator doors. Van Haas had a security detail with him. Those men weren't here to watch his back while he was at a conference. What was going on here? Were they really just to keep him protected? As an alpha, she would have thought he would shun away from having bodyguards. She knew she was capable of protecting herself; then again she had never considered herself to be in any form of danger.

Her brother Morgan had; he had been kidnapped and hunted after leaving a meeting with Roman at SeaQuence, a gene sequencing laboratory in the East Bay. Morgan had been missing for almost two full weeks. Upon his return he told the story that lone wolves, Smiths, were working with daywalkers for someone called His Lordship. Smiths were wolves that chose to leave their family structure for one reason or another. While not typically more dangerous than the next wolf, they did tend to be the more criminal element of their kind. When a wolf went rogue, they changed their name to acknowledge their break from family ties. In North

America the name they were referred to as was Smith, whether they adopted it or not.

The daywalker element was a concern. In true stereotypical form vampires and wolf shifters did not play well together; it was one thing movies and fiction got right. In fact, they typically hated each other's kind with a vengeance. Daywalkers, the biological children of male vampires and their female blood slaves, followed their parental lead and also hated wolf shifters.

Morgan's encounter with these two enemies working together had led to uncovering disturbing rumors that a powerful and long-thought-dead vampire had returned. Growing business relations with Cyan del Fuego provided confirming intel that a dangerous coven master named Lazarus had indeed returned. Morgan's kidnappers had claimed to be recruiting him to carry out a death threat against Blackston or Roman. Morgan refused, and on his return he insisted that Julia have improved security, even though they were only aware of a threat against the Aventines. But after a month without further incidences and no hint of threat, Julia had dropped the security detail.

Van Haas was an alpha, no denying that; maybe the climate for their kind in South Africa was different. Maybe there was some kind of ongoing threat she wasn't aware of. He wasn't as powerful an alpha as he projected. Could the show be for her, for the Americans?

Julia pulled out her phone and began walking. She punched in a number, then held the cell to her ear.

"Yeah, I'm going to need a shadow. You want to come out here and pretend to be all tough?"

5

"Miss Palatine? You're Julia Palatine, right?"

Julia turned to the young woman who had approached her.

"I'm Cindy Kimbro," she said, thrusting her hand out.

Julia raked the young woman's form with her gaze. About what she'd expected: lanky, thin mousy hair, thick wire-framed glasses. She fit Julia's vision of scientist but was substantially younger than what Julia had been led to believe.

"Right. Hello, Cindy. I had expected you to have called or texted." Julia held up her phone.

"I decided to just come on down and check out the conference. I saw your name on your lanyard." Cindy pointed at the ID badge hanging around Julia's neck. "And thought I would introduce myself."

"Have you registered with the conference yet?" Julia asked.

Cindy shook her head. She shifted from foot to foot, unable to stand still. Nervous energy bounced around her.

"Go ahead and sign in, then pick a session for the afternoon."

"Which session were you going to attend? I thought I would just tag along."

Cindy was rapidly no longer fitting Julia's expectations. She was too enthusiastic. Julia had envisioned someone a bit more introverted. Julia needed her to calm down; she was like some hyperactive puppy.

"You should plan on attending something different, so that we can compare notes later."

"The plan is to maximize our presence here by attending as many different sessions as possible," Roman responded when Julia paused. Cindy's smile immediately faded. Her eyes opened wide as she looked at Roman.

"Roman Aventine," he introduced himself.

"Oh, I wasn't expecting you, others," Cindy stuttered, then quickly corrected herself, her smile returning to her face. "Um, how many of us are here?"

Julia answered. "Roman, myself, and Sholto van Haas. He should be here later this afternoon. He is expected to join us for our little note-sharing session after dinner."

Julia opened the schedule. She indicated a session circled in pen. "I will be at this one. So you should..." She ran her finger down the list. "Go to this one, or this one." She selected the two she didn't fully understand, hoping that Cindy would be able to distill the information into easily understandable concepts.

"Okay, sure." Cindy nodded vigorously. "You don't have a notepad or something I could borrow to take notes on. I, um, didn't really know what to expect, so I didn't really bring much with me."

Julia's brow clenched in annoyance—exuberant and

unprepared. She reached into her bag, then handed Cindy a notepad and a pen. "Here."

"Have you had lunch yet, Cindy?" Roman asked. When she shook her head, Roman suggested she join them. Not that Julia particularly wanted to be alone with Roman; she did want to be able to focus on their strategy for the conference. If she was expected to make idle chitchat with this young lady, she doubted she would get much work done.

Julia made a mental note to check with Kathleen. Had she missed an email letting her know that Cindy Kimbro would be so young? Julia's mental image had been of an older, professionally established person. Maybe Cindy was a phenom, a child prodigy. It didn't matter as long as she could help Julia to comprehend the language and help to strategize their needs in regard to this new-to-her knowledge.

Julia slogged her way back toward her room. She had a few moments, hopefully without Cindy, to lay back and clear her mind of today's activities. She wanted a blank slate, no thoughts, no worries for just a few quiet moments before she had to dive back in.

She planned on joining Cindy and Van Haas for a dinner meeting in Roman's suite, where the four of them would review any new information they'd learned from the day, and discuss the ever-developing strategy for both spreading the news to other wolves and how to contain the information, preventing the spread about their unique DNA in the nonwolf science community.

She entered the room—good, no Cindy. An open suitcase

with clothes and random snack food wrappers was strewn across the second bed. Cindy had made it to the room all right. She already annoyed Julia, she probably didn't have the focus to be tidy. She reverberated with excitement. Julia would get that from time to time, especially when younger female shifters met her and recognized her as an alpha. It had not been the power trip today that it frequently was. Today it was exhausting. Today she needed a professional adult who could be trusted to function on her own with minimal input. Cindy was like potty training an overexcitable puppy. Constant direction, constant correction, constant affirmation that she was doing as requested. Julia dropped her pile of papers on the side table, kicked off her shoes, then collapsed face-first onto her bed. This had been a mistake. She should not have invited others to this conference.

Her phone began vibrating. Julia groaned and rolled over, trying to fish her phone from her pocket. It stopped vibrating. She looked at it. She'd missed a call from Mel.

Julia smiled. She could use some of Mel's grounding influence, a conversation that made her feel human again and not like a business automaton.

Julia hit the call back button.

"Hey, Mel."

"S'up, bitch?"

"Really? You're going to play that today?" Julia groaned.

"Spoilsport. How's Nashville? Is it crawling with hot country singers in tight jeans and cowboy hats?" Mel asked.

Julia chuckled. "No clue; haven't seen it. I'm in a hotel that's part amusement park."

"What?"

"It's actually pretty cool, but I kid you not, there is a boat ride in one of the lobby areas. It's kind of crazy."

"Pictures or it didn't happen."

"I'm out somewhere by a freeway and a mall. I don't even know where downtown is. Everybody calls me 'ma'am,' it makes me feel old."

"You are old."

"Shut up. Thirty-four isn't old. This place is huge; I probably won't end up leaving the building all week." Mel was the only person outside of her siblings and cousins who felt comfortable enough to razz her without fear. Being best friends for almost twenty years made her family.

"You work too much, Jules."

"Yeah, well, that's what I do."

"Was Mr. Dreamy Suit Porn on your flight?"

"You mean Mr. Tall Blond and Arrogant? Sat next to him on the way out."

"You two getting it on yet? Did you pack sexy things?"

"Mel!"

"Give it up, Jules; we both know you have the hots for him. Do it while you're not home; that way if he sucks, you can pull the 'what happens in Vegas stays in Vegas' routine."

"No, Mel, he's annoying, condescending, arrogant—"

"You said that one already."

"He's an ass."

"You want to bone him so bad." Melinda chuckled.

"I swear, Mel..."

"Yes, you do. Now what's the worst thing that could happen? You do the deed, and it's horrible. So move on."

"That's not the worst that could happen." Julia sighed.

"Ooh, gurl! You are not thinking the worst is you'd fall in love. Jules, that's the goal, isn't it? Grow up, meet Mr. Wonderful, fall in love."

"Love is too messy; I don't want any complications." Love hurt. Love lied. Love wanted to stifle and muzzle her.

"Liar!"

Julia pulled the phone away from her ear in reaction.

"Big fat liar liar pants on fire. Julia, you were always looking for 'the one.' 'Is he the one? How will I know if he's the one?' You are a bigger romantic mush than anyone I know. You just put up a front. You don't want to fall for blondie because you're afraid he won't fall for you."

"You're full of shit."

"I am, but I'm right. And look, you have to go out and risk getting hurt once in a while or you'll never find *the one*."

"I did that once, remember." Julia didn't want to remember.

"I do, and that was years ago, Jules. It's time to pull on your big-girl thong and move on."

"Stop being so smart," Julia chided.

"I can't help it. Smart, gorgeous, and—can you believe it?—still single. Look, if you don't do the sexy with Mr. Suit Porn soon, I'm gonna have to sit in his lap to get him to notice me."

Julia laughed.

"No, you're right; that won't work. I'd have to be naked for him to notice, and even then it would be to ask me to get off his lap so I don't mar his clothes with bodily fluids."

"I'm pretty sure he'd notice you on his lap, Mel." Julia laughed. Her friend always brightened her day. No wonder Mel had been her rock during the dark ages following Grant.

"Not if you're anywhere in the room. He has the hots for you, and you can't see it, can you? His eyes do that intense wolf-glow thing around you. No, Julia, he wouldn't notice me; I'm not you. You really should make a move."

"I'll let him make a move; then we'll see."

"Really?" Melinda squeaked. "He will; I know it. Quick, give me his phone number so I can text him a clue!"

Julia laughed. "Goofball."

"That's me. So how is the conference? Learning lots?"

"Mel, can I pay you to go back to college and learn all this DNA and genetics and gene stuff? I need someone I can trust in this."

"Sure, I can science."

"Good. I need you ready to graduate yesterday. My brain looks at this stuff and says, 'Oh, this makes sense; this is easy.' But when I try to explain it back to myself, I trip over some of these concepts. I'm not sure how much I really need to know."

"You don't need to be an expert."

"I get that; problem is I'm not sure what level of comprehension is basic and what's expert."

Mel threw the question back at her. "So when you aren't a specialist, what do you do?"

"I find a specialist. I get out there and network; I take my ass to a panel discussion. Pick out one or two of the panelists to approach later. Buy them food, ply them with drinks, grill them. Collect business cards and make appointments with them, then fly my ass out to meet them." Julia talked herself through the process.

"I can't believe I had to prompt the all-powerful Julia Palatine, youngest and first woman CEO of Truria, on how to network at a conference."

"Because you are awesome, and you know me too well. And you know I need reminding that I'm human and not a machine."

"Even the mightiest of us needs a confidant," Mel said.

"Minion."

"B-F-F."

"Sidekick."

"Bestie."

"Okay, you win. Beastie."

"Who you calling a beastie, bitch?"

"You." Julia laughed; Mel had won this round.

"We have reverted to our baser animal instincts; you know what that means?" Mel giggled.

"You're gonna tell me what you want?" Julia asked.

"Yep, I'm gonna tell you what I want, what I really really want."

"You do that. I need to go be a functional adult and get back to business," Julia replied.

"What time is it there?"

"Time for dinner." Julia groaned as she sat up. "I'm gonna be late for a meeting."

"Go be all badass and professional. I'll talk at ya later."

"Bye, Mel."

Julia's mood had drastically improved. Talking to Mel always put her in a better frame of mind. She didn't have to maintain a persona of business intellect and control; she could let her hair down. No game playing. It was as if they were perpetually sixteen and happy. Julia splashed water on her face, slipped her shoes back on, picked up her papers, and then headed out to Roman's suite to meet with the others.

6

J ulia added another dish to the pile of plates and glasses stacked on the tray outside of Roman's door. Room service would pick up the dishes at some point without disturbing their meeting.

They had been talking in circles for over an hour. Julia's head thrummed with an impending headache. She could feel it trying to take hold. She tried to ignore it, not wanting to succumb to the dull ache.

They had been arguing over how to share information and still stay safely hidden from the world at large. Julia wanted to get the information out hard and fast. Find out who else in the world had stumbled across it, or were they the first? Contacts in North America were scarce. The family in Nevada pretended they didn't know her or what she was talking about. Even though she knew they knew. Her uncle had contacts with a family in Japan. Beyond that, she really didn't have any idea how many of them there were, or in what parts of the world. The fact that she had managed to find an alpha from the Toronto area had been a fluke. She gazed across the room at Roman; he leaned against one of the side tables, his arms folded across his chest. She had seen that posture before: intent listening. He was engaged in a heated discussion with Van Haas. Van Haas had sought her out. His presence here emphasized to her just how isolated their kind had become. The only reason she knew Roman was because their families had known about each other since the beginning.

The Palatines and the Aventines, two halves of the same patronage. Descendants of the twin brothers Remus and Romulus, founders of Rome. And as far as anyone knew, the first wolf shifters. The twins' mother, Rhea Silvia, was beloved of the god Mars. Her father was imprisoned by his insane power-mad brother, who when he couldn't have her, sent Rhea Silvia to live as a Vestal Virgin. When she had proven to not be a virgin and pregnant with the war god's sons, she had been sentenced to death. Fearful of the wrath of Mars, the insane uncle of Rhea Silvia cast mother and infants into the river Tiber. The river god Tibernius saved them all. Rhea Silvia shifted into a wolf to suckle and protect her infant sons after they washed up into the swamp at the base of the Palatine Hill.

The infant boys grew into mighty warriors and wolf shifters. They freed their grandfather and fought over where to establish their new city-state. Romulus wanted to establish their stronghold on the hill where they had been safely brought to shore, the Palatine Hill. Remus preferred the neighboring Aventine Hill. In a bloody wolf battle for dominance, Romulus prevailed, killing his brother.

The Palatines and the Aventines, a family feud that had lasted centuries. They continued to keep tabs on each other and eventually followed each other to the new world. Julia was aware there had to be other family branches and groups that had eventually split off, but she did not know them. She knew the Palatines and the Aventines were enemies of old and friends of new. And she did not really want to think of what that meant for her.

"You don't even know how many there are of us in North America. Do you have any concept how big Africa is? This continent is puny in comparison. At least most of Africa is not technologically advanced. It should be easier to stay under the radar in less developed areas." Van Haas's voice was sharp.

Julia slid back into her seat at the table. Roman stood across from her.

"I think you are underestimating the reach of mobile access. Mobile computing and mobile education have a far greater reach than most people realize. I mean, mobile education is a pretty big deal in areas you are calling under-developed," Cindy volunteered.

Van Haas shook his head. "You keep using the word 'mobile' like the Sicilian used 'inconceivable.' To quote *Princess Bride*, 'I do not think that word means what you think it means,'" Van Haas attempted a Spanish accent. For a moment Julia was taken back; the man had a sense of humor. She had not expected that of him.

Rolling her eyes, Cindy glanced from Van Haas to Roman, who sported a bemused expression. Julia was the only one who seemed to not discount her theory.

"Elucidate, please." Julia nodded in encouragement. Finally Cindy was contributing.

"You need to be more familiar with what is happening in mobile availability. Education is a front-runner for bringing tech to the people. Mobile technology is reaching areas those of us in first-world regions think of as underdeveloped: Southeast Asia, India, Africa. I mean, there is better cell phone access in backwater areas of Vietnam than there are in parts of Connecticut.

"I honestly think China and North Korea are the only areas you can say connectivity is fully limited because of their governments. People are using their phones to complete college courses. If they can do that, that means they have access to the same information we do," Cindy explained with rapid fire speed.

"I thought you said you were a chemist?" Roman asked.

"I-I am," she stammered, "but my sister is in education. She is specializing in distance technologies in underdeveloped nations. She's studying mobile connectivity. There is a lot of growth in this area, especially throughout Africa." She turned to Van Haas. "You're from Pretoria, right?"

He nodded.

"Well, there is a big university there, and they are developing programs for distance mobile access."

Roman raised an eyebrow and looked at Julia.

"What kind of work does your sister do?"

"She's in university, why?" Cindy asked.

"This might be something we need to enhance our outreach. Currently we have"—Julia paused, indicating everyone at the table—"this. I've been making initial contacts, then setting up one-on-ones." Julia directed her comment to Van Haas. "As you said, we have no idea how many of us there are."

"But if we can make our information more widely available..." Cindy jumped in excitedly.

"We still need to control access to the information. We want to educate our kind, not let nonshifting humans find out about us."

"So it's a dead end?" Cindy asked, deflated.

"Not at all," Roman interjected. "It's another area to

explore. We see an area we need access to; at the moment we don't know how to get to it. Your sister might be able to help us with this new concept."

Julia picked up Roman's thought. "This is a new puzzle piece; we need to see if it fits in with our big picture. Is it going to be of use and how so? We still need to get the information out to our people while limiting the data from getting to the general public."

"How? That's easier said than done," Van Haas grumbled.

"True," Julia continued. "The concept is simple, the execution complex. We need to approach this problem not as if there is a linear solution, but as if our answer is an octopus with ten arms on LSD."

Van Haas scoffed.

"Everything is interconnected, and it's all going in what seems like a million directions at once. We will find that following one solution pathway will eventually lead us to intersect with another solution pathway; then they will split off in completely new directions." Roman gestured toward Cindy. "Ten minutes ago we didn't know about mobile computing access, and now there is a part of my brain chugging away on how this new information can be leveraged to our benefit. So, we start with what we have and expect exponential growth. We spread information by word of mouth for now."

Julia continued. "Tell the families you know to spread the word. Tell those families it's time to pull everyone in, track down family records. Follow bloodlines to see if any lineages have lost the ability to shift. Find the Smiths, the loners, and find any kids out there with questionable parentage. If there is any way they belong to us, get them situated. Make sure they know their family histories so that they aren't randomly sending in for DNA tests. And we'll be able to find a way to control what labs they do use for DNA testing."

"That's fine and good for law-abiding citizens. How do you propose handling when one of our ilk leaves DNA evidence behind?" Cindy asked.

"Police our own," Van Haas answered.

"After the fact?" she asked.

"Before the fact." Van Haas's answer was gruff.

"No." Roman's voice was sharp, his statement clipped. "When good men do evil to prevent wars, wars are started. We will not be responsible for forming death squads."

"Who said anything about death squads?" Van Haas scoffed.

"That's where it would lead," Roman explained.

"It comes back to education." Julia added, "And taking care of our people."

"Some people cannot be helped, no matter what."

"Then we figure it out case by case, one person at a time," Roman replied.

Van Haas nodded slowly, not convinced. "Easier said than done." He drew the sound of the words out slowly, making the statement an insult.

"It needs to be done. You're here for the same reason we are." Julia gestured to Van Haas and Cindy, then to Roman and herself. "You understand we need to contain the information. Van Haas, you flew in from South Africa just to listen to me explain this in person; well, this is the next step. We need to contain the DNA information, and we need to take a multipronged approach to do so." She began ticking off her fingers. "Person to person. Data containment. Education.

"Let's start with person to person. Start with family

records, send someone out pounding the pavement talking to people, tracking birth records. Reach out to other families that you know, have them do the same. Roman started by telling me, and now"—she gestured to everyone at the table —"all our families are aware of the situation. We share, we talk."

"And data containment?"

"Less straightforward." Julia continued, "That's why we're here. We need geneticists we can count on to squelch research out of our hands. We need controllable researchers and labs. People we can trust to see just how and where in the DNA wolf data resides. We need to flag DNA reports so the trait is reported to us when it does show up on a test. Aventine Industries recently acquired a gene sequencing lab in California. There are hundreds of labs all over the world. We can't possibly buy them all."

"But we could get scientists into them," Cindy interjected. "Pay for their educations, use whatever pull we have to get them into jobs. Create a network of genetic spies, as it were."

"I'm in full agreement on that." Julia nodded to Cindy. "I have a few offers out on private labs. I want one where we can conduct research and not worry about outside ownership interfering with test results, by sharing them with the scientific community at large." Julia directed her next statement to Cindy. "I will share any research I can with your alpha, but my work has been limited to the United States. There has been some Canadian crossover, but not much." Turning to Van Haas, she said, "I will send over the parameters and requirements I've been looking at. I don't know if any of it will be beneficial to your people in South Africa."

Van Haas nodded. "We have a lot of work ahead of us. I'm going to call it a night; jet lag is catching up to me." Van

Haas stood, gathering his papers and notes into an easy-to-carry pile.

"That's actually a good idea," Cindy announced. "I'll head back to our room. I want to take a shower before turning in," she said to Julia.

Julia began gathering her papers.

Roman placed a hand on top of her growing stack. "Stay for a bit. We have acquisition papers to go over."

Julia sat back down and gave Roman a side glare. She wasn't aware of any acquisitions they needed to discuss.

Roman was silent until the door clicked shut behind Cindy.

Julia watched Roman; as soon as he moved to begin speaking, she cut him off. "Don't."

"Don't what?" Roman asked innocently.

"Don't say something witty and slightly flirtatious. I don't have it in me tonight to cross words." She was exhausted. The conference meetings today had thrown her a steep learning curve, and she felt she was not keeping up as she normally would. Business acquisitions, mergers, personnel management were all easy concepts. Genomics. Alleles. Arrays. Epistasis. Heterosis. All new vocabulary, all new concepts. Julia hadn't had to deal with this much science since she was in college.

"Then don't," Roman said evenly. "Don't fight me all the time."

"I don't, Roman, I..." She wiped her hand across her brow, smoothing her hair back from her face. "I can't."

"You're right. In business you don't fight me; that's true. But you never let your guard down around me." Roman paced away from her. "I take that back. You have only let your guard down once. I would dearly like to see that Julia again."

"Seriously, Roman, it was just a kiss," Julia snapped.

"It was hardly just a kiss. It lasted forty minutes; had your brother not interrupted, I'm sure there would have been more than kissing." Roman's tone was heated.

Indignation flooded Julia with the reminder that it hadn't been a simple kiss but rather an aggressive make-out session. "We're doing it right now, arguing."

"Foreplay," Roman countered.

"I'm tired and I don't want this."

Roman stood over Julia as she slumped deeper into her chair.

"You are a smart and strong woman. I am drawn to you like a moth to a flame. You were drawn to me once, but now you fight that urge inside you, don't you? You fight me." Roman's tone was low, gravelly. "As long as you continue to play, I will happily flirt with you. Tell me to stop and I will. Tell me to leave you be and I will. But I want you, Julia, and I don't want to leave you be."

Julia looked up at Roman. Her body yearned for him; there was no denying it. She fought her body's reactions to him constantly. She stared into his eyes; and caught the beginning of an intense glow. She shook her head, not wanting to know he wanted her as much as she wanted him. She didn't know what to say. She didn't want the complication of dealing with a struggle for dominance. She didn't want the confrontations that would come when Roman decided he needed to subdue her.

"I'm tired of the fight," she confessed. "I'm tired of having to put forth a more concerted effort to be taken seriously. I'm tired of my natural dominance being second-guessed."

"I never question your lead. So why are you fighting?"

"Your father never once acknowledged that I was in the

room during the accord meetings, and I was there as Morgan's second. The board questions every other move I make. I'm tired."

"I'm not my father, Julia. And your board of directors, with a few exceptions, are all old men trying to stay relevant. Those are different fights; those are not with me. I promise." His tone was soothing. She wanted to lean toward him. She wanted to believe him.

"I'm tired of empty promises."

"Are you tired of me?"

Words were out of her mouth before her mental editor kicked in. "I like you, Roman; I like the attention." Realizing the words she'd let slip, she froze, and then sighed . "Can we call a truce this week? You back off with the overaggressive flirting, and I'll back off with the overaggressive bitchiness."

Roman held out his hand. Julia slipped her fingers into his palm, allowing him to help her stand. His hand felt warm, soft, and like a caress wrapped around hers. She stood so close she could feel warmth radiating from his body. Her gaze followed the movement as Roman slowly raised her hand to his lips and lightly brushed her knuckles with a kiss. His glowing blue eyes gazed back at her through lowered lashes.

"As you command." The tone of his voice combined with the flair of glowing passion from his eyes sent a shiver down Julia's spine. She stumbled back, noticing the faint shimmering aura surrounding Roman. Her chest tightened, and she struggled for breath. Realization of what she was looking at pierced her chest like a spear. "Oh," she said out loud. Internally she began cursing. *Damn.* Julia finally admitted to herself the meaning behind the glow. *That's what Mother meant when she said I'd know; she forgot to mention I needed to accept it for what it was.*

~

Julia sat against the pillows on her bed, typing away on her laptop. Cindy gently snored on the other one. A sharp knock sounded on the door.

"Julia." A familiar deep voice. A voice that should have been in California.

She opened the door. Tall, with a Hollywood perfect smile and curly dark hair, her cousin filled the doorway.

"Dante, what are you doing here?" she snapped.

He held up a garment bag. "Playing security, apparently. What's up?" He began to step into the room. Julia looked over her shoulder at her sleeping roommate before flipping the bar lock and stepping out into the hallway.

"I called Shane; what are you doing here, and how did you get here so fast?"

"You called Shane. Shane called me. I was closer, in Chicago, when Shane told me to grab a suit and get my butt over here to you," Dante explained.

"Chicago on business? I would have thought that would be Shane's thing," Julia responded drily.

"Yeah, no, he's headed to Peru. So he sent me. I met with an adorable little daywalker, Erica. Did you know they have fangs too? Sexy as hell. Why don't we like them again?"

"Dante, focus."

"Right, they have a gossip network you would not believe. They already know about what we're looking at with regard to Lazarus and the Del Fuegos. I'm sure they have more intel on what's going on than they are willing to share. How come the vampires are more organized than we are?"

"They rely on each other for survival and protection. Something about getting crispy in the sun." Julia smirked.

"Right," Dante drawled. "I am here to save the day, but we do have a small problem." Dante paused. "The hotel can't get me in a room for at least two days. And clearly you can't put me up in there. So now what? How am I supposed to play bodyguard if I'm staying in another hotel?"

"I have an idea." Julia dashed back into the room and grabbed her phone. She was already dialing a number by the time she returned to Dante.

"Roman, I need to borrow that couch tonight. No, not for me."

After speaking to Roman, she ducked back into the room, tossed on a hoodie, slipped her feet into Birkenstocks, and grabbed her key.

"Aventine has a suite; you can crash on his couch," she explained as she led Dante through the hallways and up to Roman's room.

"So what's the drill? I'm furniture?" Dante asked as he followed behind Julia.

"You're furniture," she confirmed.

"I've been here the entire time if anyone asks; they just haven't seen me before?"

"Exactly. Make them think they are going crazy if they try to figure out if you have or have not been here. You have, end of story."

"So you are in queen B mode? Huh?" he asked.

Julia rolled her eyes. "It looks like it."

"So why aren't we in a suite then?"

"Reality, they were booked. Let's say I'm going low profile. If I need to, we can use Roman's room as a base."

"Aventine got a suite but not you?"

Julia turned to glare at him. "Look, this was going to be a simple conference. I was perfectly okay with a normal room. I don't have to travel high on the hog all the time. It's actually why our quarterly numbers stay good. I don't support frivolous spending so that you can make the big bucks."

Dante held his hands out in mock protection. "I wasn't questioning your motives, cuz, just getting my facts straight. And for the record, thanks for having a regular room so I can live the high life. Which looks like chasing down ghosts and dead relatives after I'm done here."

"You do know why that's important; please tell me you understand."

"I completely understand, trust me. I'm not as think as you stupid I am."

She paused to glare at him.

Dante flashed a toothy grin. "I'm not some blockhead, Julia. I just play one on TV."

Julia rolled her eyes.

"Lighten up; I'm just teasing. Long day?" Dante finally asked.

She nodded. "And exhausting."

They stopped in front of a numbered door, Julia knocked. When Roman opened, Julia forgot how to speak. He wiped shaving cream from his cheeks with a towel.

Her mouth went dry. She had almost expected to see him in a suit and tie since that's all she ever saw him in. She did not expect to see his chest, his skin. She had to remember how to breathe as she took him in.

His shoulders appeared broader than when he wore a suit. That must be it, she thought, because she could see how well-defined all his muscles were. A light dusting of chest hair on his muscular pecs drew her attention to his pink nipples. She stopped breathing. Pink, against pale skin.

Her gaze continued down the center of his washboard abs. Her fingers screamed at her to let them lightly trail down the crisscross muscles over his ribs and down to the

Apollo's belt ridge above his hip bone. Dear gods, her dry mouth flooded with drool as she caught a glimpse of a thatch of dark blond hair sticking up past the waistband of his plaid pajama pants. She couldn't pull her eyes from the knotted string that held his pants up. If her gaze drifted farther downward, she might just cry with the beauty of this man's body.

Stop it, Julia! She forced her eyes back up Roman's body. His gaze locked on hers. A smirk played at his lips. Without a word he cocked a single eyebrow at her.

Julia interpreted Roman's expression to say *I saw what you did just now.*

Dante clapped Roman on the shoulder. "Hi, roomie. So where's my couch?" He brushed past Roman without a glance at the man's state of dress.

Julia hovered in the hall until Roman stepped aside, silently inviting her in.

"Straight razor?" Dante asked, nodding at Roman.

"Yes." Roman slowly ran his hand over his jaw, seeming to appreciate the feel of a fresh, clean shave. "I can get a good close shave, and it will last. If I need to, I touch it up in the morning."

"I always feel that if I shave at night, I wake up with scruff. Of course when that's the look I'm going for, I never remember to shave at night. Don't you have that problem?"

Roman chuckled. "I'm not as hairy as you."

"You don't have the Italian and Portuguese like us Palatines," Dante said.

"True, the Aventine line is more Nordic than Italian at this point," Roman admitted.

"Seriously?" Julia asked.

Roman nodded. "Definitely one of the more interesting bits to come from all the DNA testing. Always thought the blond came from Northern Italian-Swiss lines. But the amount of Scandinavian I have really caught me off guard."

Roman reached out his hand to Dante. "I believe we met at the wedding."

"Yeah, Dante. Nice to see you again."

"You bear a striking resemblance to Morgan; you're not a brother, are you?" Roman asked.

"I get that a lot; twins separated by parents. Morgan's taller; I'm the better looking one. I'm the cousin."

"You're a cousin." Julia emphasized the A. "'I'm the cousin," she mocked, "as if there is only one of you."

"Hey, there is only one of me." Dante puffed up his chest with bravado.

"Yes, thank the gods, one Dante, but not the only cousin." Julia poked him good-naturedly. Turning to Roman, she said, "Thanks. The hotel doesn't have a room I can get him into for tonight. This will add to the whole bodyguard mystique anyway."

"So what do we think Van Haas is up to? Clearly you think it's more than just a power trip or you wouldn't have brought in your cousin." Roman indicated Dante with a gesture.

"He has two bodyguards, and they leer; hell, he leers. They were acting like some TV show drug lord when I met him in his room this morning. Something about them just feels off to me. Sinister." Julia turned to Dante. "I don't actually need you to guard me, but having an extra pair of eyes at my back will allow me to focus on the business at hand and not be constantly looking over my shoulder."

7

Her phone buzzed with an incoming text from Melinda. *You do it yet?*

I'm in a conference! Julia texted in reply.

That's a no.

!!!

Call me.

Julia shook her head at her friend's persistence. Melinda wasn't going to give up. Ever since Julia admitted to making out with Roman at JoJo's wedding, Melinda had been trying to get them in bed together. There were days Julia not so secretly thought the two of them were conspiring against her. Maybe she should give in and make everyone happy. Hell, it would probably make her happy too.

Julia turned her attention back to the presenter. He was droning on about assays and DNA that stood up. This entire presentation needed a translation into English as far as Julia was concerned. The individual words may have been English, but once combined they were no longer comprehensible.

Julia made an executive decision. She did not need to

know this information or struggle with it any longer. She picked up her case and quietly exited the room. Once in the hallway she reviewed the conference schedule. No, she was not going to anything else until after lunch, she decided before making her way into the atrium to find a coffee shop.

She would sit under a patio umbrella pretending to enjoy the morning outside in fresh air while she checked her e-mail or something more productive than sitting in a presentation that gave her a headache.

She looked up when Dante joined her.

"Playing hooky?" he asked.

"Don't you know it. There wasn't anything for me in that session, so I thought a break and doing something productive was in order."

"That Cindy chick isn't around, is she?" Dante looked behind him as he sat in an empty chair.

"No, why?" Julia sipped her coffee.

"Can you please clue her in that groping the help is frowned upon."

"What?" Julia coughed. "You shying away from the advances of a woman?"

Dante smirked. "She's not a woman. She's a little girl playing dress up. She's acting like a co-ed gone wild on spring break. And believe it or not, I do know appropriate place-and-time behavior. She's got neither. Convince her I'm like a service dog. I'm at work. Look, don't touch. Admire my beauty from afar. 'Cause I swear if she tries to grab my junk again, I'm gonna bite." He paused. "And not in some giggly-foreplay kind of way."

"So it's not just me she's annoying?" Julia asked.

"Fuck no. I get that I'm irresistible, but..." Dante shook his head. "She's being handsy with Van Haas's men too. I think she'd like to get handsy with Roman and Van Haas, but they clearly intimidate her. She shrinks around the three of you."

"Shrinks? She doesn't shut up."

"That's nerves. You can't see it because you're in the direct line of fire. But a well-placed word..." He stood, nodded to Julia, and smoothed the front of his black suit.

"Want me to hang around and look pretty?"

Julia snorted. Dante enjoyed playing bodyguard. He did look good in a suit, and he knew it. But he didn't look as good as Roman, Julia thought. There was a reason she and Melinda called Roman Mr. Suit Porn.

"Nah, I won't need you showing off and tempting poor Cindy. Oh, did you find anything out from Van Haas's guys?"

"Stoic and Kiss Up were not very forthcoming with information."

"Stoic and Kiss Up?" Julia chuckled.

"Stoic's the bald one; all he does is grunt. I gather he's been with Van Haas for a while. Kiss Up—his name sounds like that; it's Cassup, Keyset... I can't figure out what he's saying with that accent, it's so thick. He's a total yes-man. A few beers and I'll know his life story, if I can understand him. So far all I've got is he's thrilled to be here, never thought he'd visit America, blah blah blah. Nothing on Van Haas yet. But I don't like the way he looks at you."

"He looks at me?" Julia asked.

Dante nodded. "Like you're in his way, or prey to be caught. Not sure which. Don't give him a peek of your sparkling personality."

Julia glared at Dante.

"Seriously, keep the real you under wraps; keep up queen B mode around him."

"Gotcha." Julia saluted. "Yes sir."

"I know you only wanted someone to play a part. I'm not

gonna waste my time standing around doing nothing. You wanted me to watch your back, so I'm watching your back; that means watching the people watching you. And I don't like how Van Haas watches you. He's up to something."

"That's why I called. Thanks, Dante, for looking out for me."

"That's what I'm here for," he said, patting her on the shoulder after he stood up. "I'll find you in an hour or so to check in; you won't see me..."

"But you'll see me. Sounds good."

Dante was right; there was something off about Van Haas.

Not wanting to do any work, Julia dialed Melinda's number.

"S'up?" Mel drawled in a deep, mocking voice.

"Really?" Julia replied a bit tersely.

"Uh-oh, one of those days already, huh?"

"My brain hurts, and I have to be a coldhearted bitch this entire trip."

"What did Roman do?"

Julia chuckled. "Not Roman. Actually he's behaving. The delegation from South Africa."

"Oh, delegation... sounds serious."

"He is entirely too serious and into power plays. So..."

"You have to outpower him?"

"Yep, and it's exhausting. Dante thinks he's up to something."

"Dante? What's he doing there?"

"Playing security."

"Playing..." Melinda emphasized the word, making it a double entendre.

Julia shook her head. At one time she knew Melinda had a thing for Dante. Then again Melinda had had a thing for most of the men they grew up around. "Any-way..." Julia pulled Melinda back onto the conversational track. "I'm in high bitch mode, and that shit is exhausting."

"Ouch, you can't be flirty with Mr. Suit Porn with Delegation Guy around, not if you're in ice queen mode."

"Ice queens don't flirt," Julia agreed. "But I'm not flirting with Roman either way." Julia paused. "Ya know, I was thinking about that offer I made you."

"About being my lesbian lover?"

"About sending you back to college to learn this gene stuff. I'm serious, if you want."

"And give up my brilliant career in social work?"

"Yeah."

"It's a nice offer, Jules, you know that. I'd science for you, but my guys need me more."Melinda hated her job but loved her work providing support and finding help for veterans with PTSD. She wanted nothing more than for her job to be obsolete, but until it was, she would be there holding hands and taking calls in the middle of the night. It was why Julia loved her best friend; her capacity for compassion was staggering and her loyalty fierce.

"Yeah, I know. You are doing good in the world; I shouldn't try to take you away from that. I'm playing hide-and-seek from the conference. So what have I temporarily lured you away from? It's, what, nine there?"

"Morning group ended early, so I'm catching up on paperwork. Shouldn't you be networking right about now?"

"I'm playing hooky. As soon as I get off the phone with you, I need to call Kathleen, make sure my family's empire still stands."

Melinda chuckled. "I'll let you go then. I hope Delegation Guy keeps out of your way, unless..." Melinda paused.

"Is he hot? Maybe you should bone him, make Roman jealous."

Julia laughed. "Not bone worthy, definitely not boneworthy."

"Oh well, work requires my attention. Call me later."

"Will do." Julia ended the call, placing the phone on the table.

She flipped open the laptop and booted up the system. Her in-box was virtually overflowing. She sorted out all the newsletters and sales offers that sneaked through the e-mail program's filter system. Messages from her assistant went into a folder for processing before she began reading messages from the few new contacts she'd made the day before. Two scientists were looking for jobs, thanks but no thanks. A few messages that were just follow-ups from having met at the conference. Nothing promising, at least not yet.

She began sorting through the messages from Kathleen. Her assistant firmly believed in, and used, an effective flagging system. Red flag urgent, orange, yellow, green flags less urgent in descending order. Only one urgent red flag. Julia opened that e-mail first.

Nothing drastic, but still very important. It was Carolyn's birthday. Kathleen had flowers sent, but Julia needed to call her sister. Julia cursed herself for being distracted and missing her sister's birthday; then again that's why she treasured her assistant; she actually paid attention to schedules and dates and birthdays.

"Happy birthday, Caro," Julia crooned as her sister groggily said hello. "Any big plans today?"

"Producing milk and changing diapers. I got the flowers; thank Kathleen for me."

"How do you know to thank her and not me directly?"

"The card says it's from you; you are on a business trip. It's okay, Julia; you've been seriously distracted lately. But you had better bring me a really cool and touristy snow globe for my collection."

Julia laughed. "I will; how's that baby?"

"He's an eating, pooping machine."

"And you love every second of it."

"I really do, Julia. I'd love to talk, but I'm exhausted. It's morning nap time. Come see me when you get home, okay?"

"Will do; happy birthday. And have a good nap."

Julia ended the call.

She was busy typing, responding to Kathleen's messages and task lists, when Roman sat down. He placed a fresh warm cup of coffee in front of her.

Julia glanced up and grinned despite herself. Mr. Suit Porn really did describe him, especially this morning. Roman looked sleek and slightly dangerous in his designer suits. It didn't help that Julia knew under the suit he was just as well put together, with perfectly defined abs and pecs. Julia wondered how many suits he'd packed for this trip. She had packed a limited module wardrobe, one where each piece had to serve double or triple duty, and she expected to wear the combinations more than once. Roman almost never appeared in the same combination twice. Today his suit was a dark storm gray with the faintest windowpane grid pattern woven in blues and paler shades. His shirt was a pale blue, his tie silver. The colors made his eyes look like a storm building on the horizon.

"The last session not useful?"

"Not at all. I don't think I'm going to get much from this conference." Julia picked up the coffee and inhaled the steaming aroma.

"You need to change your approach, Julia. I think you are too focused on learning the genomics portion. Let's start focusing on the scientists and the presenters. Who is speaking in gobbledygook; who is speaking English. Instead of the content, focus on the person explaining the content.

"There is a panel this afternoon. Why don't we see if we can get out of the sessions we signed up for and get into the panel. Send Cindy Science to the ones we want translated, send Van Haas to anything that will make his head explode."

Julia chuckled but let Roman continue.

"I've reached saturation. I can regurgitate the lectures, but it doesn't mean I actually comprehend what I'm saying. I know you've reached that point too."

Julia nodded. "I need to find a scientist I feel that I can work with before we proceed with the next step."

"I know; now find someone who can clarify for us. I think that means instead of us learning their language, we find someone already speaking ours."

"Are you being smarter than me, Roman?" She tilted her head to the side.

"Not at all, I'm seeing to your needs. Keeping the path ahead of you clear."

"Am I making this out to be a bigger deal than it is? We've really been focusing on it lately, and I'm a hamster on a spinning wheel. Lots of running and getting nowhere fast." Julia's frustration was wearing her out; she sounded tired even to herself.

"What feedback are you getting suggesting that this shouldn't be a concern? Has Morgan interfered in any way?"

Julia shook her head. "No, he's pretty much handed it over to me. He wants to focus on the construction company and his wife. His idea of managing the big picture is to divide it up and let the specialists handle their areas. So that means me handling this. Me getting Truria set up to have a stake in the DNA business." She tapped on the table in front of her. "Morgan's still involved, and he's totally supportive of it. But he has that other little issue that's also pulling on our resources."

The circumstances surrounding Morgan's abduction had started an investigation that opened a much larger can of worms than anyone could have anticipated. Lazarus was back from the dead and gathering troops. Intel revealed his goal of instigating a war between wolf families. Best guess for why was as a distraction, so Lazarus could move in on the current ruling family, the Del Fuegos.

Julia knew Roman was keenly aware of the entire situation. It involved him almost as much as it involved Morgan. No other threat had yet to surface in regards to Roman's life that she was aware of. Roman nodded, clearly aware that her brother had other areas demanding his attention.

"What does your father think of all of this?" Julia absent-mindedly waved her hand around.

"He thinks it's a bunch of hokum. He doesn't actually think that people take these DNA tests seriously, and that it's a waste of time."

"And you?"

"Julia, if I thought it was a waste of time, I never would have shown you the evidence. I think there is something important here that we need to get a grasp on," Roman explained.

"Tell me this isn't a mistake. I feel like I'm chasing a rabbit down a rabbit hole. And that it might be the wrong rabbit hole."

Roman slid out of his chair and crouched in front of Julia. He grabbed the hands that rested in her lap. "It's worth chasing. And if we run down the wrong rabbit hole, we find our way out of it and chase that sucker down another hole."

Julia looked into Roman's eyes; they were an intense blue, his gaze held hers for several heartbeats. She sighed, then closed her eyes. *Stop being so handsome; it makes it hard to maintain objectivity with you.*

"If nothing else comes from all of this, we will both have successfully learned a great deal about genetics and diversified our business holdings in a much broader scope than projected. However, I don't think that's going to be our only successful end result."

"Hiya." An exuberant voice took Julia's focus from Roman. She looked up into the cheerful face of Cindy. Cindy dropped a stack of handouts and assorted conference giveaways on the table before flopping into a chair. "This conference would be really cool if it made any sense. At least the giveaways are fun. Look at all this swag." She began picking up and showing off helix-shaped Post-it notes and pens with corporate logos.

Roman cleared his throat and slid back into his chair.

"Are you finding anything out that seems relevant?" Julia questioned their new companion.

"I'm not really sure. It's all pretty boring information. I mean, the session this morning was all about identifying..." She paused, reviewing the title on a notepad. "Mitochondrial hippo... happo... haplogroups. They showed a bunch of maps with arrows and talked about mothers and caravans and shit. I just don't see how that's going to help with tracking down how our kind is showing up as an ethnicity. So what are we doing for lunch?" Cindy flipped the notepad closed and looked up expectantly.

8

L unch had not been relaxing. Cindy and Van Haas had joined them at one of the hotel's more exclusive restaurants. Instead of planning on how to best approach the new strategy Roman had suggested, or learning more about haplogroups from Cindy, Julia felt they were relegated to idle chitchat. Cindy's inane conversation made Julia wonder exactly what kind of science she specialized in. She had been told it was chemistry, but after talking to the girl, Julia began to think it was probably kindergarten science and nothing more complex than that. Julia was fairly certain that she actually understood genomic concepts better than Cindy. Julia was also beginning to question the woman's doctor credentials.

Van Haas was in braggart mode. He discussed his ranch and other holdings. Julia really did not care about his car collection or his hunting experience. When he mentioned the acreage of his ranch for the fourth time, she had to fight the urge to lean over and offer condolences over the size of his penis. It was too much.

Cindy seemed impressed with Van Haas; then again

Cindy seemed to be impressed with everything. Especially anything that seemed to indicate money. Julia felt a bit sorry for the young woman. Her ill-fitting clothes indicated that she wore hand-me-downs or was a thrift-store shopper. Not a thrift shopper herself, Julia did think that the source of the clothing shouldn't indicate how poorly they fit. It was possible that she wasn't a scientist, not yet at least. If she was still in school and studying to be in the sciences, that might explain her overenthusiasm. Then again, if that were the case, wouldn't her alpha have mentioned that instead of saying she was a chemist? Julia couldn't quite figure the girl out yet.

Roman had been no help in the lunch conversation either. He spent his time smirking and nodding. Julia felt positively abandoned when he excused himself to leave early. He expressed his hope in being able to meet with a presenter prior to the next session. Cindy followed shortly after Roman left, leaving Julia on her own with Van Haas. Once alone, he seemed to morph from a human into a slimy toad. She couldn't put her finger on the exact differences of his actions; possibly it was a change in his breathing patterns, or how he said her name. No matter what, she recognized that her own reactions changed. She immediately became haughtier. She was in full snob mode, queen B as Dante referred to it.

"It's time to return to the conference." She placed her napkin on the table and reached for her water glass. She made no excuses, making no concessions for Van Haas's time. While she played this part, she knew she didn't have to.

Van Haas leaned across the table. "We have plenty of time. Which session will you be attending? I'm in a continuing breakout session from this morning's presentation. I will admit, this is all very interesting. I am learning much. I look forward to sharing my newly learned information with your this evening." His fingers trailed across the back of Julia's hand as she held her water glass. "Admittedly, I don't know how we will begin to track the information. But it is good to know about."

Julia stared at the back of her hand. She glared at Van Haas, making sure he was aware as she snatched her napkin back up and wiped her hands off. "Time is limited and we are currently only one step ahead in our need to be"—Julia paused, looking for a word—"contained, as it were."

"I quite agree. I am waiting to hear from a colleague back home. I may have a contact at the University of Pretoria. If this mobile learning is something we need to be concerned with, might as well get started."

She stood, trying to ignore his actions and focus on his words, as he continued to speak business. Van Haas vocalized that he was on board, in pretense if not in actuality.

One of his suited goons leaned into their conversation. "Mr. van Haas." Julia ignored the man completely, just as one would paint on the wall.

"Pardon me, Ms. Palatine," Van Haas said. Her name oozed from his lips.

A shiver rolled down Julia's spine, she felt nauseated at the sound of her name. Everything about him just felt off; he had zero appeal, and wasn't even properly dominant. If he was going to pretend to play the big alpha, he was going to have to learn how to be around subordinates. They were furniture until you wanted them. And they never interrupted.

She glanced at her phone after feeling it buzz.

Lol! These guys could really take some lessons, couldn't they?

She glanced over at Dante; his stoic expression gave nothing away, yet he was laughing in his text.

Seriously!

For Julia and Dante it was so much game playing. They knew exactly what they were doing and exactly how to be the big dog in the room. Van Haas was failing.

So which dog was that?

That's Stoic, names Kruger, build like a bulldog, about as much sense of humor.

Julia pretended not to pay attention to Van Haas and Kruger. Their heads were conspiratorially close. She was being paranoid. They were probably simply discussing nothing more nefarious than if housekeeping had given them enough towels.

Are you listening? Julia wondered why the men whispered; of course Van Haas probably had been ignoring Julia's alpha traits. As an alpha Julia had command of her shifting and senses, something that, if she were a lesser wolf, she wouldn't have. With Dante playing bodyguard, Van Haas and his men probably assumed him to also be a lesser wolf; after all, an alpha like Van Haas would never pull guard duty. Little did they know Dante was a strong alpha with full control and the ability to shift instantly.

Sure am. Missed first part. Locating someone. Bring them, Dante texted.

?

I'll see what I can find out.

"So sorry for the interruption," Van Haas said. "I regret anything that takes me away from your company." His words felt sticky to Julia, as if Van Haas was trying to touch her with his voice. He fell short. His voice was not calming nor soothing. While deep, it had greasy overtones to it. Just talking to the man made her skin itch.

The day before he hadn't seemed so oily and oozing, but today Van Haas seemed particularly attentive, and it was not a comforting prospect.

"Shall we?" He held his arm out, indicating they should begin walking.

Julia tipped her nose in the air. She had been herded. Julia made sure Van Haas knew with her visible disdain that she did not appreciate the action.

She hated these games, yet they were a necessary evil. Van Haas had to recognize her as superior, and more importantly, so did his dogs. Stupid, weak men could be dangerous, especially when they didn't fully understand their place in the hierarchy.

Julia did not like this feeling. It was foreign, strange, and uncomfortable. And, unfortunately, becoming too familiar. She sat with one leg crossed over the other with the yellow legal pad poised and ready for notes. Surrounded by the scientific community, she felt out of her element. She was not in control, nor grasping aspects of entire genomic concepts. Julia understood situations; she put puzzle pieces together and made connections. She had big-picture strategy in a way that confused others, yet here she sat dumbfounded.

The afternoon panel discussion had yet to begin. Two of the scientists on the panel sat behind name tags. After this morning's revelation that she didn't need to understand it, she just needed someone who could explain it in clear language, she'd begun to feel better. But now she was back to feeling like some wannabe poseur because "science," and "science is cool."

She felt a little ridiculous dumping her concerns on Roman, yet she knew he would understand. She trusted him. She really did, especially with this. Funny how she could admit that to herself when she was alone and nervous. She could admit Roman had her back, as it were, and it comforted her. Yet—and she knew this—if he were sitting next to her, she would have her walls of animosity up, and she would question his motives. Because the second she was around him, the back of her mind reacted as if he were Blackston, clenching and wanting to pull away.

You are messed up in the head.

Julia looked up as several more panel members stepped up on the raised platform and took their seats.

She nervously tapped her pen on the paper in front of her waiting for the session to start. Hopefully this new approach would prove to be more fruitful than any of yesterday's sessions.

The discussion began and Julia focused as different panelists, all genetic scientists, discussed various topics. Nothing made sense; everything she heard was noise and sounds. She continued to take notes as she associated letters and words to the sounds she heard. Her stomach sank, this new approach was not working.

Then she stopped. One panelist was speaking English. Clear, understandable English. It wasn't that the other panelists weren't; it was that they were using terms and jargon that Julia had a hard time remembering the meanings to. She felt like clouds cleared and rays of sunlight shone down from the heavens on this one person who made the connections between how information was stored in different gene groups and were expressed on different locations on the DNA strand. And how different gene groups associated and worked together.

Julia put her pen down and listened. Another panelist commented, and the conversation between the two made Julia feel like one spoke English and the other a foreign tongue.

She wrote his name down—Dr. Jeremy Rosemund—and she circled it several times. Every time Dr. Rosemund spoke, she drew another arrow pointing toward his name. By the end of the session Dr. Rosemund's name on Julia's notepad resembled a porcupine with hundreds of quills sticking out from it.

She would approach Dr. Rosemund at a later time during the conference; right now he was swamped. She did not want her business card to get shoved into a pocket with so many others. No, she wanted a chance to really meet and speak with him.

Julia left the panel presentation feeling good about the entire prospect for the first time since she'd begun. She didn't need to know the details of the science, she just needed to know enough, and to work with someone who explained it in understandable terms. Roman was a smart man. She could kiss him for his insight.

Julia paused. She could kiss Roman. That was not a repugnant thought. Actually kissing Roman was not a repugnant action. She recalled what it was like to press against his lips. Nice, soft, warm. Distracting. Why was she thinking about running her hands over Roman's firm anything when she should be focusing on the victory at hand, having located someone who might just be able to explain all this genomics mumbo jumbo? Julia shook her head.

No, Roman wouldn't get a kiss for this; a cup of coffee, yes. Julia was not going to let her lips get anywhere near that man.

9

Roman, unable to focus, walked through the hotel, trying to clear his head after another long conference day. He contemplated getting another drink before turning in, but knew in his current state that might not be the wisest of choices. Too many things to focus on, everything being distracted by one succulent pair of lips and large hazel eyes. Eyes that glowed amber around him. Business matters he could relegate to business hours, but Julia would not stay limited to business. He didn't want her limited to business; he wanted her in his bed. He wanted her, pure and simple. She took over his thoughts; she clouded his judgment; she messed with his senses. He would smell her and his brain would turn off as blood rushed to other body parts in anticipation of touching her. He would see her and his fingers would stop writing; instead they wanted to feel her softness, stroke her curves.

Getting women had never been a problem for him before he met Julia. Then again, Julia wasn't just any woman. She wasn't someone to conquer; she was someone to cherish. His need of her made him edgy. The physical need could be taken care of easily enough; the emotional need left him raw. Being an ass to the one he cared for the most showed his knee-jerk response to how much it scared him.

Movement, a change in the light, caught his attention. Roman's gaze was drawn upward. Julia shimmered as she leaned on the balcony above him. She watched something farther away and had not noticed him. He stared at her perfect beauty. She always commanded his attention, but something about her, relaxed and in her pajamas, shut his brain down and caused all the blood in his body to speed to his groin.

Something had spooked her in the past, but he was tired of tripping over eggshells around her. Yes, she was alpha, but so was he, damn it. She was his ideal mate, Time to stop pussyfooting around the subject and do something about it.

The room phone rang. Julia rushed from the bathroom to pick it up. Heavy breathing assaulted her ears. She slammed the receiver down and immediately called the front desk.

"Hello? Yes, this is Julia Palatine again. I'm still getting some prank phone calls, heavy breathing. Are you sure there is nothing you can do about it?"

Not pleased with being told no again, Julia grabbed a bottle of Jack Daniels from the in-room mini bar and decided to people watch from her balcony. Lights twinkled, mimicking a thousand stars over the plants of the atrium. A couple stroll past on the walkway, the woman resting her head against the man's shoulder. Julia sighed. It was a romantic setting. Perfect for a beautiful evening stroll, as if one were outdoors in the tropics without the bugs.

Love. She shook her head. Romance was so messy. Too much ego stroking, too much ego coddling. Julia wanted an equal, not someone she would lose herself to, and not someone she would constantly have to direct like a child.

Roman passed by her mind's eye. She sighed again. It was time to acknowledge what that glow was. She'd tried to ignore it; goodness knows she'd been trying for weeks. Sweeping it under the carpet as stress or needing her eyes checked. It was that "you'll know your mate when you meet him" bit of magic her mother had always told her about. But Mom had never gone into details; she must have thought she had plenty more time to explain it. Time for Julia to come to her and say, *I met a man and he glows with love.* Time to see her children married.

Julia closed her eyes and wished yet again that her parents hadn't died and were still around so that Mom could elaborate more on the whole mate-glow thing. All this time Julia had thought it was just a fairy tale Mom had told to keep her chaste. Hell, maybe if she had paid better attention, she wouldn't have wasted time or emotion on Grant. He had never glowed. Not even a little.

Did she glow for Roman? Dare she even ask? She conceded that they would be good together: an ideal power couple. But would Roman really be able to treat her as an equal? He did okay in the boardroom, but the bedroom? She shook her head. That was another issue. Emotions messed with things too much. She didn't want to make that mistake again.

But she yearned for him. She knew it. As long as he was an obnoxious flirt, she could hold her own against him. But when he stopped all that and did not put up a front, she wilted. Last night when she'd called a truce and he agreed, she hadn't realized that her resistance to him would all but disappear.

Today he had been charming, but not in a forced manner. He had been supportive without being condescending. His easy smile had set her senses all atwitter. She had lost words, and entire concepts fled her brain as she thought about kissing him. And she had thought about kissing him more than once today.

"Julia," his deep voice called to her. The sound surrounded her and brought the nerves in her skin to life.

Her gaze swept the walkway below her room. Roman stood there. She wondered if this was as disheveled as he ever got, shirtsleeves rolled up exposing his forearms, collar undone, tie gone, shirt untucked. His normally slicked-back hair mussed as if he had run his hands through it repeatedly.

She smiled down at him. The grin he returned weakened her knees.

"What light through yonder window breaks? It is the east and Julia is the sun. Arise, fair sun and kill the envious moon, who is already sick and pale with grief." Roman made a broad sweeping gesture with his arm.

Julia's smile began to hurt her cheeks; she covered her mouth, convinced she was blushing.

Roman jumped onto the walkway's railing.

"Roman!" Julia called out as he swayed, finding his balance before continuing. "You're going to get kicked out. Be careful."

"O, speak again, bright angel! For thou art as glorious to this night, being o'er my head. As is a winged messenger of heaven unto the white, upturned wondering eyes of mortals that fall back to gaze on him." As he spoke, he walked with the skill of high-wire artist along the railing's edge.

"Roman!" Julia called out again, imploring him to stop but not finding the words.

"Your line is, 'Romeo, Romeo, wherefore art thou, Romeo?' But I'll let you replace that with my name," he corrected.

"What are you doing?" she asked.

"Parkour." Roman crouched on the railing before leaping into the air. He reached out into the void with the grace of an athletic dancer. He grabbed onto a thin palm tree and let it swing him across the open space like a pole vaulter. His hand gripped the landing, and he let go of the tree. He pulled himself up using the railing before swinging a long leg over the wrought iron.

Julia gasped and stepped back as Roman joined her on her small balcony. He crowded against her, taking over her personal space.

"I've always wanted to do the balcony scene from *Romeo and Juliet*." He chuckled. "Young lovers realizing they have the world against them, but they don't care." He stepped into her, closing what little space was left between them, and slipped his arms around Julia's waist. "Deny thy father and refuse thy name," he whispered in her ear. "Or, if though not, be but sworn my love and I'll no longer be an Aventine."

"I'm pretty sure it's Capelet, or Mongue. I know that much," Julia corrected him.

"Capulet and Montague. I'm not quoting anymore, Julia." Roman's voice was soft, thick with emotion. "I'm wooing you, and I would give up my family for you."

He dipped his head down, covering her lips with his own.

Julia braced her hands against his chest; she could feel the rhythmic tattoo of his heartbeat beneath her palms. It raced as fast as hers. Roman's lips covered hers, surprising her with the fierceness of his kiss. His lips were demanding, unrelenting, claiming her own. She kissed him back with equal need. Scraping her teeth along his lower lip, plunging her tongue into his mouth, before sucking his tongue into hers. Her hands grabbed onto his shirt, pulling him closer if that were possible. Roman closed his arms around her, pressing her softness against him.

"Hello, Julia," Cindy called out as she entered their room.

Julia broke off the kiss and pushed Roman against the wall so he was hidden from Cindy's view. Her hand rested in the middle of his chest.

"I'm out here," Julia called back into the room.

Roman panted, his chest lifting against the hand Julia pressed to his chest.

"Okay, I'm gonna take a shower. You need the bathroom before I do?" Cindy asked.

Julia maintained eye contact with Roman; she knew her eyes glowed with desire as much as his eyes did. He pulled her hand up and began sucking on her fingertips, nibbling her palm. Julia closed her eyes as his lips made more than her hand tingle.

"No, I'm good," Julia called back. She looked at Roman. "Shh." She nodded her head toward her roommate.

Roman looked down from the balcony. "Meet me under the waterfall; let me continue to seduce you with words," he whispered before he leapt.

Julia gasped, watching him descend three stories to the ground floor. He landed with a crouch and a roll. His parkour skills were clearly exceptional, but a drop like that —Roman was showing off with some alpha-enhanced skills. He stood, brushed himself off, then looked up at Julia.

The fierceness of his glowing gaze made Julia's abdomen knot with anticipation. He wanted to seduce and woo her, and she was going to let him.

She turned, rushed through the room, remembering to call to Cindy that she was going out before the door closed behind her.

Curse the size of the hotel. From her balcony she was only about fifty feet from the small waterfall; from her front door it felt like miles. She ran down the long hallway to the elevators. She pushed the button; when an elevator didn't immediately appear for her, she dashed down the stairs, her feet flying until she was on the path to the waterfall. Once on the path, she slowed, mindful of her step. The aggregate pathway was rough against her bare feet. Anticipation grew as she approached the waterfall.

Roman appeared from nowhere and whisked her into a grotto behind the falls. She was in his arms with his lips covering hers again. His scent filled her; her senses reeled; they were finally getting what they wanted. Her nose breathed him in; her fingers caressed his strong muscles through the fine cotton of his shirt. Her tongue tasted him. She groaned with pleasure against his mouth.

Roman deepened the kiss, running his hands over her back and up her ribs. He paused before cupping her breast. He moaned into her mouth.

She pulled back, breaking the kiss. "I thought you were going to seduce me with words. No more Shakespeare?"

His arms still held her close. He caressed the side of her face, reaching back and pulling the hair band out of her ponytail. "I have no words for how it feels to have you in my arms. My brain can only think want, need. My tongue doesn't want to talk; it wants to taste you." Roman growled in his throat as he lowered his head for another kiss. His hand held the back of her head, buried in the thick curls of her hair.

"You want me?" Julia asked, speaking against his lips. "Then I need words of seduction."

Roman tried to kiss her again, but she pulled back. She ran her hands over his chest, feeling the firm muscles. She ran one hand over his flat stomach and down the front of his slacks, caressing his hard length under his clothes.

Roman hissed in appreciation of the stroke. "My mistress' eyes are nothing like the sun; Coral is far more red, than her lips red."

Julia continued to stroke him through his clothing.

"I can't think when you do that. I want you in my bed," Roman managed to moan.

"I don't think Shakespeare ever said that." She unzipped his fly and snaked a hand inside his trousers. Again stroking, this time only the thin cotton of his shorts separating their skin.

Roman groaned. "Words... can't... Julia."

Laughter from a group of people walking nearby stilled their movements. Julia quickly removed her hand. Roman adjusted himself, rezipping his pants. He grabbed Julia's hand and began quickly walking down the path toward the elevators. "Come on."

"Where are we going? I have a roommate, and Dante."

"He can get lost for a few hours; besides, the bedroom has a door." Roman stopped and turned to Julia. "I'm going to make love to you, then spend the rest of my life seducing you with words; forgive me if tonight I am less than eloquent."

~

The door to Roman's suite flew open. He stormed in, dragging Julia by the hand. By now she practically had to run to keep up.

"Get lost for a few hours." He growled at Dante, who lounged on the couch reading.

Dante shifted his gaze from Roman to Julia. "Only a few hours? You really think that's enough time?"

"Dante," Julia snapped.

"Well, if you're going to stay here, then—"

Julia cut him off. "I am."

Dante chuckled. "I guess I'll go find a party; there are plenty of roving hordes of bridesmaids to defile and bachelorette parties going on around here," he drawled as he put his shoes on. "Remember a condom, kids." He winked at them both as he sauntered from the room.

Roman turned a questioning glance to Julia.

"I'm covered, and neither of us gets sick, so we're good." Julia said, referring to the fact that as wolf shifters they never seemed to get ill.

"You are staying with me tonight," Roman said.

"Oh yeah?" Julia closed the distance between them, running her hands along the top edge of his waistband. "So I guess that means you should continue the seduction. Where were we?"

Roman pulled Julia into the bedroom and kicked the door closed behind him.

Julia pushed Roman backward against the bed. He sat with a thud.

"Where was I? Eyes, lips, breasts. If snow be white, why then her breasts are dun."

"I'm not sure I like this one. Dun is not an attractive color. Shouldn't you be comparing me to a summer's day?"

"Do you want high school quotes or the good stuff? It gets better, I promise."

"I want the good stuff." Julia stood in front of Roman, toying with the lower hem of her shirt. She exposed a hint of her smooth skin.

Roman continued with the sonnet.

"If hairs be wires, black wires grow on her head. I have seen roses damasked, red and white; But no such roses see I in her cheeks; And in some perfumes is there more delight Than in the breath that from my mistress reeks."

"Now you're saying I have bad breath?" Julia tugged the edge of her shirt firmly down.

Roman rushed the next lines, pausing to recite the last line slowly. "And yet by heaven, I think my love as rare, As any she belied with false compare."

Julia smiled and removed her lounge pants.

The sight of her in just a T-shirt and black panties caused Roman to hiss. He reached to unbutton his shirt.

"Uh-huh-huh," Julia chided. "That's my job. But you have to continue reciting poetry."

Roman moaned. "Vixen." His blood-starved brain searched for sonnets as his cock swelled with need.

"Or if it were, it bore not beauty's name."

Julia unbuttoned his shirt.

Roman spoke slowly, methodically. "But now is black beauty's successive heir, And beauty slandered with a bastard shame."

She removed his shirt as he continued to quote the sonnet. His words sped up as she touched him. She smoothed her hand over the tight white T-shirt he wore under his dress shirt. "Sweet beauty hath no name, no holy bower."

A quick tug and she pulled the shirt up, exposing

perfect pale abs and a broad expanse of chest. Roman paused to pull the shirt over his head before continuing. Julia's eyes flashed with a golden glow as if she were as pleased with the sight of his smooth skin as her ears were with his quotes of romantic poetry. Roman locked his gaze on Julia's before continuing. "That every tongue says beauty should look so."

Air rushed from his lungs as she pulled her shirt over her head, standing in front of him with her bare breasts exposed. Roman reached for her, barely able to control his hunger when he saw her taut brown nipples and her full round breasts. She was gorgeous. Perfect. Her skin a lush tawny tan, her coloring enhanced as she glowed with the mate aura.

Julia danced away from his reach. She trailed her finger up and down the valley between her breasts. Roman didn't know where to look—at her face with its bemused smirk, her glowing eyes that revealed her passion, her perfect body that he wanted to bury himself deep into. She was a bounty, yet she kept herself out of reach.

"More," she demanded.

"I can hardly think straight with you standing there. Can I touch you?" Roman pleaded.

"Please my ears and I'll let you please my body," Julia purred.

"As you command." Roman couldn't think of any more sonnets, so he reverted back to passages from the plays he could remember.

"Over hill, over dale, Thorough bush, thorough brier, Over park, over pale..."

Julia caressed his chest, then pushed him back so he lay against the mattress. When she began to undo his trousers, he inhaled sharply and missed large portions of the play. He skipped from one speaking part to another. Julia didn't notice. She continued to remove his clothing.

Roman's voice cracked as he attempted to recite passages from *A Midsummer Night's Dream*. Julia removed his pants; his erection sprang free. Julia was so close, and her gentle touches while removing his clothes tickled and tantalized him. He knew he was mixing up words, but he continued with as much as he could remember. When her warm mouth engulfed him, he could no longer form words. He buried his hands into the tangle of curls her hair had become.

Julia ran her tongue up the underside of Roman's thick cock. He tasted like salt and warmth and perfection. She delighted in his pale skin and pink nipples, and the pink tone of the delicate skin around his balls. She ran her hands down his firm thighs, pushing his pants off. He filled her mouth as she sucked him in. His voice continued making sounds, but the words were replaced with groans and hisses of appreciation. His hands held her head gently but with enough guiding pressure she knew he enjoyed every wet second of her lips around him.

"Julia, Julia." His voice rasped in her ears. She looked up into the piercing glow of his blue eyes. She let him pull her up his chest and to his mouth. Her panties disappeared with a hard yank, and fingers caressed her hips.

"I want to come inside of you," Roman growled into her mouth.

"Yes." She hissed as she sat up and straddled him. Their gazes locked as she impaled herself on his length. Julia lost her control as Roman began bucking thrusts into her; she grabbed his hands and held them to her breasts. She rocked and ground her hips into his as they reached a fevered pace.

Roman cried out his release. Julia grinned in triumph as she continued to ride Roman through his orgasm. She cried out her own orgasm as all her muscles seized up and she stopped moving. Roman grabbed her hips and thrust up into her as her internal muscles continued to squeeze him dry.

"You stopped reciting," Julia purred, still perched on Roman's hips.

"Lord, what fools these mortals be!" Roman drew in a ragged sigh. "I'm all out of quotes, darling; forgive me?"

She leaned down and kissed him deeply. "I think I might be the one needing forgiveness. I'm a damned fool mortal."

Roman rolled her onto her side and into his arms. "For this?" A sad tone filled his voice.

"No, for resisting you for so long." She smiled as she felt his body relax. "You are spectacular."

"Anything to please you." Roman lifted her chin to kiss her. "Anything."

Julia's head rested against his chest. Her hair cascaded over his shoulder, a fall of cool silk. Her gentle, even breaths tickled his skin. Roman traced circles on her exposed shoulder. She had proved to be the perfect lover, just as he had known she would. She had been greedy and demanding, yet sharing and giving, her body, soft and lush, responsive to his attentions.

"Can we ignore the rest of the conference and stay here, like this?" Roman asked.

"Naked, in bed, living off room service?" Julia purred.

"Sounds perfect."

Julia pushed up to look at him. "Are you a romantic, Roman?"

"Romantic, gentleman, lover. All of the above."

"I thought you were just an asshole most of the time."

"And you, my dear lady, are a cynic."

Julia lowered herself back into Roman's embrace. He sucked in a sharp breath as her hand trailed down his abdomen. She wrapped her fingers around his tumescent shaft, squeezing it back as it pulsed thicker in her grasp.

"I'm a realist, and I like to drive."

"Are you downshifting me into gear?" Roman chuckled as she toyed with his growing erection. He slid his fingers down to stroke her folds.

"I like to be in control. I like the power of a manual transmission." Julia played with him as if she were changing gears on a stick shift. "I don't have to fight for power."

"Not everything is a fight for power."

Julia's mood turned serious. Roman continued to pet her with his fingers, playing with her as she continued to fondle him.

"For me it is. Roman, I know you understand the jostling for power and authority, but at some point you are established as alpha, as boss, and it stops. For me it never stops. Especially when dealing with regular people. I constantly have to prove my worth, demonstrate my intelligence, exert my authority because I'm a woman. When was the last time you heard of a female alpha?" Julia stopped toying with his manhood.

"Well, never."

"Exactly. Have you not noticed how Van Haas always looks to you to confirm my statements?" She pulled his hand away from her.

"No, but..."

"Well start paying attention." Julia sat up, leaning over her knees.

Roman placed a hand on the small of her back. "Cindy defers to you."

"She defers to us all. She is not dominant. Men will pretend they want me in control; then they try to take over. In business"—she glanced over her shoulder at Roman—"and in bed. At some point you will try to exert dominance over me."

"Julia, I have already ceded that you are superior to me in business. I don't want to dominate you. I want you as an equal."

Julia lowered back onto her elbow, facing Roman. She traced her finger up the center of his chest, resting her fingers on his lips. "You will change your mind, and you will want me under your thumb."

Roman sucked her index finger into his mouth; he twirled his tongue around her fingertip. Julia hissed in a breath.

Roman sat up slightly, grabbing Julia and rolling her onto her back. He slid his hard length into her with a growl. "The only time I want you under me"—he pulled back before slamming his hips to hers with a forceful thrust—"is when I am driving my cock into you." He emphasized each word with a thrust.

Julia gasped as she took Roman in. She threw her head back and laughed as she counter thrust against him. "You want me on my knees in supplication."

"Only if you are in front of me with my cock in your mouth."

"You only want me as a receptacle for your lusts."

Roman's movement paused. He looked down at Julia, his

eyes blazing. He realized there was truth in her words. He needed her to know there was so much more in his need for her than merely lust.

His voice ragged with emotion, he said, "I want you, Julia. I want to be by your side. And yes, I want to make love to you. I want you on your hands and knees; I want you on your back; I want you in my mouth. I want to be in your mouth." Roman rolled onto his back, pulling her over him so that she straddled his hips.

"I want you on top; I want you from behind. I want you in every position I can have you."

She slid onto him. Roman moaned in appreciation as Julia shared her body with him again. It felt so right. The aura glow that indicated she should be his mate was not wrong. He needed to convince her of the same.

"I also need you to want me in all those ways."

Julia began rocking her hips. "You want me to do this?'

Roman groaned. "Gods yes."

Julia stopped moving. "And what if I don't want to? What if I want to be held?"

He watched her face as a tender expression crossed her features.

"Then I will hold you close and pet your back and stroke your hair." Roman trailed his fingers up her legs, then wrapped his hands around her hips.

Julia began moving again. "I can drive?"

"All you want. I'm all yours." Roman spread his arms wide.

"I like that." Julia grinned, then leaned down to suck on Roman's lower lip. She rolled off Roman. "But I think I'll let you drive this time."

Roman smirked as he shifted to the new position.

"What was that about wanting me in your mouth?" Julia crooned.

Roman chuckled; taking the hint, he adjusted himself lower between her thighs. He growled with satisfaction as he sucked at the delicate flesh between her legs. He thought she made the most delightful noises when she gave herself over to pleasure.

Pressure built in his groin as her ravaged her with his tongue and fingers. When he felt her internal muscles begin to clench and release rapidly, he replaced his fingers with his cock, deep into her, so he could enjoy her warm, wet orgasm around his shaft.

Julia bit down on a scream as she came hard around Roman's thrusting cock. Roman joined her with a roar of his own release.

Panting, he collapsed on his side so as not to crush Julia beneath him.

"Roman?"

He hummed in response, too spent to properly form words.

"I think I would like you to do that to me again."

"Give me a minute," he groaned. "I don't think I can move at the moment."

Julia laughed. "No rush, just that felt really good. I'm going to want more. A lot more."

Roman pulled her back against his chest, curling around her. "It will be my pleasure to meet your demands, but right now, I need to recharge."

Julia snuggled into Roman, content to be held by him in postcoital bliss.

~

Julia started to roll forward out of bed. Roman's strong arm gripped her tight, holding her in their warm spooning position.

"Where are you escaping to?" His warm breath caressed the side of her neck.

"Hmmm," she sighed, comfortable in his embrace. "I have to head back to my room, take a shower, get dressed. You know, all that functional morning stuff."

"It's not functional morning time. It's still early; you can stay for a bit longer."

Julia ran her hands along Roman's forearm as she snuggled against him.

"I could stay a bit longer..."

"There's a 'but' coming, isn't there?" Roman chuckled.

"Yes, but, I don't want to be seen prowling the halls in my pajamas while there are lots of people up and about. I've stayed longer than I should have."

"Nonsense, you haven't stayed long enough. Give me fifteen more minutes of you in my arms."

"I can give you fifteen minutes." Julia sighed and closed her eyes. Roman's embrace was perfectly comfortable. She actually thought she could easily stay here the entire night if it weren't for her clothes.

A deep, soothing voice rumbled near her ear. Julia squirmed her head deeper into her pillow; she was warm and comfortable and having a wonderful, sexy dream, and she did not feel like waking up just yet.

"Julia, darling, you fell back asleep."

Julia groaned. "You let me? Why didn't you wake me?'

"I feel asleep too, lambkins. I woke you when I came back around."

Julia turned in Roman's arms. Her face brushed his. Rubbing her cheek against his, she purred.

"This is nice, but did you really just call me lambkins?"

"I did." Roman smiled as her hair tickled his face. "You like it when I recite Shakespeare, remember."

"Oh, I remember." Julia's lips gently brushed Roman's nose before softly pushing against his lips.

Roman's arms wrapped tighter around her back. His hands cupped her head and neck, holding her close as he deepened the kiss.

"Do you have to leave right now?" His voice was a low grumble.

"I do."

"Then you had better stop kissing me, because"— Roman wiggled his hips closer to Julia—"I feel the need to detain you for hours and hours."

Julia giggled and squirmed away from Roman. "We have to be functional today. Remember, we are on the hunt for a geneticist we can work with."

Roman rolled onto his back and groaned.

"Yes, Ms. Palatine. You are correct. We have work to do." Roman sat up. Julia had slipped from the bed and was pulling her panties on. He hissed in appreciation of the view. "You sure I can't convince you to stay? Wilt thou leave me so unsatisfied?"

Julia finished pulling her pajamas on, then climbed onto the bed, giving Roman a quick kiss on the lips. "Not fair, I'm trying to be focused here."

"Fine. Will you meet me for breakfast?"

"Eight thirty at the coffee shop. Don't be late," Julia said.

"As you command."

Cindy looked more like a pile of blankets and empty chip bags than a sleeping person. Julia walked around to the side of her bed just to confirm that Cindy was in the pile and that she could breathe. Had the girl even noticed if Julia was gone all night? It's not that Julia cared, unless Cindy was the type to harp on her obvious absence.

Julia yawned. Her bed looked cold and uninviting. Staying in Roman's warm embrace would definitely have been the happier choice, but all her clothes and toiletries were here. She hadn't planned on spending the entire night with him, but it felt so natural.

Julia picked up the phone and ordered a coffee service and padded into the bathroom. A long hot shower would be perfect to help her get ready for the day.

Warm water ran down her bare skin—skin that still tingled from Roman's masterful touch. She began washing herself, each touch reminding her of Roman's hands. She moaned in frustration. Today is going to be a long day, she thought as she adjusted the water temperature to cold.

Julia leaned toward her reflection as she applied

mascara. Cindy hadn't stopped chattering since she woke up. Fortunately she was now in the shower, and the barrage of questions and comments had ceased, at least for the moment. If she had noticed Julia hadn't slept in her bed, she hadn't said anything, which was remarkable considering how much talking the young woman seemed to do.

The bathroom door opened. "I wish you had come dancing with me last night. The club in the hotel is really good. It was so much fun." Cindy picked up the conversation as if she hadn't stopped to breathe, let alone take a shower. "There is a group from the conference going out tonight. Apparently the hotel has a shuttle and it will take us into downtown. You want to come with me? We aren't going to have another one of those boring recap meetings you seem to like, are we? I mean, I can pretty much just give you my notes if you really want to know what they talk about in the different sessions? Please, Julia, please don't make me have to review everything after dinner."

Julia sighed; she should have stayed with Roman.

"Do we really need to go to today's session? There is a mall right over there." She pointed in the general direction of outside. "Let's go shopping instead; it will be fun. The whole point of coming to Nashville is to see the place."

"No, Cindy." Julia's voice was sharp. "The entire point of coming to Nashville was to attend a conference on genomics and to learn what we can regarding DNA and genes. You're a scientist; you're supposed to be here to help me understand what we're learning."

"Well, it's not my kind of science," Cindy whined. "Can you at least come to the sessions with me? I don't know what you want to know."

Julia had already reached her saturation point with the girl. Funny she thought of Cindy as a girl and not a professional scientist; her attitude was more like a pouty teenager. She kept her room like one, with candy wrappers and empty soda cans all over the room.

"You were highly recommended by your alpha. And that is why I am paying for you to attend this conference. You should consider behaving a little more professionally while you are here. I'm not your B-F-F for the week; we are not here to party. I'm essentially your boss for the week, and as such you need to go to the various sessions, take notes, and share what you have learned."

Cindy crossed her arms and glared at Julia.

"Maybe I wasn't clear regarding my expectations in hosting you to attend this conference. We need to learn anything and everything we can; we review the information; we refocus, narrowing in on a goal of understanding. I am here to grow my understanding of genetics and how I can approach the business of genomics to help contain information. I need your assistance in helping us determine where to target our attentions."

Cindy harrumphed. "Fine, I'll attend the sessions. But do I have to go alone? I think they are a waste of time; they are really obscure topics."

"We are all attending different sessions. Yes, some are obscure; that's what I need your help with determining." Julia didn't want to work with the young woman any more than Cindy wanted to be here. "May I suggest a compromise? You don't need to make a presentation to the entire group tonight, just me, and then you can have your evening free after that."

Julia paused with the mascara wand in her hand. She focused her eyes so as not to smudge the still damp makeup, and sighed. "I will need your session notes. And I will need you to explain them to me." Last night her notes hadn't been helpful at all, and neither had her commentary. Beyond that one little nugget regarding mobile technology the first night of the conference, as a way of connecting with people, Cindy hadn't contributed anything of value. Nothing.

Julia needed to remember to get Kathleen to arrange for Cindy to return to Toronto early. Her presence at the conference was no longer necessary and had proven to be a waste of resources.

"I can do that, but I'm still going out with that excursion to downtown tonight. Come with me. It looks like it should be a lot of fun. I'm hoping we can see some real country singers."

"I have plans." A shuttle bus full of drunken conference attendees off to have a wild touristy time was not high on her priorities list even if the promise of naked Roman in a messed-up bed wasn't the alternative. She wasn't about to tell Cindy that. Julia let her mind drift over thoughts of spending time with Roman while Cindy rambled on about activities outside of the conference that she would much rather be doing.

"Maybe your bodyguard could come. He's hot."

Julia choked on air. "My bodyguard?"

"Yeah, Dante. He's got that big sexy smile. I saw him at the nightclub last night. He's a pretty good dancer. I bet he's really good in bed."

"That's not a good idea," Julia stated.

"Why? Just because he has to work for a living doesn't make him a bad person."

Julia stopped applying her makeup and stared at Cindy, her brows pulled together in a puzzled expression. Flummoxed by the direction Cindy was taking the conversation, Julia stayed quiet.

"He probably works twice as hard as you and makes less

than half. That doesn't take away from his attractiveness. I mean, maybe for you. You don't seem to even notice all the men who are falling all over themselves every time you speak."

"Excuse me?" Julia finally asked.

"You haven't even noticed that Sholto is walking around with some kind of metaphysical hard-on for you, and Roman is always having some kind of extra paperwork for you to go over."

Julia shook her head. She did not want to think about Van Haas having any kind of hard-on. "Aventine and I are business partners on several projects. We really are going over an infinite pile of paperwork. When I said it wasn't a good idea to pursue Dante, I meant he's a bit of a dog."

"But..." Cindy began.

"But nothing. He will lure you in with big puppy dog eyes, then ditch you without a by-your-leave. I wouldn't even attempt to get his attention that way if I were you. Womanizer is spelled D-A-N-T- E."

"He just needs the right woman," Cindy purred, clearly thinking she had what it would take.

"By all means don't think you are going to be the right woman to change him; I've seen that train wreck too many times to count," Julia explained, exasperated. Cindy just wasn't cluing in. "Look, do me a favor; don't try to seduce him while he's working this conference for me. If he's interested, hook up with him afterward." She couldn't believe she was about to use his words. "Think of Dante as a service dog. You can admire him while he's at work, but it's not good form to distract or touch while he's working. Slip him your number; if he's interested, he'll come find you after the conference."

Julia looked for understanding in Cindy's eyes. When

the girl smiled, Julia knew she'd succeeded in getting Cindy to back off a bit.

"Oh, that's a good idea. Do you think he's interested?"

"No clue," Julia lied.

As soon as Julia finished with her makeup and the rest of her preparations, she slipped her feet into her shoes and picked up her case.

"Why are you off so early? Sessions don't start until after nine."

"I have a morning meeting with..." Julia paused, savoring the feel of his name on her tongue and hoping she wasn't giving away anything she felt. "Roman. I want to implement a different strategy; we'll be working that out."

"You should have told me sooner. I think I can be ready in—"

"You don't need to be there. You have your list of sessions for the day; stick to that. And we will meet up just before dinner to review your notes."

"Oh, I'll see you later then." Cindy sighed; she sounded deflated.

Julia left as Cindy flopped into her bed and buried back under her pile of covers. In the hall Julia paused to clear her mind of the incessant noise. Cindy's voice was brittle and bright and far too exuberant for Julia's nerves. No, her nerves desired the soothing tones of Roman's rumbling voice. Especially in iambic pentameter. He had been right; girls certainly do respond to words of the Shakespeare. At least she certainly had.

~

Roman sat at the cafe waiting for Julia. Two steaming cups of coffee sat on the table in front of him. Today would be a challenge in more way than one. He needed to focus on work. Yesterday he'd identified a scientist whom he thought would be beneficial to work with. Now Roman had to make a successful initial contact and establish a foundation for a working relationship. Conferences were places where networking contacts were made, yet those connections could be quite tenuous. Business cards got lost, e-mails misspelled. Roman was mostly concerned because his ability to focus on the business at hand was completely gone. Julia pervaded his entire existence. He no longer particularly cared if they succeeded in locating a geneticist who could help them navigate the ins and outs of DNA and how genes that determined ethnicity were also tied to other genes that defined shifting capabilities.

Roman didn't care. He cared that Julia glowed. He cared that her tongue took away his ability to speak. He cared about how her breasts had felt against his arm when he held her in bed this morning.

She defined beauty for him. He looked down at his hand and remembered how her hair had woven itself around his fingers.

He groaned as blood rushed to his groin. The mere thought of Julia and he was hard. Yes, today was going to be difficult. Wasn't he too old to be randomly sporting erections for pretty girls? Yet Julia wasn't any pretty girl. *My mate.* He sighed. *She's not mine yet.* He reminded himself. *No, I have to convince her to be mine, to let me be hers.*

He smiled broadly as she approached the table. Roman stood, taking her bag and holding the chair out for her. "I wasn't sure what you like for breakfast, so I didn't order, but I did get you a coffee."

"Thank you, Mr. Aventine," Julia purred. "Coffee is perfect for now."

The tone of her voice tightened his balls and made him ache for her. He leaned in and whispered as he helped to scoot her chair to the table, "If you continue to speak to me like that, there will be no breakfast. I will make a spectacle of myself by turning into a primal caveman and tossing you over my shoulder to return to my cave."

"Mr. Aventine," Julia said with a mockingly shocked tone.

"I might not make it that far. I might just take you on the table right here." He sat back in his chair.

Julia leaned across the table. "Stop being so tempting."

Roman groaned. "Tempting? Then let's take this back to my room and forget about the rest of the conference."

Julia closed her eyes. Roman couldn't help but watch as her sigh pushed her breasts against the thin fabric of her blouse.

"Conference hours are for business." Julia said.

"We're going to have to split up for the morning then. Julia, you are far too desirable, and I confess, I'd rather focus on you and your genes than anything else. You will be too distracting if we are in the same room together."

Julia laughed. "Distracting? I'm distracting?"

Roman lowered his voice. "I know how you taste, and I cannot think about anything else at the moment. With you in the room, I will remember nothing. I will count your breaths. Every time you squirm in your seat, I will wonder if you're thinking about me, and if that makes you wet."

Julia sat back; a grin spread across her lips. Roman watched a flush wash over her.

"I think that would be best then. I certainly don't want you misinterpreting the discomfort caused by sitting in a chair as arousal. However, since we are on the topic, I think you are the one who would be distracting for me. I know that you would tap your fingers or rub them together, and you would actually be thinking about touching me with them. You would be thinking about stroking my skin. You know that I would know this, and you would do it on purpose, making me desperate to be touched."

Roman closed his eyes, resting his brow against his fingers. He held his reaction in check and let out a long, steady breath. "Julia," he said, looking up at her. "We need to stop this now. I'm about to embarrass myself."

"Need a cold shower?" she teased.

"Already took one. Are you sure we should do this today?"

"Do what?"

"Attempt at being functional. I want you back in my bed with a fierceness that is hard to describe."

Julia chuckled. "We have work to do."

"Damn it, woman, do I not affect you the way you affect me?"

"Seriously, Roman, do you think I would admit to it?"

Roman leaned back and smiled wickedly.

"What?" Julia asked incredulously.

"I do." He smirked.

"You do what?"

"I affect you; you're just more focused on the conference, while I'm more focused on you."

"Roman, if I don't stay focused, nothing will get done. And we have a job to do here. So conference during the day, other pursuits during the night. Fair enough?"

"Fair enough," he agreed.

~

Julia could not find her focus. Her mind kept returning to the memories of last night, of Roman and his passionate touch. Just thinking of how he made her body tingle heated her blood. One second she was actively attempting to focus on the panel discussion; the next second she'd closed her eyes and was remembering the feel of Roman's hands caressing her skin.

He had had the better idea: stay in bed and forget all of this. Was it the smarter idea? Probably not, but it was definitely what Julia would prefer to be doing.

Julia had selected this session specifically to listen to Dr. Rosemund. Rosemund had impressed her. Would he make as much sense today as he had when she first listened to him? As soon as the session ended she should approach Rosemund, see if she could arrange a dinner or lunch during the conference. She also knew that she wouldn't.

Julia's problem was not that Rosemund wasn't speaking in terms that she understood; it was that he wasn't Roman. And right now Julia had plans for every free moment of the conference to be spent researching Roman's genetics, with her tongue. Her physical need of the man grew exponentially as the seconds ticked by.

Another panelist began a diatribe of scientific gobbledygook. Julia sighed. Rosemund added what was possibly a counterargument. And again, Julia felt lost, a feeling she did not like, yet there is was mocking her. Rosemund used words and concepts she comprehended. Hopefully he was as smart as she needed him to be.

The session dragged.

Her phone vibrated. Roman texting her.

Lunch?

She couldn't help but smile. Yes, she wanted him for lunch.

Please. She responded.

Meet at that bistro place in the garden atrium.

Julia frowned. Her idea of lunch with Roman involved room service and no clothes. Clothes were definitely required at the bistro. As the session broke up, Julia hung back and listened to a group of attendees discussing the ramifications of matching locus points in deep sequencing. For a moment she felt she understood them; they were discussing the mapping of mutations within the genome. If she was right, they were referring to being able to consistently identify a mutation in a set location in the genetics. She took quick notes with key concepts she wanted to look up later. Would wolf be considered a casual mutation? What exactly did RNA interference mean for their research? She lost the tenuous grasp she had on the concept when polymorphic nucleotides were apparently the punch line of a joke. Hopefully she could find out more from this afternoon's poster sessions, or for when she got around to speaking with Dr. Rosemund directly.

As she approached the arranged lunch location, Julia saw Roman chuckling; there was another person with him at the table. Damn and double damn.

The smile on Roman's face when he saw Julia made her tingle.

"Ms. Palatine, I'm so pleased you could join us." Roman stood, guiding Julia to her chair. "This is Dr. Rosemund; I believe you may have attended one of his panel discussions yesterday. I met him in a breakout session late yesterday."

Julia shot Roman a glare. He was at least a full step ahead of her. She sighed as she stuck her hand out to Dr. Rosemund.

"Yes, I also sat in on the panel this morning; I was

hoping to make an appointment with you. This is fortuitous that you already have met Mr. Aventine."

"I'm sorry I can't give you my entire lunch hour, but Mr. Aventine's pitch was intriguing. I look forward to learning more."

Julia smiled, relieved that Rosemund didn't expect to take up too much time.

Lunch discussion touched on the edges of Julia's and Roman's goals of acquiring labs and only hinted at the reasoning behind this new direction in their businesses.

Julia kept casting furtive glances at Roman. She wanted to ditch Rosemund and proceed with undressing Roman with more than her eyes and imagination. Roman's insistence on referring to her only as Ms. Palatine annoyed her at first; when she realized it was his form of subversive flirting, it made her squirm with arousal. The seating arrangement frustrated her; there would be no slipping her foot up his pant leg under that table.

She unbuttoned the top button on her red silk blouse, absentmindedly toying with the button. Waiting for Roman to pay the bill and ditch the doctor began to grate on her nerves. She felt raw with need. Her lust threatened to take over, leaving all decency behind. The humidity of the indoor rainforest began to wear on Julia. She watched everything through a warm-wet haze.

"Your project sounds interesting. But it strikes me more as a fairly basic research project really. Tracking a mutation is time intensive but not inherently complex. Do you really need to invest in a dedicated lab?" Rosemund asked.

"We feel the importance of this warrants such an undertaking." Julia watched Roman's lips form his answer. Julia continued eyeing Roman. She hadn't realized that when he talked business, it was a complete turn-on.

"After all, is it a simple genetic anomaly or not? The scientist who brought this to our attention, as it appears both of our families possess this mutation, believes it to be more," Roman explained.

"I wonder, why not bring this to a university research department. Why approach you?" Rosemund looked from Roman to Julia.

"Several reasons," Roman responded. "Primarily funding. As a private organization we can provide an opportunity that will allow the scientists time to focus on their research without having to write justification reports seeking out grants. The other reasons are all proprietary at the moment."

"You do understand that you can no longer patent a gene?" Rosemund asked.

Roman chuckled. Julia lost the thread of the conversation as frustration mounted in her core. Roman would not look at her; a quick glance and then his attention would land somewhere else.

"Wait." Julia's attention flashed back to Rosemund. "Repeat that please."

"It is no longer possible to patent a gene. After all, they exist in the human genome and are not designed. At least not yet. Science fiction may be making movies about genetic design and inserting engineered genes into a human for enhanced function, but we are nowhere near that level yet. Science is still working on successfully mapping the entire genome and identifying the connections within the system."

Julia deflated. "Damn, I was hoping we were going to be able to lock up some of our research that way. This is exactly why we need to bring someone like you on board. We need someone who is familiar with the business end of the science as well as the science."

"I'm not sure how much help I will be regarding the business part of things, but I can definitely help you to navigate the science." Rosemund offered a genial smile.

"If you are interested in taking this to the next level, I would like to draw up a standard nondisclosure agreement," Roman added.

Rosemund nodded. "I think that would be good. And if this is something I personally can't take on, knowing what your goals are will help me to help you find someone more suitable."

Inviting the scientist to lunch had been a good idea at the time. At least he had thought so until he saw Julia. Roman sucked back the need to drool as he watched her. The expression of raw lust on her face kicked him in the groin with how bad of an idea this lunch meeting was.

He had focused on establishing a potential business relationship. It had been hard work, especially since his brain was starved for oxygen, all blood flow in his body having redirected to his erection.

Not willing to brush Dr. Rosemund off after extending the invitation, Roman mentally reprimanded himself every time Julia directed a subtle tongue lashing in his direction.

Julia undid another button on her blouse. She already revealed more cleavage than she typically exposed. Roman's cock throbbed. Why hadn't he considered a nooner to be an option? Right. Julia had said conference during the day. But even she was acting contrary to her own directives.

He needed to get rid of Rosemund. The man was already providing valuable information. Hell, Roman hadn't been aware that Julia was entertaining pursuing patents on the genetic mutations that defined wolf shifter. It made sense; that was what she did; she protected her business interests.

Roman signaled for the check. Thank gods the doctor was only available for a short lunch.

Julia leaned in. "Mr. Aventine, I believe I left some paperwork in your suite yesterday evening. I think the notes I need for this afternoon's sessions are there." Gods, she was purring.

Roman leaned forward, placing his coffee cup down on the table, his languid motions hiding his tension and need to grab Julia and take her right now on the table. He used the change in position as an opportunity to adjust himself.

"We have plenty of time, Ms. Palatine." His slow grin added to the farce of his words. Roman toyed with Julia, wanting to see how brazen with her flirting she would get around the doctor.

She left out a small harrumph and sat back. Roman watched her delicate fingers stroke the stem of a wineglass. Did she realize how sexually blatant she was being? Did she realize he replaced the wineglass with his cock, imagining her fingers running up and down his length? He hoped Rosemund wasn't reading sexual overtones into every little thing Julia did, as he was.

Roman was distracted by how her breathing forced her breasts against the thin silk of her blouse when cold water spilled across the table and flooded onto his lap. Roman couldn't be certain if it was an innocent accident or a not so innocent attempt to get him out of his pants faster. In either case Roman silently applauded Julia for her quick thinking.

The accident gave them a perfect excuse to speed along the ending their lunch meeting. Julia's need for her paperwork was her excuse to follow the soaking wet Roman. They ended their short lunch with an agreement to meet again for a longer breakfast meeting.

~

"So, Ms. Palatine, are you expecting me to stroll slowly down the hall with a wet spot that looks like I have pissed myself, or do you expect me to toss you over my shoulder and run?"

"I really don't understand what you are insinuating, Mr. Aventine?" Julia's shorter legs moved quickly to keep up with Roman's long strides.

"Could you have been any more obvious?"

Julia laughed. "And here I thought you weren't getting the hint."

"You spilled the hint all over me. However, I did think this was a business trip. You made it fairly clear this morning that conference activities were for daylight hours."

"Potentially I could have been mistaken there."

"Ms. Palatine, I think it is most definite that you were mistaken there. This morning's sessions have been a complete and total waste of time. I could have spent my morning in more worthwhile pursuits."

"Such as?"

Roman slid the card key into the door; he held it open for Julia to pass through. She began kicking off her shoes and unbuttoning her blouse. Roman loosened his tie and unfastened his belt.

"I could have spent my time with you and not trying to focus on concepts that did not involve your breasts."

"My breasts?" Julia left a trail of clothing behind her as she made her way to the bed. "And here I thought you might be a little more interested in this." Julia slid her panties off before climbing up onto the bed on her hands and knees. She stopped and looked over her shoulder at Roman, then rotated her hips, lifting her butt high.

Roman hissed at the sight of her inviting rear. He dropped his trousers, grabbed her thighs, and pulled her back as he thrust into her.

Julia gasped as he filled her.

His large hands bit into the flesh of her legs.

"Oh, that's it, baby, nice and hard."

Roman pulled her back against his hips as he pounded into her. "You are a demanding woman."

"Some men need to be told what to do."

"Command me." Roman growled as he continued to thrust into her forcefully. He reached around and began toying with her clit, drawing circles over her peak in time with his thrusts.

Julia pushed against the mattress, forcing her hips back and up.

"More," she groaned, practically a whimper of need.

Roman sped up his tempo, increasing his drive with her demand.

Julia spasmed around him. Her arms gave way as she succumbed to the ecstasy of Roman's ministrations.

Roman pulled her tight against him as she throbbed in orgasmic delight. He reached forward and pinched her nipples through the shear fabric of her bra.

"More," Julia barely whispered, rolling over, spreading her knees in invitation.

"As you command." Roman climbed between her legs.

His mouth was hot against her skin through her bra; his teeth scraped and toyed with her nipples. Julia moaned with continued passion. "More." She thrust her hips up toward his, urging him to return to her.

Roman lifted up on his elbows; he gazed into Julia's face, her cheeks flush with excitement, her eyes glowing amber with passion. His lips in dire need of her mouth, he claimed her lips, thrusting his tongue as he thrust his cock deep into her. She cried out against his mouth, and she renewed its orgasmic convulsions.

He roared as his own release was sucked from him by her body. Roman held his hips tight against hers, waiting for his own spasms to ebb.

He collapsed on his side, pulling Julia into his embrace.

"Did that serve your purposes, Ms. Palatine?" He chuckled against her lips.

Julia smiled into his kisses. "Well served, Mr. Aventine. Well served."

"Do we have to go back to the conference? I think we both proved to ourselves it was a futile effort this morning. I know all I could think about was this." Roman's voice was thick with continued desire.

"Being half dressed in bed after a rather satisfying quickie?"

"Bed, yes, you in my arms, yes, satisfactorily making love to you, yes. Half dressed, not so much, quickie, definitely not so much." Roman let out a low, humming growl. "I would like to remove the rest of your clothes, and all of mine, and start all over again."

"How about we bow out on this evening's activities and order room service? I can be back in my room by a not so scandalous hour. And I won't have to feel guilty for kicking my cousin out all night."

"Dante is a big boy; he can take care of himself."

"Oh, what do you know that I don't? Is there something you should tell me about you and my cousin?"

"Funny, Julia." Roman sat up. He removed his tie and

finished unbuttoning his shirt. "I want you with me now. You've accepted me as your mate; we should be together."

"Whoa, whoa, whoa. Who said anything about being mates? This is fun, Roman, but…"

"No buts, Julia. We're mates. Why do you think the sex is this good? Because we should be together. We belong to each other. You have the glowing mate aura when I look at you. I know you see it when you look at me."

"Is this open for discussion?"

"Of course it is. But why fight it?"

Julia began buttoning her blouse. "I wasn't signing up for the whole mate situation when you and I started all of this." She whipped her finger around in a circle. Julia slid off the bed and began gathering her clothes.

Roman pulled off his shoes and socks.

Roman followed Julia to the bathroom. "What were you signing up for?" He stood outside the closed door as she cleaned up inside.

"A good time, a really good time," Julia called out through the door.

"Fine, then this is a good time. But it's a good time I would like to be long-term and not something for just this conference."

Julia opened the door.

"What are you saying?"

"I want a relationship with you, Julia."

"What if I'm not ready for a relationship? Relationships are messy; they mean emotions; they mean egos. You'll want to be in charge and control me." Julia turned around in the middle of the seating area. "Where the hell is my earring?"

"How many times do I have to tell you? How can I show you I don't want to control you? I want to be by your side, equals as a couple." Roman followed her back through the room as she searched for the missing earring.

He leaned over, retrieving a small glinting object from the floor. Roman took Julia's hand in his, turning her palm to faceup. "You trust me enough to share your business concerns and fears, yet"—he delicately placed the earring in the palm of her hand—"you say you don't want to be dominated, that you expect me to try to control you." As Roman spoke, he closed her fingers one at a time over the object in her palm. "I have yet to take advantage of your weaknesses, using them against you. Don't you think maybe you can trust me on this too?"

Roman held her hand, protected, in his tender grasp. Julia closed her eyes against the piercing gaze that Roman bored into her soul. She pulled her hand away from Roman's.

"Gods, you're good in bed, Roman; why can't we just be friends who scratch a need when we need scratching?"

"I need you constantly, Julia." His voice was thick with emotion.

"I don't want a relationship right now, Roman."

"And I don't want to be a tool you use for scratching an itch."

Julia looked up into his face. His normally smooth brow was furrowed, his eyes storm dark. She cupped her hand against the side of his face. "Can we please talk about this later?"

Roman held her hand against his face, leaning into it. "Yes, we can talk about this later."

Julia rushed out the door.

Roman turned, calmly walking back into his suite, before he slammed a lamp across the room in frustration.

~

Julia rushed to the elevators. Crap, what had she done? She had panicked like a fool idiot and ran out on the one man who probably would be the perfect mate for her. What was she thinking, *probably*? He was. He glowed. She knew what that meant. She wanted to ignore it and play dumb. But he glowed for her. And he just now openly admitted it, no games, no manipulations, no power struggle. Just raw emotion—and she ran like a scared rabbit.

She needed to get her head on straight. Melinda had called her on it earlier. Julia had been a hopeless romantic as a teen and young adult, but one bad relationship with Grant had given way to cynicism and taking care of urges.

What she was feeling for Roman wasn't some urge that a quick grunt and thrust would take care of. If that was all it was, she wouldn't have practically thrown herself across the table at him at lunch earlier. Gods, she hadn't even taken all her clothes off before she needed him inside her.

She should turn around and beg for forgiveness right now.

No, she needed to be strong on this one. She groaned; who was playing games now? She would give him a chance to clean up and get dressed; then she would text him. Yes, that was what she would do.

They'd already agreed to talk about it later this evening. She wasn't going to back out on that. No, what she was going to do was go shopping. She needed something a bit more seductive than the red and black separates she'd packed for this trip.

Tonight they would discuss this mate situation, start the planning process on how to proceed with a future as business partners and as lovers; then they would fall into bed and make love all night long. A perfect plan. Right now she would go to the poster session, try to get some answers regarding the connection between deep sequencing and casual mutations, see if she was on a path she should continue on. And then she would skip out early to find a dress. Fortunately there were plenty of shops in the hotel, and if that didn't work out, a mall lay just beyond the parking lot, as Cindy had pointed out earlier.

11

Julia turned, trying to look at her backside in the mirror. Not too bad, she thought. The mall had provided more than enough shopping options after she found the hotel just didn't have anything that suited her figure. She returned to her room with a selection of dresses. While trying them on, she had texted Mel photos of herself in dressing room mirrors wearing different looks. Melinda hadn't responded to any of her texts. Julia knew better than to take it personally. Mel was a working professional; there were just times, like now, when Julia needed her for fashion consultations, that she wished Mel would reply instantly.

Unable to make up her mind regarding a few of the dresses, Julia had purchased them and was now trying to decide on her own which dress was more seductive. The red wrap dress she wore accentuated her curves and was a bold statement color.

Her phone rang with Melinda's ringtone.

"Not the red dress," Mel announced.

"Why not?"

"What colors are you wearing for the conference?" Mel asked.

Confused, Julia told her that she'd packed a red, gray, and black modular wardrobe for this trip.

"That's why," Melinda announced. "We are talking about Suit Porn, right? You said you wanted something seductive for him? Well, he's seen you in red. He sees you in red all the time."

"Red's my default color."

"Exactly," Melinda explained. "You texted you needed help with something seductive—red, as your default color, is not seductive."

"Not even a hot red dress?"

"Not even a hot red dress; that only works when red is a shock of a color. You're always in red; it's not a shock. I liked the teal one; how does it make your ass look?"

"Big," Julia said with a touch of disappointment. "Body contour dresses just don't work on me; the stretchy material shows off too much of the wrong things."

"Shut up already; your butt is awesome. I bet Roman really likes your butt and would love an opportunity to ogle it and manhandle it."

Julia was uncharacteristically quiet.

"Jules." Melinda dragged out her name. "What are you not telling me? Did you finally...?"

Julia made a positive uh-hum sound.

"Gurl! Tell me—wait, no, I don't want to know, 'cause that will be awkward. Looking him in the face, knowing stuff. Okay, I do need to know. Is he as good as he looks?"

Julia twirled in a circle before flopping down on her bed. "He's better." She felt butterflies in her abdomen thinking about him.

Melinda cackled with delight at Julia's confession.

"Why do you need a seductive dress if you've already caught him?"

"I want to keep him. I want to make some effort, you know, not just assume that we're going to be together." Julia suffered pangs of guilt for having run out on Roman as soon as he said the word *relationship*. He had made her body feel so wonderful, and she had wanted to get naked and not move from his bed all afternoon, but then it all fell apart. Roman had mentioned being mates, and she panicked. There was no other word for it: sheer unadulterated panic. The look of pain on his face as she had gotten dressed to leave had broken her.

"We had sex; it's not exactly a done deal. I want to show him I'm willing for this to be more."

"Wow, Jules. What does Roman think of all that?"

"He's the one who used the word 'relationship.' I'm not one-hundred percent ready for that, but I might be ready to consider it, to move in that direction. You know what I mean?"

Melinda sighed. "Yeah, I think I do. It sounds nice, Jules. I knew you were still a romantic. You need a dress that says, all this could be yours if you play your cards right."

"Right." Julia chuckled. "I want him focusing on my assets, not my ass."

"Okay, not the first black dress, neckline too high and it looks like some weird uni-boob thing is going on in the picture you sent. What other choices are we left with?"

"I didn't get the teal one; it made my butt look huge, like a VW Bug. You said no to the red one. I didn't buy the first black one—exactly, total uni-boob. So that leaves me with the black lace one and the gold one."

"Okay, being realistic, 'cause gold can either make you look sick, or it can make you glow. How's the color?"

"I think it's okay. I didn't look sick under dressing room lights."

"Send me a picture in better lighting."

"Sure. Give me a minute; I have to change."

"Which one did you think you were going to wear?"

"The red one," Julia said flatly.

She rang off and changed dresses. The silk fabric had a warm golden hue, with a hint of hot pink shimmer woven throughout.

Julia ran her hands down the cinched waistline of the dress. The tailored bodice emphasized her breasts and narrow middle. The skirt was a slender pencil-line cut, yet the dress had a slinky shape without making Julia feel as if she wore a stretchy sausage casing of a dress.

She posed in the mirror and took a picture. A few button clicks on her phone and the image was sent to Melinda. The phone rang.

"That makes you look positively sexy in a James Bond babe kind of way," Melinda announced when Julia answered the phone.

"It is kind of giving me that bullet-boob look. I'm okay with that. And the color looks much better in this light. My skin looks amazing, and my eyes look seriously gold in this dress."

"I think that's Roman making your eyes look gold. They have that laser glow to them in your pictures. Let's talk makeup and hair."

Melinda convinced Julia she needed to play up the 1960's spy appeal of the outfit with cat-eye makeup. Her hair, they decided, needed to be big and full, allowing her natural curls to do their thing. Julia did admit, they seemed to respond well to the humid climate inside the hotel.

Julia dusted a pale shimmering gold across her eyelids

and meticulously drew a single line wing of black eyeliner across her upper lid. Hot red lipstick finished the look.

She sent another picture to Melinda.

YES! Melinda texted in reply.

She wanted Roman to see that she wasn't all business; she wanted him to see that she was willing to be a woman with him. To accept that they were mates. She could not make that commitment to herself; how was she going to convince him?

Hi, Roman, I think I might be ready to consider maybe. Seriously? She berated herself. Why was it so hard to accept that they were mates? They would be so good together. They already were, yet her fear of someone taking over, wrenching control away from her, prevented her from taking that last step.

Julia needed to stop comparing Roman to her past. If anything, he had proven above and beyond that he was not like anyone she had ever encountered before. She knew it was her baggage and hers alone that she kept overlaying on him.

So why did she expect him to try and supersede her in business and in this relationship? Was it even a relationship yet? Yes, it was; she wanted it to be. Fighting her in business was what she had come to expect from the Aventines. Maybe because she grew up with "Aventine" always being the "them" in us-against-them situations. Maybe because before they had met face-to-face, Roman Aventine had been the name on the documents when the two companies played tug-of-war games with each other over clients and commodities. Maybe because she had met with such resistance from Blackston acknowledging that she, a woman, was Morgan's second when it came to Palatine affairs. But Roman was clearly not his father. He was also not Sholto van Haas, trying to impress her with a show of impotent, slimy power. Roman had proven open to sharing concerns that impacted both of their families, hell, all shifter families.

And Roman had said all the things she needed to hear when it came to her heart. Tonight Julia needed to brush aside business and focus on emotion. Mel was right; one bad relationship did not need to ruin all chances of love for the future.

She needed to stop allowing Grant power over her life. He was gone now, had been for years; she needed to erase him fully. But he still threaded uncertainty around her soul like a virus, a virus one could never recover from but simply learned to live with. Had he damaged her so completely that even now, she doubted her ability to trust Roman?

Julia closed her eyes and focused on Grant's face in her mind. Maybe if she could conjure his image one last time, she could banish him from her thoughts. He had been lovely before his personality overwhelmed his physical beauty—thick dark hair, piercing black eyes. And a sense of mischief she first took for carefree, wild, and fun. Even though he had been almost twenty years older, he was young in mind and body. He'd had the spirit of an artist, completely unpredictable and bohemian. That was before she realized he was truly dangerous and manipulative.

She had needed his wild abandonment after the death of her parents. He had pulled her from a dark pit of despair. It took her months to realize he had only pulled her from the pan and into the fire. It had been exciting, fun, and then it had hurt. It burned. Adventure quickly turned to abuse and power struggles.

Young and not fully realized as an alpha, Julia had happily followed Grant's lead. At first it started off with suggestions. Then he grew more insistent, telling Julia that if she loved him, she would do as he asked, in everything from how she dressed to where and when she could go out on the town, when she could call him, what she was willing to do in the bedroom. He pushed her past her comfort zone. She'd actually thought he was good for her, that he was helping her to grow. He was, but not in the way she'd thought. Thank all the gods she never revealed her true nature to him. She had wanted to, wanted to share everything wonderful about the world with him. But something had kept her from confessing. He hadn't handled monthly feminine changes very well; she had suspected he wouldn't handle her shifter skills at all.

Too late, she'd put two and two together. Grant had isolated her from her family. All she knew was Grant and grad school. Julia had been convinced that neither of her siblings saw what was going on. Morgan never liked anyone she dated, especially nonshifters, so that hadn't been new. How was she to see past her own insecurities to understand that her brother had been trying to pull her from an abusive situation?

She would never forgive Grant—he could rot in hell for all she cared—but she needed to forgive herself for getting into that situation. She needed to let go of the pain and the fear. "Leave me alone, Grant. You no longer have control over me." She spoke out loud, as if releasing the thoughts and the image in her mind to the air would untangle the last threads of uncertainty from around her heart.

In the end Grant had fought her over everything, but she had been strong enough to walk away. Roman challenged her at every turn. No. Roman didn't challenge, Roman encouraged. Roman pushed. Roman accepted.

How had Julia gotten so wrapped up in her expectations of male reactions that she'd misinterpreted Roman's actions so badly? She sat on the edge of her bed thinking over all the times she'd had to deal with Roman, trying to identify one single time he had fought her for the sake of fighting her. They debated, but Roman never really forced his opinion or choices on her. He would goad her, but that may have been just to get a reaction from her when she was cold as stone toward him.

She shook her head. She had been so blind toward him; she really had. Except of course at JoJo's wedding. He had been hard to resist in that black tux. So she hadn't. She had wanted to kiss him, and she had. And he had kissed her back. Maybe it was a good thing Morgan had stumbled across them making out. She had been rapidly on track to taking Roman back to her room and having her way with him that evening. But she had run away, and yet he had continued to flirt with her, even when she was an outright bitch to him. He was never the asshole she'd called him. He'd let her drool on his shoulder while she slept on the plane, and he recited Shakespeare for her.

Relationship; that was a big word for her. That meant she trusted him. She already trusted him. They were successfully working together, so why not extend that trust into a personal sphere of influence?

Why not?

Julia got stuck on that question. She could not find an answer that stopped her. He made her stomach knot up not from dread, she realized, but from anticipation and excitement. He had followed through with his commitments. He had strength and power. He had compassion. There was no answer forthcoming for *why not?*

There were plenty of answers for why. He made her body tingle. Her lips didn't want to belong to her anymore; they wanted to be consumed by him. She felt protected in his arms while not having to give up any of her personal fortitude. He came from a strong family line; he was a success in business. He quoted Romeo and Juliet's balcony scene for her. He had blue eyes that broadcast his moods like clouds in the sky. He glowed.

And he was still willing to talk to her after she ran out on him this afternoon. Who was she kidding? Talking was not on her mind. She would see him, apologize profusely for being stupid, agree they should be in a relationship. Then beg him to make love to her again. She would be in this dress for less time than it had taken for her to get ready. Her makeup would be smeared across both their faces, and her hair would become a frizz farm. Dinner would be room service in bed. She wouldn't care as long as he agreed to wrap his arms around her again.

12

Throbbing music grew louder as they approached the nightclub. Dante trailed next to her, a self-appointed wingman. He said he was there to witness the surrender of Roman. But Julia felt she was the one surrendering. Colored lights danced across the floor of the entrance. Conference attendees packed the club. Half of everyone still had their identifying lanyards and ID badges hanging around their necks. Julia noted, based on the various levels of business dress, there were several conferences worth of people inside.

Julia paused just inside the entrance, searching for Roman. She saw him; he hadn't seen her yet. Mr. Suit Porn had not disappointed in the dressing department. There was something in the cut of his clothes—or the way he wore them—that made a suit positively the sexiest way for a man to dress. Julia realized it had more to do with the person wearing the clothes more than the actual clothes. This evening Roman wore a pale suit. Expecting him in a crisp shirt and tie, Julia sucked in her breath when she saw he wore a black shirt, unbuttoned, showing off the column of his long neck. The dark collar of his shirt framed the hollow at the base of his throat. She felt the urge to lick from that concave indent up and over his Adam's apple to his strong square jaw. Her heartbeat a little faster when she saw he had a single stem rose on the table next to him.

She waited for him to see her, to make eye contact. He stopped looking around, his gaze locked on someone or something off to her left. Julia followed his stern look to a woman in a red dress sashaying toward Roman. Julia shook her head. It had to be a coincidence; the club was crowded. The bitch in red was not walking toward Roman, and Roman was not eyeing her like a hungry kid longing after cotton candy. Julia clenched her fists and growled low in her throat when she saw the woman in red pick up the rose and apply herself to Roman like he was supposed to wear her.

Julia's vision blurred and tunneled; Roman and that woman were all she could see. She vaguely heard Dante comment something about white on rice. Julia closed her eyes and counted to four. She never made it to the intended ten. She stepped in front of Roman. The guilty expression on his face told her everything she needed to know. The relationship they were supposed to discuss was going to be a set up for how Roman would control her, what he would and wouldn't allow her to do, all while he had his cake and some cupcake on the side. He was no better than Grant. Roman was just like him.

"Roman." Julia drew out his name like an insult.

"Oh hi, you must be Roman's business associate. I'm his wife. His mother sent me down to remind him we need to start making her some grandbabies." The announcement from the bitch in red wasn't so much a statement as it was a battering ram to Julia's gut.

It became difficult to breathe. A clamp seized her chest,

and Julia's heart felt like it would pound its way out of her rib cage. "Wife?" she barely whispered.

She slowly turned around and walked out of the club before she did something she'd regret. She already had; Roman was married. She now wanted to avoid bloodshed, since the only thing she wanted to do to his neck involved ripping it out, as he had just done to her heart.

Dante caught her arm as she passed him. "Who's the blonde?"

"His wife," Julia hissed, then tore her arm away from him and left.

Roman could not believe what he was seeing. The coincidence was impossible. There was no reason for his ex-wife Britt to be in this nightclub. Something was up, and not something good. His brow furrowed as he glared at her. She slunk toward him, a walk that when he was twenty had lit his body up like a firecracker. A walk that, by the time he was twenty-one, told him she wanted something, usually money.

His skin crawled when she draped herself around him for a hug and a hello.

"What are you doing here?" he snarled.

"I was invited to come see you."

Roman started to pull her arms away from him. He froze when he saw Julia standing before him.

She was stunning, and the anger that radiated from her told him that she had just witnessed Britt's over-exuberant greeting. He was stunned senseless by the combination of the situation and Julia's beauty. Before he could say anything, Britt introduced herself "Oh hi, you must be

Roman's business associate. I'm his wife. His mother sent me down to remind him we need to start making her some grandbabies."

Julia had blanched, her glow diminished by the shock. She mumbled something and left.

"Get off," he hissed at Britt as he finally succeeded in shoving her away from him.

He turned to run after Julia, to explain. The glare Dante gave him before he turned and followed Julia was well deserved. A large hand clamped down on his shoulder and pulled him back onto his chair. Roman helplessly watched as Julia hurried away from him. Roman turned to see the hand belonged to Van Haas's man Kruger. Van Haas appeared like a cheap magician's trick.

"I think we should have a little discussion right now, Mr. Aventine." Van Haas scowled.

Van Haas held his hand out to Britt. "Miss Jackson has been telling me how the two of you were married yet never managed to make the grandchildren your parents so desired. Do you have a potency problem? Should you maybe consult a doctor?"

Britt leaned against Van Haas, toying with his lapel.

Van Haas shook his head at her. "He is your prize, not me." Van Haas looked down at his watch. "I'm giving her a ten-minute head start; then I will go be her knight in shining armor."

"What?" Roman asked incredulously.

"Ms. Palatine. Clearly she has an unfortunate misguided affection toward you. I promised Miss Jackson a good deal of money and the opportunity to reconnect with her beloved ex-husband as a way to remove you from the equation."

"Don't make me out to sound like some kind of prostitute, accepting money to flirt and seduce Roman," Britt spit.

"You're the one saying prostitute, not me." Van Haas looked down his nose at the woman. "Good night, Mr. Aventine. Kruger will see to it you stay here for a while." At those words Kruger exerted downward pressure while he squeezed Roman's shoulder.

"Miss Jackson, your services are no longer needed. I am sure you are capable of finding your own way back. I believe your return ticket is for the morning. You will understand if I do not see you off."

Britt huffed.

Roman fumed. He needed a plan. Kruger's fingers dug into his shoulder. His ex-wife lounged in the chair across from him. "Get me a drink, Roman; we really should consider that making-babies idea."

"Go away, Britt; you've already done enough damage."

Julia had to hate him. He couldn't even begin to think what she must feel like right now. The look on her face when Britt said *wife*; all the color drained from her face. She'd looked like her legs were about to go out from under her. And then she ran.

And this asshole prevented him from running after her. Van Haas thought he was going to win her affections by stepping in while he, her mate, was detained in the middle of a crowded club. Van Haas clearly counted on Roman not showing his fangs in public, but Roman couldn't think straight. His instinct was to lash out and run after his mate. She was worth fighting for; she was worth fighting with. Roman followed his instincts; he could still lash without exposing his true nature.

Roman shifted just enough to bring out his claws. He grabbed Kruger's wrist and sank one claw into the thin flesh. Simultaneously he reached behind him and grabbed the other man's crotch. Claws bit into Kruger's privates. As

Kruger collapsed into himself, Roman stood, twisting his grip and wrenching the man's reproductive organs. Kruger dropped to the floor, holding himself and moaning.

Britt began to coo something at Roman.

He growled wordlessly at her before she said anything more.

Roman was out of the club and sprinting toward Julia's room. He didn't believe for a second that Van Haas would successfully seduce her.

Dante stalked back toward Roman.

"Where is she?" Roman asked, running up to him.

Dante shoved both hands against Roman's chest. "Keep away from her."

Roman staggered back. Dante's eyes blazed with fury.

"Let me talk to her; it's not what she thinks."

"She's not going to talk to you tonight. Leave her alone."

"Fine," he barked. Roman raked his hand through his hair. He walked in a wide circle. Dante stood between him and the direction Julia had run. Roman paused, pointing his arm down the hall toward where Julia was.

"No," Dante snarled.

Roman let out a hard sigh. "Van Haas is up to something; go watch her back."

"I will as soon as I see you walk away."

Reluctantly Roman turned and slowly walked away. He turned to make sure Dante began following Julia.

Roman pulled out his cell. He texted Julia.

Not my wife.

Please talk to me.

He knew better than to berate her with texts. She would respond if she was going to respond. Anger pulled his wolf to just under the surface of his skin. Roman stalked back toward the nightclub. Britt would give him answers if he had to rip them from her throat.

He stared into the throng of the club, his control barely in check.

A light touch snaked up the middle of Roman's back.

Roman snarled. He whipped around and faced Britt. Claws extended of their own accord. He was tempted to wrap a hand around her scrawny neck while he still had opposable thumbs. Instead he wrapped a hand around her upper arm, not caring if he bruised her, and dragged her away from the noise. The laughter of drunken conference attendees kept his claws in.

"You're hurting me," Britt whined.

Roman growled. "Tell me." He tossed her away from him.

"I was paid to come make trouble," she replied in a singsong voice. She shimmied to stand in front of him before reaching out. "That was easier than I expected. Now that I see you, it's not such a bad idea. You and me."

Roman squeezed her wrists harder than necessary as he pulled her arms from him. Britt winced. Roman felt no remorse. "We"—he spat the word—"were over years ago. There is no, and will never be, a you and me."

Britt whimpered.

"How did he find you? What are you playing at?" When she didn't answer immediately, he shook her. "What was your price?"

"Some PI called me, said I had a ticket waiting to take me to Nashville. Fifty large and all I needed to do was keep you occupied for a night. If there is one thing I know, it's how to keep you occupied." She attempted to sound seductive and not fearful.

Roman was scaring her; fear rolled off her. He didn't

need a wolf's nose to smell it. "I paid you a couple of million to stay away from me."

"You know I can't do that. You're my family. I can't go out on my own and be a Smith," Britt whined.

"And that's why I tolerate you staying in Boston. No more, Britt. Stay away from me; stay away from the family. If I even catch whiff of you anywhere near me, I will have you forcibly relocated."

"Boston isn't that big of a city, Roman. We're bound to bump into—"

"The fucking country isn't big enough as far as I'm concerned. If this situation is not salvageable, I will hunt you down and make your life a living hell."

"Jeez, Roman, I just got in the middle of a date. The girl wasn't even your type really."

The squeal Britt started to make was cut off as Roman rushed her. He slammed his fists into the wall on either side of her head, caging her in between his body and the wall. To the casual observer it would look like he was leaning in for a kiss. He let his jaw lengthen and teeth grow. He snarled. "Leave while you still can."

Her eyes popped open wide with terror. Roman, realizing all his rage and murderous anger for Van Haas was directed at Britt, dropped his arms. "Go."

Britt slumped to the floor.

Julia ran back to her room. She hadn't expected to be back here until much later, if at all. Her stomach lurched as she realized that she'd had an affair with a married man. One-night stands were all fine and good, but never with a married man. Never. That was the line she would not cross.

Roman had never once indicated that he had a wife; then again she had never asked. She wanted to throw up. Not again.

A thin figure in a black suit stood outside her room. She did not have the time nor the inclination to deal with Van Haas or his bodyguards tonight. She ignored Kezzup and slid her card key into the lock.

"Mr. van Haas would like a moment of your time."

"Not tonight; Van Haas can talk to me in the morning."

A rough hand covered hers as she put her hand on the doorknob.

Julia stared at the hand covering hers. "Get your paw off me. I said not tonight," she snarled.

"I think you misunderstood; it was not a request."

Julia closed her eyes and inhaled a ragged breath through her nose. "I said no."

In a fluid motion Julia grabbed the hand that was on hers, twisting the arm up. Simultaneously she stomped back on Kezzup's instep and mule kicked him in the groin. She hit Kezzup in the elbow, forcing the arm the wrong direction. While still holding his arm, she spun and flipped him over her back.

His twisted arm still in her grasp, Julia placed the toe of her shoe on his neck and pressed down. "I said not tonight. If you ever touch me again, I will remove this arm." She yanked on the arm in emphasis.

Leaving the man in a pile on the floor, she stepped over him and into her room.

Julia walked straight to the mini bar. She emptied a small bottle down her throat before picking up the phone and directing the front desk to not allow any calls through tonight. Grabbing three more mini bottles of alcohol, she headed to the bathroom and turned on the shower.

The catch of a latch froze her in her tracks. She stepped back into the room and glared at the room door; it was still shut. She flipped the bar latch to make sure it stayed locked.

"Julia." Roman's voice was quiet and came from the opposite side of the room.

She whipped around and hurled one of the bottles at him.

He deflected it, knocking it to the floor. She grabbed several bottles of shampoo and the hair dryer and threw each of them at him. He knocked each object out of the way.

She reached down and removed a shoe, hurling it at him in a fluid move. "You're married!" she yelled.

She had forgotten to lock the patio door, never thinking that anyone would be able to get in that way, even though Roman had proven to have the physical skills necessary to make it to the balcony.

"Get out of my room," she hissed. She felt the change surge against her skin. She wanted to hide and lick her wounds, but now she was cornered, and she would fight. She threw her other shoe at him.

"Listen, please," he pleaded.

"You're married!" she screamed and lunged across the room at him.

Roman threw his arms up to protect his face, but he made no attempt to stop the pummeling as she beat fists against him. "I'm not married, Julia. I'm not married."

Julia hit him a few more times before her hands fell to her sides in drained defeat. Her body followed as she slumped against the foot of the nearest bed. Her heart hurt; her head throbbed.

"I'll give you five minutes. If I like what I hear, we can talk more. If I don't, you're gone, and you are never to attempt to talk to me again."

"I'm not married."

"Then who is that woman, and why is she here?" She felt her voice catch in her throat. She growled. She did not want Roman to see how badly this had affected her.

Roman rubbed at his forehead as if he were also developing a headache.

"I screwed up. I was married, but that was years ago. For some reason, somehow that bastard Van Haas found out about my ex-wife and had Britt flown down here. I haven't spoken to her in a long time. I had no idea or expectation that she would be here. Julia, I..."

Julia help up her hand; Roman stopped talking.

"If you didn't expect her, why did you give her that rose?" The hurt in her voice was obvious.

He shook his head. "That rose was for you. She picked it up. I didn't give it to her. What I gave her was a lot of money to not bother me or my family again. Apparently it wasn't enough. I hadn't yet had an opportunity to tell you."

"What do you mean, you hadn't had an opportunity?"

"It hadn't come up. We hadn't gotten to that point of discussing and comparing relationship horror stories from our past."

"Roman, I thought you were married."

"I know. I know."

"I never... I thought I had an affair with a married man. Do you have any idea how that made me feel? I know my past isn't perfect, but I would never..."

"I know you wouldn't, Julia. You have integrity; that's never been in doubt."

"I doubted myself."

Roman stepped to her, and she let him pull her into his embrace. "I never wanted to hurt you like this." He stroked her hair. It eased the tension and pain she felt building up her neck and across her skull. "You looked so beautiful tonight, my brain didn't know how to function. I handled that poorly."

"You said Van Haas is behind this. He had Kezzup waiting for me when I got back here. What's he up to?"

"He's into playing the power games, showing off his money, showing off his control. He must see you as some kind of prize. You know how trophy hunters want to take down the biggest, baddest, most beautiful creature. Well, you're being very alpha around him, not your typical more laid-back, easy, controlled self. I think he sees you as some big game prize, as it were. 'Look at me, big hunter alpha, I have claimed the beautiful female alpha; she follows me now.'" Roman mocked a bad accent.

"So you're telling me you don't want me for the same reasons? Hmm? You're not going to try to tame the alpha in me?"

"You are," Roman sighed, "superior to me in every way. Why would I want to cage such beauty and power?"

"I don't know, Roman; this still hurts." Julia tapped her fist against her chest.

"I understand; me too. You ran away, and I felt my lifeblood leave with you." He dipped his head to kiss her.

Julia pushed him away. "No, not yet. I'm still stuck on you being married."

"But I'm not."

"It doesn't matter, Roman. I thought you were. I thought I had done the unimaginable. I need to recover from that." She wrapped her arms around her body; she hated admitting her stupidity, even if it was in the past. "I had a relationship with a married man once. It was all my fault. At least at the time I thought it was. I was naive. And I thought he loved me. When his wife came after me and blamed me for everything, I thought she was right." Julia shifted uneasily.

"It couldn't have been your fault."

"I was raised Catholic. So yes, it was. I should have known better. I should have asked. I mean, what the hell was a man in his forties doing with some twinkie in grad school? When I confronted him, he told me I was being stupid and they were divorced. It turns out they weren't. They weren't even separated. I was subpoenaed; I had to give statements to lawyers."

"Oh, Julia."

"The whole thing was awful. Grant never had my back. I found out later he said I seduced him knowing he was married. That he was a victim of his own desires, and I was some evil agent of depraved sexual needs."

She stared at Roman, her eyes boring into him, but she couldn't see anything, couldn't see into his soul. She continued, "I don't touch married men. Ever. Not even if they are separated."

"We were married at the end of college. We were divorced less than two years later. I haven't had contact with her or even thought about her for years. I can get you the documents, or you can simply trust me."

"Trust," Julia scoffed. "I'm having some problems with that right now, okay? I don't have words for what I'm feeling, other than it hurts." She couldn't tell him she was scared. "That trust needs rebuilding and repair. It's not completely broken, but it hurts, and right now I need to decide if it's worth the pain."

"I'm worth the pain, Julia. I know you are." Roman's voice was a growl.

He lifted her with ease and settled onto the bed. Julia

burrowed into his chest, letting the sound of his heartbeat lure her to feeling protected and cared for.

"Roman, I..." She didn't know if she was ready for more at the moment.

"Let me hold you. Don't make me go away." His hand gently smoothed the hair down her shoulders. He stroked her back in long calming motions.

Quietly they lay, Roman holding Julia, her hands resting curled up against herself. Her body settled, but her brain would not. Roman had come after her, he had risked jumping to her balcony again. He hadn't even tried to stop her when she loosed her frustration and rage against him. And now he just wanted to be with her, holding her. He wasn't trying to kiss her or touch her seductively. He would never pressure her when she was feeling uncertain.

"You're not married?" she whispered with a sigh.

"No, sweetheart, I'm not." He placed a soft kiss on the top of her head.

Julia tried to rest. Being this close to Roman, feeling his warmth, being surrounded by his smell made her body want to do more than cuddle with him. Breathing him in, Julia nuzzled into his neck. She wanted to feel his strength. Her tongue flicked out, and she licked his skin. She ran her hand over his chest, feeling the shape of him under his clothes.

"Julia." His voice was ragged and raw.

She tugged his shirt from his pants and snaked her hand underneath to feel his skin, warm and smooth, against her fingertips. She pulled at the zipper to his slacks and unfastened the button, allowing room for her hand to reach in and fondle his growing desire for her.

"Julia?" He said her name again, and this time it was full of question. Did she want to do this? Did she need him? Did this mean she agreed to be his mate? Maybe the questions were all in her head.

Roman's hand that had been caressing her hair and back, slid down and cupped her ass, shifting her so her breasts pressed into him.

Julia continued moving so that she straddled him. Her lips found his. A low moan escaped her throat.

"I don't have words for you tonight other than this is where you belong. To me. With me." Roman trailed his teeth along her jaw. His hands caressed her hips and ass through the silk of the dress, working it up until he could reach the skin of her legs. He hissed when his fingers encountered the straps of stockings and a garter belt. "Oh gods, woman, you wore these?" He tugged at the straps along her legs.

"I came to surrender to you tonight." Julia sat back on her haunches, looking down at him. What was left of her lipstick was smeared across his face, and traces of tear-smudged mascara had transferred from her cheeks to his. She began unbuttoning her dress.

Roman's hands stilled hers. "Julia, there is no surrendering. You have conquered me. Does this mean you accept me for your mate?"

She traced a finger over his features. A laugh escaped her lips as he caught her finger in his teeth before he began to suck on the digit. She closed her eyes as his tongue on her finger pulled deep in her core. Her body wept with need for him. "Yes." The word was a breathy release, a sound of need and want more than a word.

Roman growled; he lifted her and flipped her onto the bed so that she was now under him. "Then let me worship you."

There were no more words as he removed his own

clothes before he began reverently removing hers. Julia hissed and moaned as his fingers grazed the skin of her thigh. Roman unclipped the first stocking and rolled it down her leg. He paused only to kiss the flesh of her knee. When his mouth sucked and licked the back of her knee, she squirmed and let out a small squeal of tickled delight. Every time Roman put his mouth on her, it made her body yearn for him more. His hands caressed down her legs after the hosiery was gone.

Julia reached for the buttons of her dress again. "No, let me." Roman knelt between her thighs. Her skirt bunched over her hips. Roman's hands caressed her midsection as he eased them toward her breasts. He skimmed over her, barely touching before he undid the buttons at the front of her dress. Julia arched her chest up toward him as he pulled the fabric open, exposing the black lace bra and her ample breasts.

The sound he made was primordial and deep in his throat as he buried his face into her softness. Julia lost her focus. Roman's mouth was consuming her, sucking on her, pulling her into him. Hot and wet, his lips surrounded a nipple that was freed from the confines of the lace. Her dress made a ripping noise as it was pulled from her. She didn't care; it had served its function. She had Roman, and he knew she was his.

His hands felt like they were everywhere before they were where she needed them most. She whimpered as his fingers found her delicate flesh and slid over her swollen clit. Fingers plunged into her depths, and she moaned out as her body began sucking on them in rhythmic desire.

"I love your sexy underwear, but I want you naked." Roman's voice was thick and gravelly with lust. He pulled back and slid her lace panties from her hips, tossing them behind him. He stared appreciatively at the garter before unclipping it. "If you want to bring me to my knees, wear one of these. I will do anything for you."

"You really want to give me that much power?" Julia twisted so Roman could unclasp and pull her bra off.

"You already have it." Roman paused to look down at her. Their eyes locked together. "You already have me."

Roman lowered himself to her and pressed his warmth against her. Julia wrapped her legs around him and cried out with a smile as he slid in where he belonged. Skin on skin, and so warm, Roman made Julia forget the world. All that mattered was right here, right now, in this bed. This was worth the messy emotions; this was worth everything.

Julia cried with release at the same time Roman exploded into her. She wanted this orgasm to last forever. She wanted Roman deep inside of her forever.

13

Julia leaned her head against the tile wall and let the water run over her. Her entire body thrummed. The intensity of last night's fight and lovemaking invigorated every cell. She let the water caress her, and she missed Roman's hands and lips.

Roman had held her and soothed her fears. The makeup sex was mind-blowing. But the hurt had been so raw. She could still feel a bit of it, dark and lurking, in the pit of her uncertainty. He'd kissed her so gently and left her to sleep alone in the early hours. She should have held him close and kept him with her. Now she knew the sense of abandonment he must have felt when she sneaked back to her room after their first night together.

They were going to have to figure out a living arrangement back home, and soon. She wasn't going to want to be without him. She understood Morgan now, and why he wanted to give up everything and go into hiding with his wife, Honey, for months on end. No distractions, just the two of them.

She didn't feel like being a professional this morning.

But being a dauntless businesswoman was who she was. Coldhearted and focused when she needed to be. She knew she had a well-earned bitch reputation in some circles, but she didn't feel like living up to that hard-ass façade anymore, at least not when doing business with Roman.

Julia delicately stepped from the shower, her body a little sore from hours of Roman's glorious lovemaking. It was probably best he had left early, they both needed to be professional today and not act like horny, hormonal, love-sick teenagers. They had compromised—work during the conference, lunches together in private, and take a few extra days when it was over to stay in bed and live off each other and room service.

She ran a towel over her hair. The hair dryer, an unlikely victim in last night's fight, had been damaged when she hurled it across the room at Roman. She smiled, glad he had come to fight her, to fight for her.

The light indicating she had messages blinked. Cindy hadn't come in last night; possibly she'd left a message on the room phone. Of course Julia had completely locked her out, and if Dante had stayed out there all night, he would have made some excuse and gotten her a room. Julia paused, a wash of embarrassment sweeping over her. If Dante had stayed outside her room playing guard all night, he certainly had to have heard an earful. He would let her know in his own snarky fashion if their performance met his approval.

Julia punched in the code to retrieve the voice mail for the room. "Hiya, Julia!" Cindy's grating voice blared through the receiver. She was having a good time from the sound of it. "You should have come, downtown was so cute! It's all old and bricks and shit. And there's a river right there. Did you know there's a river?" Julia rolled her eyes at the slurred words in Cindy's message. "I found the cutest cowboy boots. And there are some really good bars here with music. I didn't see anyone famous. I got some postcards to send home, but I'll get home before the mail does." Cindy began whispering, "I'm staying with a new friend tonight; I'm calling from his room. I'm not coming to the conference in the morning. It's stupid and boring, and I don't want you telling me what to do anymore. Okay, I'm gonna go no—" The message ended midword. Cindy probably never even tried to get in last night. Good. So she found another bed to sleep in, and she wasn't going to be attending the conference today. Damn it, in all the distraction with Roman, Julia forgot to have Kathleen make arrangements for Cindy to fly back a few days early.

Great, for someone who was highly recommended as being a good asset for the endeavor, she had been disappointing. Julia pressed delete. She would need to call the alpha from Toronto. Julia wasn't Cindy's babysitter, and from a business standpoint, her manager, her alpha, should know about her performance. It reflected back on him rather poorly, especially considering she was here on Julia's dime based on his referral.

Breathing, heavy breathing. Julia slammed down the receiver. She was tired of the hotel not doing anything about the prank calls. They'd evolved from creepy to annoying. She picked up the phone to retrieve the rest of her messages and to make sure she deleted the most recent breathing call.

Dante stood, bodyguard cool in his black suit, just in front of her door, waiting for when she stepped into the hall. The smirk on his face told her he had heard plenty last night. Julia held up her hand, indicating she didn't want to talk about it, at least not with him. She had an appointment with Dr. Rosemund, a confrontation with Van Haas, and she wanted to find Roman. She wanted to be done with this conference and its genetics so she could focus on Roman and his.

~

"Dr. Rosemund." Julia approached the scientist, extending her hand. "I'm glad you could meet for breakfast."

Rosemund shook the offered hand.

"I'm sorry our lunch was so short, clumsy of me to have spilled my water all over everything. I know we won't even begin to come close to tackling what we need to discuss this morning. Can we set up some more extensive meetings over the next few weeks? Your ability to communicate the concepts surrounding genetics is impressive. I hate to admit it, but I feel as if I have been running to catch up when it comes to all the scientific terminology."

"I should be able to fit in a phone conversation here and there. I won't be available for a few weeks to do any traveling. What kind of consulting are we talking about exactly?" Rosemund asked.

"As mentioned yesterday, we are looking to acquire genetics labs as part of an expansion for a joint project between our families' businesses. Think of it as genealogy taken to an extreme and obsessive level."

"I haven't signed any nondisclosure agreements. Mr. Aventine mentioned those yesterday. Are you okay with continuing this conversation?" Rosemund asked.

"We aren't going to delve too deeply into those areas this morning; at least I don't think we will. But honestly, do you need to sign a piece of paper in order for us to have a confidential discussion?" Julia asked.

"Of course not. Based on what you told me yesterday, it

sounds like you want to be able to track a common anomaly that both families share back to a point of origin. Is that correct?"

Julia nodded. "That's just part of it. We are also interested in being able to use the genetic information to track down extended family throughout the world. Personally I wouldn't mind dispelling some family myths along the way, but I doubt we'll ever be able to track our family back thousands of years."

"You mean your family's genetic routes and origins?" Rosemund asked. "There are a couple of ways we can do that. We can track through the study of mitochondrial haplogroups. Haplogroups are matrilineal, meaning they are passed through the mother, which can make family origins a little messy, since for so many centuries western cultural norms were patrilineal." Rosemund nodded. "Tricky but not impossible. We can also do something similar and track the male heritage through the Y-chromosome."

Julia sat back. Haplogroups? Where had she heard that before, and why was she thinking that the term was not pertinent? She bit her lip, thinking. She had felt that she had finally hit the groove with deep sequencing, and now it sounded like she had been completely off.

"Dr. Rosemund, haplogroups, they are from a specific type of DNA, right?" She pointed to her head. "I'm thinking I've heard this before, but that it wasn't relevant. Or I was told it wasn't."

"Oh no, based on what you're telling me, mitochondrial haplogroup identification is definitely something you're going to want to look at. You see, they help to identify time and location of the DNA's origins. We can track migration patterns. Did you not attend the session I gave the other morning?"

"No, ah." Julia realized that Cindy had been the one to attend that session, and she had reported it as interesting but not relevant. "I'm not sure how much Mr. Aventine explained before I joined you yesterday. The acquisition of having access to research is vitally important. We are trying to gather as much information as we can so we know in what areas we need to focus. We invited a few associates with us to divide and conquer, as it were, so that we could maximize session attendance and compare notes, to help us determine in which areas we should be focusing. I think the information from that session was a bit beyond my associate who did attend." It shouldn't have been, not if Dr. Rosemund was the one presenting. Cindy should have made the connection between haplogroups and the need to track lineage if she had actually attended that session, and if she had paid attention. Wouldn't she? Frustration bubbled up more and more in Julia regarding Cindy Science.

"I am sorry to hear that. I presented it in the most understandable language I could. I'm not a fan of using obscure terminology. But just because I can understand it does not mean everyone can."

Julia nodded. "That, Dr. Rosemund, is precisely why I want us to talk more extensively. Screw it, I'm going to go ahead and ask if you are open to consultation work. So far you have been able to distill the information into terms I can readily grasp. I am not a stupid woman, but to be fair, genomic concepts are just not something my brain is easily wrapping itself around. I would like to bring you in."

Rosemund smiled; their waitress interrupted to take their breakfast order.

"Getting back to this haplogroup thing. We would be able to track migration patterns?" Julia asked.

"Yes, but only of the mother's line. And there is some genetic tracking we can do from the Y-chromosome—completely different from the haplogroup tracking. Of course, being female you don't have a Y-chromosome. We could compare and track similarities and patterns between the two sets of data from you and Mr. Aventine. Do you have any brothers, Ms. Palatine?"

Julia shifted in her chair, leaning in; this information was exactly what she was looking for. "Yes, I have a brother. And I have male cousins."

Dr. Rosemund rubbed his jaw. "It could be interesting. But you are interested in more than just tracking the movement of your ancestors? You want information on the mutation itself, right?"

Finally, for the first time in days Julia actually felt like she was understanding the connections she needed. "Right, we know about a marker in one location, but my understanding is there are frequently related genes in other locations, and we need to identify those. From what I've been picking up, I think we need to also consider deep sequencing?"

"You're talking about linkage disequilibrium."

"Am I?"

Rosemund nodded. "Yes, you are. That's when two genes, in different loci, excuse me, different areas in the genome, are associated together. They are not necessarily in close approximation, and they don't necessarily appear at first to be related, but there is some genetic linkage between them."

Julia felt her brows creeping toward each other as she

focused on understanding his words. "Can you give me an example? I think I get what you are saying."

"Of course. Um, probably the most simple is the correlation between certain skin, hair, and eye colors with different health concerns. Do you know any redheads? They tend to have sensitivities to opioid drugs. For years that correlation had only anecdotal evidence to support it, but now we have identifiable genomic data regarding the gene MC1R."

Julia nodded slowly as the connections in her brain were plugging in together. "Why can't they just say that? Instead it's all values of R to the second power, and decay rates of frequencies. N sample group equals pi to the V X, what the hell? As soon as I think I understand, the conversation takes a left and I'm lost again." She chuckled at her own inability to keep up.

"Oh, I fully understand. I work with this stuff every day, all day. They are concepts that come easily to me, but please don't ask me to explain the stock market. We all have specialties for a reason. It's what makes a dancer so wonderful to watch, and how a singer can bring tears to our eyes. It would be a dull world indeed if we were all the same."

Julia actually felt like smiling; yes, this man understood, and he spoke her language, as it were. She wished Roman were here. This was the information she felt they needed to proceed. She grinned inwardly when he asked if Roman would continue to be involved. Julia had to admit, she did not know to what extent, but he would be involved. They made arrangements to have additional extended discussions over the phone, exchanging numbers, so that they could coordinate for in-person meetings that would fit both of their schedules.

14

Julia stared at the laptop monitor. Every time she began to strategize how to move forward with Rosemund, her attention drifted. She couldn't focus. All she could think about was that she had let Roman seduce her and it had been gloriously wonderful. And now she needed to focus on business these genetic concepts were finally clicking together.

She slammed the laptop shut and placed her forehead against the smooth surface. Slowly she bumped her head against the computer.

"Damn, damn, damn."

Recovering her composure, she sat upright and looked to make sure no one had noticed her. Not many people were around, and every single one of them seemed to have their nose in their phone. Including Dante, who was supposed to be acting as bodyguard.

She opened the computer and double clicked her e-mail icon. Julia quickly sorted and trashed the messages she had no use for this morning.

Kathleen, precise as always, had prioritized the messages she sent. One red flag.

Julia clicked it open. The message was simple: the alpha in Canada was concerned about something, please call him, and his phone number was listed.

Nothing else, and no reason beyond "concerned."

She continued to check her messages. Several from her agent regarding a lab in central California that was looking for a buyer. Julia quickly typed out a response directing her agent to send more details and numbers.

Julia didn't recognize the e-mail as being from the alpha in Canada when she clicked it open. It was a simple request: *please have Dr. Cynthia Kimbro check in; her parents are concerned.*

Julia shook her head. That seemed to fit the character of the young woman she was rooming with. A little excited by everything shiny and new, her first big trip on her own, and she forgot to check in.

Julia typed out a quick response: she would remind Cindy the next time she saw her.

"Well, that's done," she said out loud. She had to focus to stay out of her own head this morning. Every time she started to quietly think, she thought about Roman. She missed his comfort, and that opened a crack for doubt to seep back in. He had felt so good to her heart, she had been ready to discuss a relationship, and yet...

He said he wasn't married. Julia focused her breathing, concentrating on not crying. Crying was for wimps, not for queen Bs or alphas. But damn it hurt. She had to admit it; she was emotionally involved, but would Roman still be? That tiny pit of dark despair attempted to surge back to life. Of course Roman was still involved; she needed to trust.

Her phone buzzed.

That guy from Toronto insists on speaking with you. Been calling all morning.

Julia frowned at the text message from Kathleen. She didn't want to talk to Meyers; she wanted to talk to Roman.

What's his number?

Julia tapped the illuminated digits of the phone number Kathleen texted. A call window launched on her cell phone.

Julia listened carefully to the voice-mail greeting.

At the sound of the beep, she left her name and number.

If this was because Cindy hadn't called her mother the night before, Julia was going to be more than a bit annoyed. She wasn't the girl's babysitter, and she had not agreed to be anyone's chaperone. If this became an issue between the two families, hers and the Canadians, well, she was not against having to travel internationally to put them in their place. Julia chuckled. Yeah. Right. She was not going to go to Canada and have a smackdown of epic proportions. She would be terse and authoritative in a conference call. Kicking butts and taking names would be delegated to Dante or Shane. This was not a situation that would warrant such extreme behaviors.

Her phone rang; it was the number she had just dialed. Ah, he called her back.

"This is Julia," she answered sharply.

"Ms. Palatine?" the male voice on the other end asked.

"Yes, how can I help you?"

"This is Jeffrey Meyers," the voice introduced himself.

"Yes, hello," Julia said, letting the tone of her voice warm up and become more friendly.

"Cynthia Kimbro hasn't checked in since she left for the conference. Her parents are worried. She is their caretaker and typically checks in with them frequently."

"Well, no one told me I was going to have to remind her to call in. She should be expected to take care of that on her own," Julia explained, not hiding her contempt for the situation.

"Is she nearby right now? Could I possibly talk to her?"

"I haven't seen her this morning. I really can't be responsible for the girl."

"That's a bit derogatory, don't you think? I would expect a professional in this day and age to use less pejorative terms." Meyers's tone became terse.

"I hardly think calling her a girl is derogatory; it's hard to think of her as a young woman with her behaviors. She is substantially younger than I was led to believe. She is too young and irresponsible to have made this trip on her own. Especially without having warned me or requested that I act as a chaperone."

"Young? I wouldn't say Dr. Kimbro"—there was a distinct edge to Meyers's voice as he enunciated the word *doctor*— "is old by any means, but she is hardly a young woman."

"Did you just say 'doctor'? Are you sure about that? Cindy is barely old enough to be out of college. Unless she's some protégé, there is no way she is a doctor. You said she was a scientist with an active professional interest in genetics. As an alpha, I trusted your word. I will take the responsibility of not vetting her properly for this conference, but beyond that..." Julia paused. "That's on you, for sending me an unqualified individual. I expected that she would have a better grasp on the concepts being discussed here, and she clearly does not. She barely seems to grasp basic science." Julia no longer controlled the anger in her voice.

"I'm finding this hard to believe. Dr. Kimbro is a very smart woman; she indicated to me that she already had a foundational understanding of genetics as it applies to her work in pharmaceuticals and that this would be an excellent opportunity to not only learn more about the subject, but to meet more like us and to be able to contribute to something that could really help our kind."

"That is what you told me." Julia slowly shook her head side to side. "But that is very much not how she is behaving here. She is barely interested in the conference itself, other than the party opportunities. I doubt she can even spell 'pharmaceutical.' She has complained about pretty much every meeting we have had to discuss how we are going to take and use this information. She contributes nothing. No, I take that back. She was able to contribute something regarding mobile computing for education, something she said her sister was currently studying. Now if her sis—"

"Ms. Palatine," Meyers interrupted. "Dr. Kimbro doesn't have a sister."

"It sounds like we are talking about two different Cindy Kimbros then," Julia scoffed.

"What's the saying? 'When you eliminate the impossible, whatever remains, however improbable, must be the truth.' Would you please describe the woman at the conference with you?" Meyers's voice was low, and he formed the words slowly.

"Like I said, she's young, early twenties, not yet twenty-five. Tall, thin, lanky hair. Wears clothes that don't fit her particularly well."

"Lanky hair? I can't say I've heard it called that before. What color did you say her hair is?"

"You've not heard 'lanky' before? Long and stringy, straight, and it looks like it needs to be washed, even after she's just finished washing it. I'd say its dark blond, you might call it light brown."

"Ms. Palatine, Dr. Cynthia Kimbro is a black woman in her later forties. Her hair has always been black since I've known her."

"Shit," Julia spit.

"I would have probably used something stronger than 'shit,' Ms. Palatine."

Julia began thinking out loud. "We have a very serious problem, don't we? I think you might need to fly down here as soon as possible. We need to identify this young woman, since she is clearly not Cynthia Kimbro. And we need to find out where the real Cynthia Kimbro is currently located."

"I have to agree."

"This falls straight into one of those situations we discussed the other night, policing our own versus when to call in the outside authorities. Especially if at any time we think DNA is going to be used as evidence. Please tell me you have investigators who can start tracing Dr. Kimbro's actions. Let's see if she ever made it out of Canada. I have someone here who I can start looking into who arrived at the airport under her name. Hopefully we can find out who this impostor is and why she is here. And..."

"Hopefully we can find Dr. Kimbro alive," Meyers finished her thought.

"Looks like we have work to do. I'll call you back." Julia ended the call. Damn, damn, damn. Shit and damn. Julia wasn't going to be able to leave the conference just yet. She swiveled in her chair. Dante leaned on a column a few feet behind her.

"We have trouble, Cousin," she said.

Dante stood up. "Trouble, sounds like fun." He stepped over to Julia, an expectant look on his face.

"Sit. Looks like it's time for you get chummy with Cindy Science."

Dante grimaced. "Too late, I saw her all friendly like with Kezzup last night. They were both drunk; I could smell the booze stench they left in their wake. He was so out of it, she was was supporting him as they staggered down the hall."

15

Today turned out to be nothing more than back-to-back meetings and putting out fires. She wanted to be done with all of this, and karma laughed and finally put all the pieces in place. The science was clicking, and Roman had clicked. It was amazing how much stress she didn't feel now that she had acknowledged he was her mate. But he was still frustrating, now that she wanted to be surrounded by him, he was all business and off at the conference networking.

She approached Van Haas; a bottle of wine with two glasses sat on the table in front of him. Julia eyed the bottle of wine. Something was off; this didn't feel like business.

"I had much preferred for us to meet last night," Van Haas said, pouring the wine.

"Are you planning on explaining what that was about? I'm not exactly sure I want to listen to anything you might have to say until I understand this. Oh, and educate your men never to touch me," Julia snapped. She had agreed to meet Van Haas earlier for a brief meeting. She was angry about his interference in her life, this wasn't a business lunch set up and the information surrounding Cindy had her on edge.

"What do you mean, not to touch you?" Van Haas asked, seeming confused.

"Just that. I defeated him rather humiliatingly. I really couldn't be bothered to find out how much damage was inflicted." Julia drained her glass.

"Kezzup is a strong man. I'm sure you didn't harm him." Van Haas's tone dripped with oily condemnation.

"Kezzup may be a strong man, but he is a man who does not know how to access his wolf without fully shifting. And he is a stupid man to ever touch a woman without her consent, and a more stupid wolf for not recognizing an alpha." Julia's patience for Van Haas had already evaporated. Roman had said Van Haas was interested in her because she had constantly been in high-bitch mode. That would explain the wine.

Van Haas chuckled. "That might be why he disappeared on me last night. Lying low to lick his wounds. Of course at the time I thought he had just decided to go off with the girl, to ensure she was out of our way. Your man said you were not to be disturbed and that he had not seen Kezzup at all."

"Does Kezzup have something going on with Cindy?"

"I believe so. Kruger reported that she was trying to get with all of the men. Kezzup, he is not as well disciplined when it comes to these matters. I believe she was with him two nights ago, I assumed last night as well," Van Haas explained.

"That might be a problem. It seems the Cindy Kimbro we have here is not the same woman whom the Meyers's alpha from Canada sent down to us. Dante is currently checking a few things out, seeing if he can dig anything up at the airport. Any information we can get out of Kezzup would be helpful."

"Fine, I'll send Kruger." Van Haas flicked his finger, and Kruger was by his shoulder. The men exchanged a few words before Kruger nodded, then left. "That's better; I prefer to be alone while we discuss matters."

Julia closed her eyes. Alone. Damn it. She should have known better.

"Now about this female alpha nonsense. We both know—"

Julia let her face transform instantly. Her brow thickened, her jaw and teeth elongating. It was not a visage of beauty but of terror as her human features quickly morphed to a snarling wolf, then back again. "We both know just how rare it is and can appreciate it for what it's worth. If you ever nonsense me again, you will find out just how dominant I am. Now continue while I still have the patience to listen to you."

Van Haas's face blanched, then blushed a ruddy hue as shock, then embarrassment crossed his features. "Ms. Palatine, Julia." Van Haas's voice dropped when he said her name. "I am in a position of great power and wealth. I have extensive lands and many people follow me within my organization. You are too lovely and should not be expected to participate in the masculine world of business, you—"

"I am going to stop you right there, before you say any more that you will regret. I do not know the feminist climate of South Africa, but I can tell you right now, since you are dealing with a woman in business, that you will never get anywhere by telling a woman she should or should not do something."

"Forget I said anything about business." Van Haas waved his hand dismissively. "I am leaving here soon. We have not had any time to be alone together. I would just like to spend some time with you. You invited me here. And it's been all business and genetics the entire time."

"Because I invited you to a genetics conference."

"Yes, well, you invited me, and I came. You have spent too much of my time with other people. I think we should return to my suite and..."

Julia held up her hands in front of her, stopping Van Haas from continuing. "No. Clearly you are misunderstanding." This explained his oily demeanor when the others weren't around. "I am not... no." She let out a breath. "I don't want to assume anything; however I have a very strong feeling that you are about to make a claim with emotional expectations. I am not, I have not done anything that should warrant these expectations from you."

"You invited me."

"I also invited the alpha of the Meyers family in Canada. They sent Cindy as their representative regarding our situation."

"You would love South Africa; it is very much like your Northern California. Don't discount me so readily, Julia. My head was not so easily turned by you, and I won't be so easily dissuaded."

"I'm not discounting you, Mr. van Haas. I am saying no."

"Sholto," he cut in.

"Mr. van Haas, what part of 'no' are you missing?"

"I would think you could at least give me the same consideration you have been giving Aventine," Van Haas countered.

"You are out of line." Had Van Haas figured out that she had started an affair with Roman, or was he trying to weasel in and start one of his own? "Aventine Industries is actively partnering with my company in this. I do not need to explain myself to you. But you do need to explain why you paid his ex-wife to show up uninvited."

Julia stood, glaring at Van Haas. When he didn't speak she started to walk past him.

"I don't know what you are insinuating about my actions regarding last night." He grabbed her arm, stopping her exit. "Two can play this game, Julia."

"Remove your hand immediately, or I will remove it for you," Julia growled. She let her teeth elongate. She wrenched her arm away from his grasp. "You shouldn't lie, Sholto; it's not becoming of an alpha. I did more than kick your man in the balls last night. I'm sure he won't bother to tell you the details. After all, alpha or not, getting dropped by a woman is always hard on you men. When Kruger finds him, ask him how his shoulder is feeling. I'm sure once he got it relocated, it stopped hurting him considerably."

Julia stopped as they made eye contact. Her smile was electrical, lighting his entire body up. He crossed the atrium to her; his own smile felt as if it would break his face. He couldn't remember a time he had been happier.

"Where have you been?" Her voice quavered. She couldn't still be shook up over the fight last night? Or maybe the meeting with Van Haas had unnerved her. Roman knew if it was him and his voice was shaking like that, it would be because he was a Julia junky desperate for a fix.

"Divide and conquer. I had a breakfast meeting with a Dr. Fredrick. That's why I left you to deal with Rosemund."

"And Van Haas." She let out a heavy, ragged sigh. "Was yours a successful meeting?"

Roman took that as a sign and enfolded her in his arms.

"Not particularly. I should have come back for you after breakfast. I thought staying away would be easier for focusing."

"Are we okay?" She looked up at him, and he was overcome with the need to kiss her. Her lips were warm and soft and welcoming to his.

When the kiss ended, Roman gazed into her eyes. He could live there forever, in the hazel depths. "Haply I think on thee, and then my state, like to the lark at break of day arising, from sullen earth, sings hymns at heaven's gate; for thy sweet love remember'd such wealth brings, that then I scorn to change my state with kings."

"Are you trying to seduce me?" Her voice was a tinkling giggle that shot straight to his groin.

"Always, yes." He chuckled. "What are you doing for the rest of the day? I want to show you how all right we really are."

"That sounds glorious." She smiled.

"Don't say it; I can hear the 'but' in your voice."

Julia grimaced. "Uh huh. There's a 'but.' We have a problem with Cindy. Not only has she hooked up with Van Haas's man, Kezzup, she's not who she says she is."

"I don't see the problem with her getting together with that man. They are adults; that's between the two of them."

"That's not the real problem. We don't know who she is exactly. Meyers has got his people looking for the real Dr. Cynthia Kimbro. We need to find this chick and find out who she is and why she's here."

"Damn. Have you looked through her bags? Maybe she left her ID or passport. If she flew in from Canada, she'll have a passport."

Julia kissed him. "Smart man."

Roman wanted her lips again. He didn't feel very smart

right now. Julia was going to leave him to track down information on Cindy and send him away again.

"Kiss me before you send me out into the trenches."

"You don't mind that people might see?" Julia asked, twisting his tie around her fingers. Did she know she had him wound up like that?

"I'm all for public displays of affection, but you have a cold exterior facade to maintain, Ms. Palatine." He smirked.

She huffed at him. "There you go talking all hot and dirty, Mr. Aventine." She stopped toying with his clothes. "I like this, Roman. I like this a lot."

He cocked an eyebrow up.

"Knowing where we are with each other. Knowing where we will end up tonight. Thank you."

"For what exactly?"

"Not giving up on me." Julia looked up at him through her lashes. Roman's cock kicked into gear as blood left his brain.

He growled in response and crushed her to him. Public displays be damned. His lips bruised hers. His tongue twined and danced with hers. They consumed each other.

"You sure we don't have time for a quickie?" he asked as his lips left hers.

Julia shook her head. "I think we need to find out what the hell is going on. Would you head up to Van Haas's suite and see if Kruger has found anything out? I'll go see what I can find out about Cindy Lu whoever the fuck she is."

"I'd rather beat the shit out of him for last night." He smiled at the glare Julia leveled at him. "But I'm the bigger alpha and the better man. I will go find out what they know. Meet me at the coffee shop in an hour?"

"Yeah, I'm going to head over to the Delta Atrium when I'm done. I thought I saw a small raggedy wolf down there the other morning. Maybe I can poke around and see if I can find any trace of it. I bet that was Cindy Science not knowing what to make of herself."

~

Julia stalked back toward her room. Her phone was low on charge, and her backup battery pack was not in her bag. She just hoped she could find it before her phone died. She needed Dante to get back to her on what he'd found by now. She hoped Roman would be a little uncivil. Who was she kidding? He would be the epitome of civility. Van Haas would grovel, begging for forgiveness. Roman's diplomacy was that good. She smiled. It had worked on her, hadn't it?

She needed Kathleen to follow up with Meyers and his timetable to get here. She also needed Kathleen to follow up and get Rosemund to California as soon as he was available. She did not want to lose traction on the genetic situation.

She felt as if she had really dropped the ball big-time. She should have taken more time to vet Dr. Kimbro, at least spoken to her once on the phone. She had flown Cindy down and shared a room with an unknown. *Sloppy work, Palatine. Sloppy work.* She had been raised to trust the word of an alpha. Then again, she had been raised around trustworthy men. She needed to do better.

She fumbled for her card key, finally managing to get the door to open.

Cindy's bed was an unmade mess. The maids weren't allowed to do anything to it while personal items remained on top. The bed Julia and Roman had nearly broken in their enthusiasm was neat and tidy. Julia grinned; she looked forward to messing up his bed tonight.

Where to begin? There was no way to tell from the mess

if Cindy had been back to the room or not. Her suitcase, more of a duffel bag, spilled across the pile of blankets. Julia lifted the case and checked the central compartment. Nothing.

After unzipping several side compartments, she found what she was looking for. A boarding pass and a passport. The ticket said Kimbro, the passport said Cartwright, same first name. How the hell did that work? Airport security wouldn't let her travel if her documents didn't match. She kept rummaging. An envelope revealed how that had happened. Julia unfolded a marriage certificate. It looked official. Whoever had done the forgery was a professional. It couldn't be real, but it did look like a government document indicating that Cynthia Meyers Cartwright recently became Mrs. Cynthia Kimbro. With it slipped out two IDs. One, old and beat up, with the Cartwright name, and a shiny new ID for Cynthia Kimbro. That was probably enough documentation to get her from Canada into the United States. Hell, it wasn't that long ago that travel between the two countries hadn't required any papers.

Julia slid the papers into her purse. She needed to call the Meyers alpha and find out exactly what Cindy Science's relationship to him was.

She continued to poke through pockets. Julia tossed aside a sheaf of e-mail printouts. A quick glance and she dismissed them as nothing as soon as she saw the series of emojis on the page. Sitting on the edge of the bed, she glared at the items she had pulled out of the bag. Was there a connection here she was missing?

The folded and wadded-up papers fell to the floor when she stood. Julia bent over and retrieved them. A set of highlights caught her attention. These were not the stupid nothings of a simpering fool.

"Fuck." Julia sat heavily on her bed. The top two pages were kissy-faced and full of emojis and flirtatious words, what she expected from Cindy. The rest were printouts of transcribed telephone conversations. Julia's telephone conversations. Highlighted and commented on. This wad of papers only revealed a few recent conversations. There had to be more.

Julia tossed the blankets aside, unearthing the backpack Cindy had been carrying. More printouts, some going as far back as...

Morgan had been right; someone was watching her. And Roman.

Julia spread the papers out on the floor. To her right the conversations with Meyers, to the left conversations with Roman. Discussions over acquiring a lab were circled with comments such as *Let Lordship know* and *Does this mean what I think it does?* The tap was on her business line. Julia stared wide-eyed at the documents; who else had they listened in on?

The notes next to the other highlights included everything from instructions on what to do with the information, to descriptions of her and Roman. Several of Julia's conversations with the Meyers's alpha were heavily noted. Someone had pressed hard with a pen, tearing through paper as they developed a plan to get Cindy here. Julia flipped the page over, reading the scrawled notes across the back of the page. Julia had provided an opening; all they needed was to find someone in Canada to take this on if the Kimbro woman wouldn't.

Who wrote these notes? Julia sniffed the papers. She wrinkled her nose and flinched. The paper was soaked in the smell of stale pot. She would never get any identifying scent from them.

Julia continued to read from the notes. This had to do with Lazarus. The timing was too close to when Morgan had been kidnapped, and the focus too tight on Roman not to be the threat against him. Julia laughed at one note, *She hates him. Perfect opportunity.* Julia far from hated Roman, but perfect opportunity for what?

Was her cell phone clean?

Julia picked up the room phone and began to dial; she needed Kathleen to have the office swept immediately. She needed—

She stopped. How would she know this phone wasn't compromised? Dante would be able to figure it out, but she couldn't call him just in case her cell was.

Julia began placing the pages in chronological order with the most recent one on top. The stupid emojis. Whoever this was, they had seduced Cindy. The top page said, *See you there, love bites.*

Did that mean they were here?

If Cindy was that wolf... and the hotel was sold out... that would mean they had a place to hide.

Julia began her mental list: Find Roman. Do they know where Kezzup and Cindy are? Have Dante sweep the room for bugs and check her cell. Call Kathleen, not from the room phone; have her do the same at the office. Follow up with Meyers...

The list was growing, and her gut told her she was running out of time if she was going to get any answers from Cindy and find out who set this all up.

Julia looked at her phone—no battery, and she couldn't trust it. She left it and headed to the main lobby; they would have phones. She already had a plan to meet Roman, and she would just have to count on Dante to find her.

"This is Melinda." Her tone was cool and professional, not at all like any conversation Julia ever had with her.

"Mel, I need your help."

"Jules, what's wrong? Whose phone are you calling me from?"

"I just found out my office phone has been bugged for the past seven or eight weeks. I haven't had a chance to have my cell checked; this was the safest way I could think of making sure I had a secure line."

"Oh shit! Are you serious? A phone tap? That's, like, all kinds of illegal. What do you need me to do? Do I get to seduce a spy?" Melinda asked jokingly.

Julia sighed. "I don't think you'd like any of them. From what I can tell, the bug was placed by daywalkers. I need you to go—do not call, but *go*—to my office and tell Kathleen. Then I need you to call the house and see if anyone can get a message to Morgan. Let him know my phone was tapped, and they have clearly been targeting conversations with Roman Aventine."

"Who else needs to know? Will Kathleen know who to bring in? What about Roman's office?" Mel fired off questions.

Julia knew she was taking notes on the other end of the line. Mel liked to play, but she could be completely relied on when it was time to get to work.

"Tell Kathleen I suggest she contact Cyan del Fuego about this, but not on the office phone. She is going to want to be involved. Kathleen will know who at Aventine Industries to contact to alert them their phones may be bugged. What else?"

"How did you find out?"

"Oh, you're going to love this; I found transcriptions of conversations, highlighted and annotated with running commentary in that little twit Cindy's luggage."

"What does she have to do with this? Oh crap! Does this have to do with that mess Morgan got caught up in a few months ago?"

"Yeah, based on the timelines from those transcripts, definitely. Look, I have to go meet Roman. I'm going to be late. I'll call you as soon as I can. And I will tell you everything as soon as I get this all figured out. Thanks a ton, Mel. I owe you."

"You owe me tickets to the next Fernando show." Mel chuckled.

"I'll do you one better. I'll get Cyan del Fuego to introduce you to him."

"How would she be able to do that?" Melinda asked incredulously.

"She's his sister." Julia ended the call.

Roman strolled down the hallway back toward the atrium and the café. His meeting with Van Haas had been tense but uneventful. No, they did not know where Kezzup was, or the girl. Neither man brought up the incident of the previous night. But from the look about Van Haas's gills, Roman was pretty sure Julia had let loose on him. Good, he deserved it. Roman would have given the man more than a little smackdown if he hadn't promised Julia he would play nice.

He had a few extra minutes before he needed to be at the café and waiting for Julia. Smiling, he decided he should buy her a present. But what? He knew what he would want —Julia in more garter belts and lace panties. But that was really more a gift for himself. Julia should be dripping with gems. He smirked—and nothing else. She needed an amethyst. A touch of deep purple at the base of her throat. She looked heavenly in purple. Or a ruby; she wore a lot of red. He stepped into a high-end jewelry shop in the Delta Atrium's shopping area.

Roman browsed, looking into the cases that flashed

bright with diamonds under halogen lamps. He stopped at the counter with the colored stones; a thumbnail-sized yellow citrine framed with small diamonds glinted up at him. It was a little larger than he thought she would wear on a daily basis, but she could carry it off. The color would work as a neutral, and she would be able to wear it when she wore purple or red. He knew it would make her skin glow; after all, it was the color of the dress he'd torn from her last night.

Roman left the shop, whistling, and headed toward the café.

"Roman!" Cindy called out as she walked toward him.

"Are you all right? People have been looking for you," Roman replied, not wanting to startle the young lady into feeling like she needed to run away. If he could get her to wait for Julia at the café with him, all their problems could be cleaned up in a nice little package.

"I'm good, but I need your help. David is hurt and I can't get him up."

"Who?"

"Mr. van Haas's security guard, Kezzup." Cindy whined.

"Kezzup, right, take me to him." He followed Cindy as she took the stairs to the lower level, turned into a hallway that led behind the fast-food restaurants, and farther back through a service door. Roman blamed his inability to clearly think the situation through on the dazzle of the gems and the lack of blood in his brain as soon as he saw the vampire.

A second later a rock-hard fist slammed into his jaw. His arms were pinned behind him; he was pulled backward. Roman couldn't move. His focus blurred, and he saw nothing as he was punched repeatedly over the next few minutes. His mouth filled with blood, and the pain began to numb with each new blow.

He felt someone rummage through his pockets. It smelled like Cindy Science. His phone was pulled from his pocket before he heard it crunch under someone's foot. The wallet was removed and tossed aside. "Oh, this is pretty. Mine now." He heard her coo as she pulled the gift for Julia out of his front pocket. Her hand returned and fished around in his pants again. "Well, damn. Why haven't you been sharing this." Cindy chuckled as she squeezed his manhood.

Roman growled and jerked away as she groped him through the pocket. He had underestimated the girl. Where had his brain been? Classic example of a love-sick idiot. Roman chided himself once his mental fog began to clear. His lip was swollen and split in at least two places. He carefully examined the interior of his mouth with his tongue. Gums were bleeding; teeth were loose; one particularly caused him concern. His cheek was tight, but the bone didn't feel damaged. His eye was already starting to swell shut. A change and things would begin to heal. A change and he should be able to slip out of these clumsy restraints. He pulled the wolf forward.

"Stop it," a crisp voice snapped.

Roman's gaze focused on a thin man, dressed in all black and wearing too much eyeliner. He would have laughed if he hadn't also seen the gun trained on him. Roman let his wolf subside, but not before allowing the genetic shift to creep along his gums to stabilize that worrisome tooth.

~

Julia paced back and forth at the café. Roman was never late. Never. The man was punctual or early to a fault. An irritating, annoying-as-hell habit. Julia softened in her aggravation as she realized the habit was flirtatious, an opportunity to be with her before anyone else arrived for meetings.

Dante strolled up, hands casually deep in his pockets. He looked too relaxed for her level of agitation. "I've been looking for you. Haven't you gotten any of my texts?"

"Did you find anything?" she snapped.

He shook his head. "Not really. We have no answers, but the Dr. Cynthia Kimbro that Meyers texted me a photo of" —he pulled out his phone and showed Julia a picture of a face that did not match Cindy Science—"has not been in the Nashville airport at all. I got them to check video footage forty-eight hours on either side of her scheduled arrival."

"You were able to check how many days of footage in just a few hours? That was fast."

"They have some fantastic facial recognition software. Also we were able to really narrow it down. There are only so many ways you can get to Nashville from Toronto," Dante explained.

"You haven't seen Roman at all, have you? He's late."

"Are you sure he isn't in his suite?"

"No, he was supposed to check to see if Van Haas had found Kezzup yet, and then meet me here. And he's late." Julia fidgeted. She looked at the expression on Dante's face. "We made up."

Dante grinned. "I know; I heard. Over and over..."

Julia began to puff up with indignation.

"Chill, I'm glad you two made up. You yell loudly; once it got all quiet, I figured out what was going on and made myself scarce. So, text him."

"I can't," Julia said, deflating. "My office phone was tapped, and I don't know if my cell is clean. I need you to check it out."

Dante nodded. He tapped his finger on his chin.

"Okay, so you were supposed to meet him when?"

"About forty-five minutes ago." She looked up at him expectantly. After all, this was what he did; he found people.

"And you said he went to have a confab with Van Haas?"

Julia nodded.

"You let him go up there alone after last night? Not worried he'll rip into the South Africans?" Dante gave her a sideways grin.

"He'll behave. He's a better man."

"Then let's go see if your better man has been detained by some lesser men." Dante turned and started walking in the direction of Van Haas's suite.

Van Haas's door was slightly ajar, caught on an expensive handmade leather shoe. Neither of his men stood guard. Dante gently pushed the door open, kicking the shoe back into the room. Julia followed him inside. The room was a wreck. Upturned furniture, broken tables, blood smeared on a broken lamp base. It looked like there had been one hell of a fight.

Julia followed as Dante stepped farther into the suite. She found the foot that was missing the shoe. The foot was still attached to its unconscious owner, Van Haas's man Kruger. From the gash on his head, it appeared as if the blood on the lamp was also his. Dante leaned down and checked Kruger's pulse. He gave a sharp nod indicating the unconscious man was still alive.

A groan coming from the bedroom area caught Julia's attention. Van Haas lay on the floor, holding his head. Julia knelt in front of him and helped him to sit up. "What happened?"

"That mompie Kezzup, and that stupid bint..." Van Haas groaned again.

"What about Roman?" she asked.

"He..." Van Haas braced himself with a hand against the floor. His eyes focused on Julia. "He's your man?"

"Yes," she growled.

Van Haas nodded. "You're one hell of a woman. I don't know; I was knocked out at some point. Roman came in to ask if we had seen either the girl or Kezzup. I think he would have preferred to have crushed my windpipe. But he got his answers and left. Last thing I recall, that girlie was arguing with Kezzup, something about..." He groaned again. "I think I was hit by a brick."

Dante stepped into the room and stood over them. "Well, your man Kruger is out; looks like they hit him with a lamp, but I don't think that's what took him down. If you can get up, see to him. I should go look for Roman."

Julia stood and pulled Dante back into the living area of the suite, leaving Van Haas clutching his head and grumbling.

"You stay here, help Van Haas; I'll go find Roman," Julia said.

"I don't think that's a good idea."

Julia pointed her finger at Dante before poking herself in the chest. "You don't think; I do." Her voice was loud and growly. "And I'm telling you to—"

"I'm bigger than you, and I'm a better tracker than you are." His voice was also on the verge of yelling.

"He's my mate!" Julia shoved Dante with both hands.

He didn't flinch; he held up a finger. "How many people are you going after?"

Julia paused; she took a deep breath and thought. She pulled on her wolf senses. She could smell beer and fear. Another deep inhale—Cindy's sweet body wash. "Just Cindy and Kezzup." Julia's tone had calmed.

Dante shook his head. "Check again. If you go, know what you are going into."

This time Julia closed her eyes; she let her face change, taking on the features of her wolf. Allowing her full range of olfactory senses to work. "Cigarettes. Beer. That's from Kezzup. So is... is that? No. It's faint but..." Julia opened her eyes and searched the floor near Kruger. She picked up the thin scarf she had seen Cindy wearing the other day. She flinched as the new smell hit her. "Vampire."

Dante nodded. "Exactly."

Julia's face slid back to human; she rushed back to Van Haas's side; she fell down onto her knees. "Listen to me, Sholto. Was there anybody else with Cindy and Kezzup when they were here?"

Van Haas winced. "No, not that I know. Maybe. I was hit immediately, so I don't know if there was someone else with them. I only saw Kezzup and heard the girl."

She nodded and stood.

"Julia, I still think it should be me. They were able to take these two down, and Van Haas is an alpha, and Kruger is damn close to being one. Please. Morgan will kill me if I let you go."

"And I'll kill you if you don't."

17

Julia headed back to the café. Dante was right, he was better at this, but Roman was hers, and damn it, no one was going to take him from her now. Not some lying little flibbertigibbet or some dead vampire with a superiority complex.

The crowd of people that had been here during the day was all but gone. There were still too many people milling about for her to lock in on any scent.

She sat with a thud on a bench and glanced up. It was already dark beyond the glass canopy. In a place like this, where would a vampire hide? They could hole up in a room until late afternoon when the light would be so filtered it wouldn't have much impact. But the hotel was sold out. Dante hadn't been able to get a room at all. And if the vamp could get a room, then Cindy would have had her own room as well.

Not a room.

A place like this had to have miles of service tunnels. That would be logical. But where to start? Where she saw that wolf the other morning. It wasn't some early sleep-deprived hallucination; it had to have been Cindy Science.

Julia headed toward the lower Delta.

A food court, a boat ride, lots of gardens... Julia rotated as she took in what was around her. If she continued in the direction in front of her, that would take her back to the conference center portion of the hotel. A vampire and wolf hiding out wouldn't want to constantly deal with lost conference attendees looking for the nearest bathroom or place to get coffee. That area was too populated with all the different meetings going on. She crossed that off her mental list.

The gardens didn't lead anywhere, just filled what would be otherwise empty spaces. The boat ride, on the other hand... The boathouse and a service hall blocked by double doors were a very good bet on where to start looking.

Julia pushed into the service area and tried to pick up any familiar smells. Nothing. It was all antiseptic and... Wait, that was the cloying scent that Cindy washed in.

Julia stalked along the hallway and then turned, following the smell. Stacks of chairs and wheeled service carts lined the new hall. She picked up fresh cigarette smoke. That was promising; a vampire in hiding who smoked wouldn't really abide by the local rules of a smoking-free building. It could always be someone risking losing their job over a cigarette, but she doubted it.

She heard voices; at first she didn't recognize them, and then Cindy started ranting. Julia slowed her pace and carefully stepped forward. The door to the room was ajar. The smells oozing from the room washed over Julia. Cigarette smoke masked almost everything else, but she was able to pick up vampire, Cindy's wash, and the smell of sex. She equated Roman's scent with sex, something she hadn't realized until this second. He was here. She relaxed.

Julia leaned against the wall. She was the big-picture planner and then take-action type. She was a strategist, and she was flying by the seat of her pants here, not her typical mode of operating. She creeped against the wall until she could see into the room. Through the crack in the door she could see Roman's back. His head listed to the side as if he were unconscious. He was tied to a dilapidated wooden chair. She focused on his shoulders, waiting to see any movement. He was still, but he was breathing. She could also, just barely, see the side of Kezzup's face. He looked peaked, like he was sick. Arm still out of socket. She smirked. Easing away from the line of sight, she slid down the wall, resting on her haunches, listening.

"Stop whining already. I told you I don't know how to fix your shoulder. I thought you tough guys all knew this stuff. Don't you watch movies? Can't you just slam up against a doorframe or something and force it back in?" Cindy whined.

Julia couldn't hear Kezzup's reply. He had to be exhausted by now, between having a dislocated shoulder for almost twenty-four hours and putting up with the incessant blather and harping of Cindy.

"Okay, I'll try again. Last time you passed out for over an hour, and it didn't work." There was a pause. "Don't call me that. I tried. No, I'm not some doctor. I already told you I took that doctor woman's place; don't you remember?" Another pause. "Okay, it's hard to remember when you're in pain. Can't you just switch? Transforming is always supposed to speed healing."

Julia carefully crawled closer to the door. She could finally hear Kezzup's pain-ravaged voice.

"I'm not an alpha; I can't change on the spot like that. It takes time. And..." Kezzup paused, breathing hard. "I think if I try to force a change with my arm like this, I'll just be a gimpy wolf with a leg out of socket, and that would be even worse."

"You should have more power by now. Unless that didn't kill him. That should have killed him. So you should be getting his powers."

"Cindy..." He hissed; it sounded like talking hurt him. "I've never heard that before."

"Tell him, pain; tell him how it works. It worked for me." Cindy hadn't sounded this eager about anything since the first night of the conference. And how would his pain be able to tell him? That made no sense.

A third voice answered. Lilting, with some affectatious accent Julia recognized from midcentury movies. That must be the vampire. "As I told Cynthia, you can rise through your strength by absorbing the power of other wolves by killing them."

Ah, Payne—how fitting of a vampire to choose a name like that. How very old-school. She bet he even spelled *vampire* with a Y-R-E. But the information was wrong, so incredibly far from the truth that either he was as clueless as the girl, or... No, he was manipulating her. Had to be.

"Well, I've never heard it before," Kezzup barked. "If Sholto isn't dead, then I am when he finds me."

"Shh, I heard the crunch when you hit him. No way he would survive that. Are you sure you haven't felt a surge of energy?"

"Why did you go after the South African, Cynthia?" The disdain in the voice told Julia the vampire was getting sick of her as well.

"I told you. David needs to become more powerful so he can heal." She pronounced it *Dah-veed*.

"Just knock his shoulder back into place." Payne sounded tired of her.

"It's not that easy. I tried," Cindy whined.

"You've been wasting time. Fine. I'll do it." There was a groan, a yelp, and then whimpers.

Cindy cooed, "Change; you'll feel better." Scraping sounds, like furniture being moved around, and then a relieved sigh. Kezzup must have finally gotten into a position to relax.

"Better? Good." Cindy's tone changed from protective cooing to shrill. "Why didn't you do that earlier?" Cindy yelled; Julia assumed it was at Payne.

"You didn't ask." How very vampire of him.

"You could have volunteered to do that at any time. You're just mad at me because I'm picking David over you."

Julia smirked at the sound he made in reply. If there ever was a sound associated with an eye roll, that was the sound. Cindy must hear it a lot; she inspired a lot of eye rolling.

"At least you finally brought me Roman Aventine. He is not what I expected. Why His Lordship wants this man, I'll never understand. Mine is not to question but to deliver."

Shit, there it was, Lordship. This guy was working for Lazarus. Julia's gut clenched; she needed to see what was going on.

"I couldn't just drag him away. That control freak Julia has been telling everybody where to go and what to do, and they all listen to her. I told you before that it was hard to get away from her. She expected notes on all those lectures, and I don't know enough about this gene crap to fake that. This was the first time I was alone with him."

"This isn't going as I expected." There was a heavy sigh from the vampire.

Cindy was getting on his nerves. Julia resisted the urge to laugh.

"I got him here; he's all tied up. So what are you complaining about?" Cindy harped on the vampire.

"We need them both." Payne's voice rose in volume. It sounded like he had explained this before.

"Well, Julia is hard; she's got a bodyguard, or she's always with Roman or Sholto."

"You were sleeping with her." The vampire's voice was even louder. Julia smirked; it really sounded like the guy wanted to throttle Cindy.

"Don't be nasty. We were just sharing a room."

Another huff from the vampire.

Kezzup groaned loudly. Julia peeked through the door. He was out of sight now. Possibly on the floor attempting a change.

Now would be the best time to act. Kezzup would be out of it for a while, injured wolves changed slower than they typically could. She didn't know what condition Roman was in. Cindy would be easy, but that vampire was an unknown.

Roman's jaw throbbed. Every time he tried to bring the shift forward, the vampire sneered at him from the other end of a gun. He couldn't think straight. The pounding had rattled his brain. He figured he was mildly concussed from all the blows to the head. He took a deep breath; pretending to be unconscious was not getting him anywhere, but it stopped the beatings.

Payne and the girl had spent the entire time arguing about everything from her inability to entrap Roman with her feminine wiles to this odd concept she had that killing a more powerful wolf—in this case Van Haas—would transfer his strength and abilities to Kezzup.

He took a deep breath and wished he actually could pass out.

"Why isn't it working, Payne? Payne? It worked for me when I hit that bitch back in Toronto. I felt such a surge of power."

To Roman it sounded more like an adrenaline rush than anything else.

"You didn't need to hook up with him. This only complicates things," the vampire scoffed.

"Don't be mad at me, Payne. I know I said I would do anything for you. I still will. But he's my mate."

Roman cracked open his eyes and looked at Cindy before glancing at the pile of skin and fur that was David Kezzup. Mates; well go figure. He hadn't really put any thought toward the man, but now he decidedly did not like him.

Kezzup with his arm relocated had finally stopped moaning. Of course, that may have been a better option. His change was slow and clearly painful as he whimpered through the transition. Roman couldn't decide which sound was worse. Gods, if it hurt that much, why bother? Right—it sped up the healing process; it brought on wolf powers. It was addictive.

"Will I still be able to have babies after you, you know, turn me?"

"Female vampires do not give birth. But you will be the strongest of us all."

Was Cindy talking about being turned to vampire? Roman hoped Julia was listening.

He could hear Julia lurking in the hallway behind him. Her heart pounded loudly to his ears. He was actually surprised the others weren't alerted to her presence. Too bad the mate bond didn't come with more than fabulous sex and a personal connection. He could really use a telepathic mental link right about now. She was behind him; his hands were behind him; this would be perfect if he only knew sign language.

But he knew his mate, and she would be assessing the situation. Making a plan. She wouldn't come barging in here without one.

"I don't know, Payne," Cindy hemmed and hawed. "I mean, I've met my mate. I kind of want to go with him and have kids and stuff like that. And I'll be strong through the mate connection, especially after he's alpha."

"We are getting nowhere." Roman listened as the vampire shuffled. "I'm done. David is in the way, and that Palatine woman isn't going to just walk down here because you texted her to meet you."

"Oh my God, Payne, put that away; he's unconscious," Cindy snapped. Her voice suddenly turned shrill. "You can't shoot David; he's defenseless; he's changing. He's on our side."

Roman's eyes flew open. Cindy was grabbing at Payne, struggling over what he assumed was the gun. He threw himself backward, and the chair fell with him onto the floor.

Julia crashed through the door and jumped to him.

"He's got a gun," Roman hissed as Julia pulled on the bindings at his elbows.

The sound of the gun firing in such an enclosed space deafened Julia. Everyone froze in stunned silence. She regained her focus and continued to untie Roman; right now as long as it wasn't him or herself who had been shot, she didn't care.

The ringing in her ears was replaced by Cindy's screams. Julia's fingers continued to work at the knots, but she directed her attention to the action in front of her.

Payne looked in shocked horror at the blood on his hands. Cindy flung the gun across the room and backed away from the vampire. She was crying. "I'm sorry; I'm so sorry."

Payne slumped to the floor, still in shock from the shot.

Cindy rushed back, clamoring to assist him. She tried to prop him against a table.

"Payne, baby, it'll be okay. I'll get you help. You can drink my blood; that will work, right?"

"You shot me." Blood dripped from the corner of his mouth. He must have bitten the inside of his mouth at the same time. The effect was exceptionally dramatic.

The shot wouldn't kill the vampire, but he did need to have the bullet removed, and then a lot of transfusions. Or he could drink blood. He was up to something.

Cindy cast about looking for something in her panic; she was clearly lost and scared. Her gaze landed on Julia. "Help me. He's dying."

"Good." Julia stood and held out a hand to Roman to help him up. "Less work for me."

"What's your plan?" Roman whispered.

Julia kept Payne in her vision. She didn't trust him. She and Roman stepped slowly to the side. "I'm winging it." Julia kept her voice low, not wanting to call attention to herself just yet.

"That's not like you."

Julia smiled at Roman's observation. The vampire should be able to function just fine with that bullet wound.

That was the thing about vampires—what typically killed everybody else, merely tickled.

"Look, baby, Julia came. I told you she would." Cindy tried to get the vampire to look up.

"I've got him," Roman whispered, his presence warm against Julia's back. He slid his hand into hers and squeezed. "Get her away from his body."

Payne's eyes rolled back, exposing the whites.

"No!" Cindy cried. She turned a tear-streaked face to Julia. "Look what you made me do! This is all your fault!"

Julia returned the squeeze to Roman's hand. There were too many unknowns right now. But at least they were between the gun and everyone else.

"Cindy, how do you know a vampire? Does Meyers know about this guy?" Julia asked as she carefully continued to sidestep closer to Cindy.

"That big fat asshole Meyers doesn't know anything. My friends hooked up with some daywalkers; that's how I found out vampires were even real. They wanted to know about other wolves, but I told them there weren't others. They didn't believe me, but then it turns out they were right. I always thought we only lived in Canada."

Cindy started talking a mile a minute, her hands flying as she continued to divulge the information she had.

"They told me there were more wolf kin around, and if I wanted to move up in power, to be stronger I needed to be an alpha's mate. So all I needed to do was marry an alpha. But I can't 'cause Meyers is icky; plus he's my uncle, so ew. That's about when Payne showed up, and he had a plan. He said he could make me great. And now he's dead," she wailed.

"How was he going to make you great?" Julia prodded. She was torn between finding out as much as she could and jumping in and ripping the girl's throat out so she would stop talking. Knowing Roman had his attention on the vampire, Julia needed to get the girl away from Payne and, if possible, away from the shifting wolf as well.

"Those daywalkers were really boring; they just wanted to get stoned, and have sex all the time. And okay, it was fun for a while. But I'm more ambitious than that. I don't want to waste my life partying in dingy holes. I belong in grander places, kind of like this hotel. I mean, I fit in here. And Payne knew that the second he saw me. He said if I helped him and his boss, some Lord guy, he would use his magic to turn me into a wolf-vampire. The first one ever. And I would be amazing."

"He was lying to you, Cindy. Wolves can't become vampires."

"What do you know, bitch?" Cindy spit at Julia. "It can't happen now anyway. Can it? Does that make you happy?" Cindy directed her attention back to Payne. He lay still. She looked at his face with an expression that made Julia think the girl's heart was truly broken. Her voice was softer when she continued.

"I went back to Meyers to ask him about other werewolves. He told me to never mind about other wolves and not to run off again like that. It could be dangerous. I had to be careful and shit like that. I hung around when that pharmacist showed up, just like Payne told me to do. He said I would learn something very useful, and I did. She was going to get to come here and meet other alphas. Payne told me I should take her place. Some friends and me jumped her for her plane ticket. Payne said you wouldn't know, that you trusted Meyers. I could replace her at the conference. And oh my God, you didn't have a fucking clue. How dumb are you? So focused on this lame-ass gene shit that's not going to do or mean anything."

Julia sighed. Cindy did have ambition, but she was ignorant. Part of that was definitely on her alpha for keeping her in the dark, but the rest was her own willful stupidity.

"It doesn't work that way." Julia's gaze shifted to Kezzup; he was almost done shifting. He would be up in a minute. "You don't understand how things work. Payne was going to kill you. There is no magic. We can't become vampires; that's why there have never been any wolf-vamps before."

"Shut up!" Cindy yelled and stepped in closer to Julia. Julia stepped back; Cindy advanced. "Stop trying to tell me lies." She flung her arms wide, putting herself between Julia and Payne as if she could protect him. "You are all the same; you are trying to control the rest of us. You want us to kowtow to your rule. You want us to hide from the humans. The vampires have it right. They know they are superior."

"Cindy, you can't..." Julia stopped. She retreated in hopes that Cindy would continue to advance.

"God, will you stop trying to tell me what to do. Seriously, you are as bad as Meyers. He's such a controlling bastard. And you with the constantly telling me what I can and can't do. I can't go to the mall. I have to go to the conference and take notes. How come I didn't get to have lunch with that hottie doctor, huh? No, you and Roman got to do that. You got to sit and have coffee with your bodyguard, but I wasn't supposed to talk to him? David and Kruger never sat and had coffee with Sholto. Oh." Cindy's jaw dropped open. "You and Dante are doing it. That makes so much sense, why he wasn't interested in me. Why you told me to back off. So you and the bodyguard..." she said with surprise and delight.

Julia bit her lip; the thought of her and Dante sleeping

together was comical. Cindy had not clued in to the fact that they were related. She wasn't going to correct that piece of misinformation now. She glanced over at Roman. He was closing in on Payne. It was clear that he didn't believe the vampire was dead either.

"You sound like a petulant child." Julia rolled her eyes.

"You fucking rolled your eyes at me? Who's the petulant child now? We are wolf kin; we are the stronger species. We should be dominating the world, yet for centuries all we do is hide from humans. That's all your kind wants us to do. The families are afraid of humans; the families want us all to be afraid of humans."

"You did not just call us wolf kin," Julia scoffed, barely suppressing a laugh.

"You make me sick; we are superior to these measly humans, and you still—"

"Shut up, you stupid twat." Julia's voice boomed. She could no longer take the noise. She now had Cindy in the position she wanted, away from the two men. Cindy shrank away as Julia advanced on her, driving her toward the hallway. "We are human. Have you not been paying attention to all this genetic data we have been discussing? We. Are. Genetically. Human. There is no magic; there is no superior species. We are human—with a mutation we don't understand, but nonetheless human."

"Then why are we trying to hide from everyone. If we're so human, why not be out of the shifter closet?" Cindy's tone was whining as she tried to find the upper hand in the conversation.

"You really are an idiot." Julia sneered. "Have you ever taken a history lesson? Ever? Humans do not do well with differences. We lose our shit over different skin colors, different languages, different religions, different genders.

How the hell do you think people as a whole are going to react to humans who can change their shape? I'll tell you right now, it will not be to worship us as gods. No. We'll end up dissected on a stainless steel examination table. You want to be the next alien autopsy? Personally, that is something I would like to avoid."

Kezzup was up on all fours, growling. He lunged for Julia.

Julia fell back, letting the thin wolf roll over her. She kicked, flipping him over onto his back. By the time he found his footing again, he faced Julia's wolf. Growling she shook what was left of her clothes off, most has shredded with the instant change. Kezzup ran out the door.

Realization washed across Cindy's expression. "Damn, you did that fast. You're a female alpha. Well hell, maybe I should have been trying to hook up with you."

Cindy screamed as Payne took that moment to act. One second he was playing dead, the next he hung from the utility pipes and hissed. Cindy looked in horror from Payne on the ceiling to Julia's wolf. She ran.

Roman barked at Julia, "Go! I've got this one."

She was beautiful; of course his mate would be an exceptional wolf—she was an exceptional woman. Now was not the time to admire her thick, warm brown coat or her marking patterns or the touch of auburn behind each ear. Now was the time to deal with the freak on the ceiling.

Payne wouldn't be able to last long up there; he had lost a lot of blood. And while the entire hotel was full of replenishing stock, Roman was going to make sure Payne didn't get access to any of it.

The vampire taunted Roman. "Poor puppy can't come up here and get me."

Roman smirked. He righted the chair he had previously been tied to, sat, and crossed his arms. "Nope, not even going to try. As long as you are up there, you can't get to me either."

He chuckled as this realization caused the vampire noticeable perturbation. Payne clearly wanted to goad Roman into doing something stupid. Roman didn't feel like playing. He wanted to eliminate this threat. And after the constant noise of Cindy's talking, he didn't particularly care to find out what this guy's motive was. Payne worked for someone he referred to as His Lordship; that was enough of a confession of working for Lazarus as Roman needed.

He shifted his weight in the chair. Everything was about how he wanted it. Now it was a waiting game. Roman was fairly certain he had the upper hand when it came to patience. He let the wolf seep into his being, not enough to affect a complete change, but enough to alter his features; his ears lengthened; his brow thickened; his jaws elongated. His countenance changed from elegant bone structure to one that would frighten. So now monster faced off against monster.

It took a few seconds longer than he anticipated, but as expected, Payne launched himself with a scream at Roman.

With wolf-enhanced speed Roman jumped, kicking the leg from the chair. He knocked Payne from the air with enough force to slam what little air there was out of the vampire's lungs. With a spin Roman finished breaking the chair and slammed the sharp broken edge into the vampire's chest.

Payne didn't thrash, and this time the blood bubbling out from his mouth was not for dramatic effect.

18

G lass crunched under Roman's feet. Quickly he looked around. Several of the shop windows had been broken, the interiors in disarray. Clearly the two wolves had been actively fighting before he found them. But the area was clear now. Where were they?

He cocked his ears; the ambient sound of the atrium made it difficult to focus his hearing. He listened for uneven patterns in the white noise, subtle sounds that weren't made by the river or air vents. He caught something and followed what he thought was panting. Tables and chairs were scattered and knocked on their sides. Fortunately the atrium was deserted and eerily dark. How long had he been trussed up? He turned the corner and saw the wolves. He looked at his mate; blood matted the fur on her shoulder. He shouldn't have taken so long with that vampire, he should have been here as Julia's backup as she faced down Kezzup, now a tall, thin wolf.

Roman let his wolf finish sliding over his skin. His face elongated farther, and his limbs shortened. While he still had thumbs, he unfastened his clothing so that his unbuttoned slacks slid from his haunches as he completed the change, he shook off his shirt. Roman left the pile of clothes behind as he, now a large white timber wolf with pale gray markings, charged the thin wolf. A human body slammed into Roman's ribs. Together they slid across the walkway and collided with a brick wall. Roman shook off his attacker and stood, head lowered, teeth exposed. Cindy screamed as she slid across the floor and scrambled away from Roman.

Kezzup made a lunge for Julia. She reared up on her haunches and came down with her jaws snapping, barely missing the other wolf's muzzle. He backed off.

Roman slinked up alongside Julia. She never took her focus from Kezzup. He inched closer, lowering his head. Roman saw that Kezzup was going to make a try for Julia. Roman positioned his own head lower. To an outsider it would appear as if he were cowering under Julia's protection, when in fact he had flanked her and was ready to lunge at the underside of her attacker.

Julia shifted her weight; Roman retreated and she lunged forward. Both she and Kezzup stood on their hind legs. The force of Julia's attack slammed the other wolf backward and down. He rolled; she pounced. She stood over his back, teeth buried into the back of his neck. He weakly turned his head to her, whimpering.

Roman leaped past them, cornering Cindy, who had tried to slink off.

Dante and Van Haas ran into the middle of the confrontation. A trickle of blood slowly oozed down the side of Van Haas's neck. He swiped at it.

He slowly approached Julia and the wolf at her feet. Hands out in supplication so she would know he meant no harm, Van Haas stopped a few feet from her. Julia growled, her teeth still clamped around the other wolf.

Van Haas lowered himself to the floor. Crouching in front of the wolves, he made eye contact with the conquered animal.

"David, what do you think you are doing? I should let her kill you. But I will bargain for your release. I will protect you until we land in Pretoria." He looked up into Julia's eyes. "And he will return to Pretoria with me."

Julia growled, then released her grip on Kezzup's neck. Kezzup moved as if he considered making a lunge for her. Her teeth were back on his neck; at the same time Van Haas's hand clamped around his muzzle.

"You will not," he hissed. Plastic strips landed on his shoulder; Van Haas glanced up; Dante nodded, handing him zip ties.

Van Haas nodded in acknowledgment of the impromptu muzzle restraint.

"We need to leave before other humans find this," Van Haas announced as he wrapped and pulled the zips ties around the wolf's snout.

Dante dug his fist into the hair at the back of Cindy's head. "Don't even think about making a sound."

Knowing Dante had this one, Roman leaped back to Julia.

He nudged Julia in the side. She snapped at him, letting go of Kezzup.

Instantly he was human, nude, crouching in front of her, burying his hands and face in the ruff at her neck.

He pulled her into his embrace. "You're hurt."

She began licking his face.

Roman sighed.

"Dude, clothes, we need to leave," Dante reminded Roman.

Van Haas led the injured Kezzup away, having utilized a belt as an impromptu leash.

Julia whined and nudged at Roman. He retrieved his clothes. Julia stayed by his side as he dressed.

Julia shifted and began dressing in Roman's dress shirt. He handed her his boxers, realizing her clothes must be back in the storage room. Roman pulled her into his arms, then claimed her lips with his own. Julia didn't protest; she melted against his chest, letting him take control of the kiss. When the kiss ended, she rested her head against his chest, snuggling into him. They stood like that, in each other's embrace for several minutes. Slowly, with arms around each other, they followed Van Haas back to his suite.

Kruger still lay unconscious on the floor behind the couch, though he had been placed in a more comfortable position. Kezzup sat, nude and still shifting in a chair, his hands and feet bound with zip ties, a hand towel shoved into his mouth, his eyes wide with fear as he watched everyone in the room.

"Can't ship him in a crate as a dog because of my country's quarantine issues," Van Haas complained. "He will have to travel as a human. Of course two weeks in a kennel might actually do him some good. I don't know if I can keep Kruger from him for that long."

Cindy sat in a corner, whimpering. Dante stood over her.

A loud groan followed by a large almost black wolf came from behind the couch. Van Haas nodded at him. "Good to see you feeling better."

Kruger crouched in front of Kezzup, a low growl coming from deep in the animal's chest.

"You will have to wait for home, my friend."

Turning to Julia, Van Haas apologized. "I am sorry for my part in your troubles. Miss Jackson was brought in as a distraction. I will admit I wanted you for myself. But I see you have made your choice. I will not challenge you." He held his hand out to Roman. "Good luck; you have a fine woman."

Roman shook the offered hand, keeping a protective arm around Julia.

"He will do anything for you. Don't be too hard on him. I will count myself lucky if I ever meet another woman with your fortitude. And if I am smart enough, I will go to her side and not expect to control her."

Julia smiled. "I think you might just be smart enough for a female alpha."

"Not how I expected to spend my last night in America. Good night; our flight leaves early." After exchanging good-byes, Roman led Julia back to his suite. Dante followed, dragging Cindy along.

Dante pushed Cindy into a chair. "I can think of several things to do with this one. What's the plan?"

"First," Roman said as he approached Cindy, "this doesn't belong to you." He removed the citrine pendant from her neck and gently placed it around Julia's. "It belongs to her."

"It's beautiful," Julia whispered as she wrapped her fingers around the gift. She let out a deep sigh.

Roman smiled at Julia before turning to Dante. "We need to do something with the vampire before someone finds him. There's lots of blood to clean up."

"Based on her story"— Julia pointed at Cindy—"Dr. Kimbro was mugged and hit on the head. Either this one did it, or she knows the people who did. I need to share what I know with Meyers. It could help him to locate Dr. Kimbro. I'm concerned she may not have survived the attack. Again, hard to know. Cindy Science here is a bit confused on what wolf shifters are actually capable of," Julia said, her voice full of scorn.

"She's been fed a lot of misinformation by that vampire, Payne. I'm pretty sure her alpha didn't think it necessary for her, as a lesser wolf, to know much about their family," Roman added.

"Stop calling me Cindy Science, and stop talking like I'm not here," Cindy whined.

"We need to muzzle her. It's late, but I'm sure Meyers would be interested in any information as soon as possible." Roman tossed a towel to Dante.

Julia shook her head slowly. "I don't have my laptop, and I still don't know if my phone is clean. I have no way of contacting him right now."

"You forgot that I do." Dante held up his phone. He handed it to Julia. "This is clean; I checked."

Julia stared at the phone, too tired to place the call. Roman took the phone from her dialed. "Sorry to disturb you so late; we have some information that might help in locating Dr. Kimbro." He handed the phone to Julia.

Julia repeated everything she could remember from Cindy's explanation of how she took the ticket from Dr. Kimbro and how a local group of daywalkers was involved. "Yes, we will be in touch in the morning." Julia handed the phone back to Dante. "Meyers said he'll help figure out how to get Cindy back to Canada in the morning. He's going to share this information with his people." Julia winced as the pain in her shoulder flared.

Roman gently took Julia's arm in his hands. "Let me see it," he said as he began peeling his shirt away from her neck to look at the wound on her shoulder. As wolf it had bled profusely; the turn to human had accelerated the healing process. However, it was still a process;

Roman looked to ensure it wouldn't need medical attention.

He hissed as he pulled fabric away from a bloody gash. "Take the shirt off; I'm going to clean that." He stepped into the bathroom and returned with a wet cloth.

Julia followed directions and held the shirt in front of her chest while Roman gently washed the wound. With the blood cleaned away, Roman could see it was a shallow cut, most likely from a piece of glass. "It looks worse than it is. See if the bathroom has any first-aid supplies," he directed Dante.

Dante returned with a pack of antiseptic ointment and self-adhesive bandages. "This is all they have," he said, handing the supplies to Roman.

"Better than nothing." Roman squeezed the ointment onto the cut, lay some tissue over the ointment, then taped the tissue into place using the bandages.

Julia eased back into the shirt.

The room phone rang.

"Aventine. No, I'm sorry, my cell phone broke. I understand." His face went ashen. He dropped into a chair as his legs gave out.

Julia watched Roman with concern as he silently listened to the speaker on the other end.

He closed his eyes, then lowered the receiver.

"Get out," he whispered.

Violently he got to his feet, hurled the phone across the room, ripping its cord from the wall. He roared, "Get out of here!"

He slammed the door behind him as he stormed into the bedroom.

Wide-eyed, Julia stared at the closed door, then back to Dante.

"I'll take her back to your room; then I'll deal with the vamp. You check on him." Dante nodded at the closed door.

~

"Roman?" she asked tentatively as she opened the door. He sat on the bed, seeming despondent, staring at the floor.

Tears streamed from his eyes as he looked up at her. He said nothing. Julia stepped to him. Roman clutched at her, pulling her close. He buried his face in her stomach, clinging to her as if she were a lifeline.

She said nothing as she gently stroked his hair, not knowing what was wrong or how to fix it for him.

Roman's breathing eased, yet he still clung to Julia. She gently climbed into the bed, then pulled Roman to lie next to her. She cradled him against her chest.

Julia woke with Roman wrapped around her. At some point during the night one of them had pulled the covers up. Julia turned in his grasp so she could see his face. Even in sleep it was full of pain. His brow was creased, and his lips pulled down into a frown. Gently laying her hand on the side of his face, Julia kissed his forehead, then tucked herself against his chest under his chin.

He was her mate, and she would protect him, just as he had protected her. For now that meant holding him while he slept. There would be time for him to tell her what demons had attacked last night, what nightmare he would be waking to this morning.

Roman stirred. "Julia." Her name was a rumble low in his chest.

She peered up at him.

"I need to go to Boston. My mother died last night."

"You need to go home? I understand."

"No, I need to go to Boston. You are my home. Will you please come with me?"

"Of course. You don't have to ask. I'll have arrangements made for us. We can leave this afternoon."

"Thank you. I don't want to think right now. Thinking hurts."

"Don't think; just let me hold you."

They lay quietly together until Roman fell back asleep.

Careful not to wake him, Julia slipped from his embrace. She unplugged the bedroom phone and padded into the sitting area. After removing the remnants of the damaged phone and cord, she plugged the phone into the jack and dialed her room.

"His mother died last night."

"Oh, I'm sorry; that's a tough one," Dante answered.

"Yeah. Look, we're going to head out to Boston this afternoon or tonight, whenever I can get a flight. I'll let you manage getting Cindy back to Canada. I'm sorry I'm ditching this on you, but—" Julia broke off.

"But nothing, Julia. His mother died. We both know what it's like to lose a parent. He needs all the support you can give him right now. I can coordinate with Meyers. I handled that little cleanup project, and I already have thoughts on how to best get this one back to Canada with minimum fuss. Right now my biggest challenge is getting her to shut up."

"Hand towel?" she asked.

"She spits it out. I wish we had a way to magically suppress the change, you know, like a silver cage or something. I'd keep her in wolf form."

Julia laughed. "That only works in the movies. Hey, don't sleep with her."

"Really, Julia? I never liked her, and I'm inclined to like

her even less now. I am not as much of a man-whore as you seem to think I am."

"I'm yanking your chain, but sometimes I can't tell."

"You've been blinded by your mate's glow." Dante chuckled.

"Okay, so does everyone know about this mate-glow thing except for me?"

"Didn't Aunt Debs ever tell you?"

"She only ever said I would just know," Julia explained.

"Are you sure she hadn't said they would just glow?"

Julia sighed; it would be horrible to have misunderstood her mother all those years ago. But even Morgan hadn't mentioned the glow when he found his mate, Honey. Maybe nonwolf humans didn't glow. She shrugged.

"By the way, your phone is clean. But speaking of dirty phones, have you been getting heavy breathing phone calls?" Dante asked.

"All freakin' week, and no one would do anything about it. I'm kind of pissed. Why, did you get one?"

"Yep, and then I got an apology. Apparently the kids making the calls were caught by their mom, and she made them call back and apologize immediately."

"Did you growl at them?"

"Julia," he said, exacerbated. "No, I did not growl; they were kids. But I did caution them on doing it again, and I could hear mom in the background. She sounded pretty mad."

"Well, good, they deserve to be grounded or on a time-out or strung up by their toes."

"Overreacting much?" Dante laughed.

"No, it did creep me out. Glad that mystery is solved."

A few moments later Julia tapped at the door to what

had been her room. Dante opened to allow her in. "Nice outfit," he teased, indicating Roman's clothes on her.

"Shut up; my clothes are all here." Julia pushed her way into the room.

Cindy sat on the bed, restrained with electrical cords.

"I had to use the bathroom; otherwise I just keep her closed up in there." Julia nodded as Dante led the girl back to the bathroom.

She looked at the other bed. Her suitcase lay open. Toiletries and assorted items were lying on the bed, clearly waiting to be placed into the bag.

"Thank you," Julia sighed as she realized Dante had gathered all her belongings.

"I was just going to grab my phone and pack later, but this is"—she paused—"this is perfect. Thanks, cuz."

"I was looking over these." Dante waved at the stack of phone conversation printouts. "These date back to a few weeks after Morgan's little adventure. There are probably hours and hours of conversations they have notes on, but the notes on these definitely focus on this trip. Based on what's here, it just reads like Truria is moving fast and hard into the genetics biz and you were trying to get a consultation with Meyers. But I have no idea what's not included. There are no notes or mentions of Van Haas."

"He was all e-mail, and Roman and I tended to not go into details unless we were face-to-face or by cell." Julia packed her items into the open case.

"That could be a saving grace. What I'm still not clear on, is how did the vamps manage to get a hookup in Canada so fast?"

"You said it yourself; they have a better network than we do." Julia shrugged and zipped her suitcase closed. "I'm hoping we find out that Payne was handling the whole project; he just needed to ask who was who in Toronto. He said something that made me think he was trying to move up the vampire ladder as hard and fast as Cindy was trying to climb the alpha ladder."

"Well, based on the email address on these first few print outs, I'm betting the notes were emailed to Cindy from Payne's account. I'm forwarding all of this on to Shane and the Aventine contact, Winters. Let them see what they can make of it." Dante nodded toward the bathroom door indicating Cindy. "She's not being helpful. I can't get a straight answer from her, but I'm sure at some point she will divulge. Whatever the guy was up to he picked the wrong vampire to work for."

"Yes, he did." Julia hauled her suitcase off the bed.

"Give Aventine my condolences. I'm truly sorry for his loss."

19

The empty pit in his chest threatened to overwhelm him. His mother. At least she had known about Julia. He remembered sitting with his mother at the shore. She had been exhausted from chemo treatment that morning. But she'd wanted to sit by the water. She said the ocean waves revitalized her. Roman had driven her over the hill to the coast. It had been slightly overcast once they reached the water. The sky had been a thin blue gray, and the ocean reflected the color with a deeper gray. They found a bench above the rocks. She sat with her eyes closed, listening to the waves. Roman sat quietly with her. He had been surprised when she spoke. "Tell me about your mate." She had sounded so tired.

"How did you know?" Roman asked.

"There's something different about you—smug, happy, nervous. You act like you're in love but completely terrified, like you're fifteen again and about to ask a girl out for the first time."

Roman told her all about Julia, from her strength as a female alpha to her prowess in business, to her glorious hair and beautiful eyes. He did not tell his mother how she kissed with abandon, had a body made for sex, or how she made it hard for him to think.

"Was she why you went to that wedding?"

Roman chuckled. "I went to that wedding because we need to be friends with the Palatines. Relations building, networking, all of that. I didn't go because she would be there. But yes, she was there."

"And how would the Palatines react if you were to take away one of their daughters?"

"I'm not sure I would be taking Julia away from her family, or if I would be joining her."

His mother had known all about Julia. He wished they had gotten to meet.

He reached for the comforting warmth of Julia. She was gone. Julia was no longer in bed. He needed her presence. She reminded him that life continued, even in the face of the death of his mother. When he couldn't find Julia in the rest of the suite, the pit collapsed into a singularity threatening to consume him; breathing became difficult as he felt himself being pulled into nothingness. He couldn't have lost her too. Not after last night, not after this.

He crashed out the door and sprinted down the hall toward the elevators. Julia stepped out of one as Roman approached. He swept her into his grasp, causing her to drop her bags.

"Roman," she gasped at the fierceness of his embrace.

"I panicked," he said, easing his grip around her. "Not very manly. Sorry."

"No need to apologize." She smiled wanly at him. "It's okay, and I think it's very manly to admit to your emotions."

She picked up the handle and began pulling her bag.

"You were asleep; I was getting my things. I'll order us

some breakfast; why don't you take a shower." Julia kept an arm around Roman's hips and guided him back toward the suite.

Roman nodded. "As you command."

"Hey." She stopped him. "It's not like that; you know that, right? I'm not here to boss you around."

Roman nodded. "I know that. Easier to fall back on old habits than it is to think right now."

Julia reached up to pull him down for a kiss. "I'll accept that, but we're partners in this mate thing."

"So you accept that we're mates?" Roman asked.

"I do; look, I'm the one that owes you an apology. I'm sorry I played into Van Haas's attempt to drive us apart."

He made a noise in his throat. "And I should have told you about my ex-wife."

"You sure you're not married?" Julia asked with a soft chuckle, laughing at herself that she needed to hear it again.

"Definitely not married," Roman confirmed.

"So you're single?" she asked with a tease in her tone.

"Definitely not single. Julia, I've known you were my mate for a while. I needed for you to see it for yourself."

"Do I still glow for you?" Julia asked, seeming concerned. "You're glowing right now."

Roman let out a half laugh. "Yes, you glow; it's the mate's aura. You don't always glow, and the more strongly bonded we are, the less I will see it. But you glow. Didn't you know what it was?"

"More along the lines of I didn't want to accept it."

Roman cocked an eyebrow at her.

"You infuriate me, Roman, and I don't want to give up my alpha status to anyone."

Roman began to speak; Julia covered his mouth with her fingers.

"You will probably continue to infuriate me, and I you. I do enjoy it at times. I'm weird that way. I'm sorry I didn't listen when you said you wouldn't try to dominate me, that you would be by my side. Last night in that fight, you did just that. You were by my side; you protected me; you never tried to take over and fight my fight for me."

"I will fight your fight whenever you ask, but you don't need me to do that. I desire nothing more than to be your knight in shining armor, but you are no damsel in distress. You kick ass and don't take names. I am the lucky one, if you'll have me."

"You'll beta to my alpha?"

"No." Roman shook his head. "We are an alpha pair, equals, supporters."

Julia nodded in understanding. She would never take over his fight for him, just as he did not take over her fight. "We take care of each other. Right now I'm taking care of you. Go shower, and I'll order breakfast and make arrangements to get to Boston." She pushed him toward the bathroom.

"Thank you, Julia."

Following him, she asked, "Will we need a car, and where should I make arrangements for staying?"

Roman nodded. "Yes, car, and we'll stay at the house."

Roman guided the car up the freeway. Dark shadows indicated tree-covered hills outside of Julia's window. She let him drive; he knew where they were going without having to worry about giving Julia directions. The flight into Logan Airport had been uneventful and quiet. Roman had been introspective the entire flight.

Julia let him be; she was there to support him, and she would be by his side the entire time. When he decided it was time to talk, she would be here to listen and to hold him.

His family's home was located in New Hampshire, about an hour north of Boston. Julia never appreciated how close the states in New England were until Roman mentioned they might be able to head over to Maine in the next day or two, after she said she had never been there.

When they pulled up the drive, Julia was not surprised to see a rather sedate mansion of gray stone. She had expected the Aventine's estate to be reserved yet large. The Palatine estate was predominantly one large building with wings and extensions. This was more of a compound, a gathering of buildings and other houses.

A tired old man, withered and gray, came to let them in. He had no greeting for Roman or Julia. She thought from his expression, and his look, that he was somehow related to Roman, possibly an uncle.

"Can I see her?" Roman asked.

Silently the man turned. They followed him to an upstairs room.

Julia tightened her grip on Roman's hand. She had seen a dead body before, but not a parent. Her own parents' bodies had been so badly damaged she had not been allowed to see them. This was Roman's mother; though Julia had never met her, she was important to Roman, and therefore important to Julia. She gripped Roman's hand a little tighter. He squeezed back.

The old man left them in front of a closed door. Roman slowly opened the door.

The woman was laid out on a bed, surrounded by flowers. She looked calm, as if she were asleep and not dead.

Julia stared at her chest, expecting it to rise and lower with breath, but there was no movement in the body that had clearly been ravaged by disease.

Roman picked up his mother's hand and brought it to his face. "Mother, Mom." He fell to his knees, still holding her hand. He was quiet for a long time. Julia, not certain what to do, stood at his back, resting her hand on his shoulder, soothing him the best she could.

Roman took a ragged breath, then stood up. "Mom, this is Julia. I told you about her once. You laughed and said she sounded like a good match. She finally agreed to be my mate. You'd like her; you would call her feisty. Not sure how Father will take to her, but she'll hold her own against him. I thought you were doing better. I guess you just told me that so I wouldn't worry. I guess you wanted to be home when this happened and not so far away. I can understand that. I hope you understand that this isn't my home anymore. Julia is my home. I wish you could see her. Her smile would have made you feel better, taken away some of the pain. She has that kind of smile. You two would have been allies. I guess Father is taking this pretty hard. He's going to be even more angry now than he has been. I'll try not to be too hard on him, and I will try to remember he's angry because he's hurting. But I can't make any promises. I'm angry too." He turned to Julia as she slipped her hand back into his.

"I'm going to miss you, Mom, more than I can ever tell you. More than I think I realize." He leaned over and kissed his mother on the cheek. "I'm glad you are no longer in pain, but I wish there could have been another way, not you having to leave us. I love you."

Tears slipped from his eyes as he turned toward Julia.

Still holding her hand, he led her down the hall to another room. Their suitcases had been placed on the bed.

Julia looked around. It appeared as if this had been a teenage boy's room, but cleaned up. Several sporting trophies sat on book-lined shelves. An old teddy bear had a prominent position in the middle of a double bed. Stacks of CDs occupied shelves next to an old multi-CD changer stereo unit. It took Julia a moment to realize this had been Roman's room. It had never fully made the transition to guest room or adult Roman's room.

Julia examined one of the trophies. "Track?"

Roman nodded. "Jumper. I did track until I discovered drama. The girls were friendlier in drama."

"You gave up track because of girls?"

"I did a lot of things because of girls; that is pretty much the number one motivator of most teenage boys." Roman pulled Julia into an embrace. "It still is pretty much my primary motivator. However, now it's only one girl I'm interested in impressing." He kissed her gently. "I'm sorry you had to come under these circumstances. I had hoped you would be able to meet my mother, and well, my father... I'm sorry you had to see him this way."

"I haven't seen your father yet, Roman."

"Sure you have; that was him." Roman pointed over his shoulder, indicating the man they had seen earlier.

Julia placed her hand over her mouth. "I didn't recognize him; he looks so much older than I remembered."

"Mom's illness has taken a lot out of him. He's not the friendliest even when he isn't dealing with..." Roman shook his head. "Maybe he'll be more inclined to speak tomorrow. I'll find out what the funeral arrangements are tomorrow. You okay if we stay a few days?"

"I'm here with you as long as you need to stay. I have a laptop; I can work remotely if I need to."

Roman pulled Julia's hand to his lips. He kissed her

knuckles, then held her hand to his chest. She gently cupped the side of his face. "Come on; let's get ready for bed. Today has been a long day, and I'm tired. I like the idea of sleeping in your arms, even if it's on a rickety old bed."

Julia was pleased to learn that Roman's old bedroom had its own en suite bath.

Not expecting Roman to do much more than want to be held, she changed into her lounge pants and T-shirt.

He was already in bed, leaning against the pillows, blankets pulled up to his waist. His bare chest and broad shoulders gave her pause. She quietly sucked in her breath as she admired his physique.

"You aren't planning on wearing that?" he asked.

"These are my pajamas; what else am I supposed to sleep in?"

Roman tossed back the covers, revealing a smooth, uninterrupted view of skin from his leg to his hip bone and up his side, showing that he wasn't wearing anything at all. "I was hoping me," he said playfully.

Julia slowly approached the bed. "I didn't think you'd be in the mood."

"I'm always in the mood for you, Julia; sometimes other emotions take over. I need to feel you tonight." All playfulness was gone from his voice.

Julia crawled in and next to Roman, allowing him to pull the covers over her. She lay stiffly next to Roman's warm body. "Well, this is awkward."

"Do I need to quote Shakespeare?"

"No." Julia chuckled. "I'm suddenly nervous and feel like we're getting ready to 'do it' in your room with your parents in the other room."

"Well, we are, aren't we?" Roman chuckled.

"Yeah, but I feel like I'm sixteen and sneaking around for some reason."

"If you're that uncomfortable, I'll go put on some pants." Roman slipped out of bed, walking over to pull a pair of shorts from his suitcase.

Julia watched him move, taking in the fine musculature of his backside. Roman had long, lean muscles in his legs; his butt was firm, his waist slim. Her gaze followed up the smooth curve of his back to his wide shoulders. He had the build of a swimmer, long and strong. She watched the side of his face, admiring the bone structure. She particularly liked the way his brow ridge framed his eye and transitioned into prominent high cheekbones. He turned; her gaze followed along his cheek and down his aquiline nose to his full lips. She watched as they spread into a soft grin.

"What are you looking at?" he asked, settling the waistband around his hips.

"I'm admiring my choice of mate. You are exquisitely handsome."

"Thank you. You do have excellent taste; then again, you are exceptionally smart."

"I'm smart?" The tone of Julia's voice indicated that was not the word choice she had expected to hear.

"Yes, you are," Roman said as he slid back into the bed. He pulled Julia into his embrace. "And the most beautiful woman I have ever set eyes on." He dipped his head to hers. He slid his lips across her cheek, placing small kisses on her face. "Why do you think I've been so persistent? Hmm?" He placed more small kisses along her temple.

"I glowed?"

"You really didn't start glowing until after I developed a bit of a thing for you. The aura isn't a predestined 'here's your match, make it work' beacon; it's more of a confirmation that this would work amazingly, beautifully, wonderfully well. You'd be an idiot not to take this cosmic hint." Roman returned to placing small kisses down Julia's cheek and along her jaw.

Julia angled her head away so Roman's lips could trail down her neck. Roman sucked on the flesh at the crook of her neck and shoulder.

"I thought you were a wolf, not a vampire," she teased.

Roman growled and bit, gently scraping his teeth along the top of her shoulder. His arms pulled her to him. He caressed her back, moving his hand under the hem of her shirt, easing his hands along her ribs; then he cupped one full breast in his hand. He teased her with his thumb, strumming across the tight nipple.

Julia sucked in her breath. She ran her leg up Roman's, aggravated that cotton separated their skin.

"I should have taken these off," Julia moaned.

"That will be my pleasure, to unwrap you like the present you are," Roman whispered roughly, his voice thick with emotion.

Julia pushed up and away. "If you were still planning on seducing me, why did you get dressed?"

Roman sat up in front of her; reaching for the hem of her shirt, he pulled it up. Julia's arms lifted, and he removed the shirt. Roman lowered his gaze to her breasts. His eyes glowed an intense blue as he looked at her. She directed her own gaze to his body. His cock tented his shorts, indicating he wanted her. Tonight she would make love to him, and maybe he would find succor in her embrace. He leaned in to kiss her collarbone. "To make you more comfortable." He kissed down along her breastbone, running his face across the soft flesh of her breasts.

Julia sighed and pulled him down with her as she lay

back. Roman reverently kissed and suckled her, laving her nipples into hard peaks. His hands caressed and massaged Julia. He delighted in her large, soft breasts, and her narrow waist. Roman nipped his way along her side where her waist flared into ample hips. "I have never seen a more perfect specimen of feminine beauty. You are the perfect shape, the perfect size." He palmed her breast with his large hands. "Your skin tastes like orange and spice. You fit into my arms like a missing part found."

Roman yanked the pajamas from her before removing his own. Julia hissed as Roman ran his engorged cock over her delicate feminine flesh. She reached down between them and took over that teasing action. Wrapping her hand around Roman's hot, hard length, she teased her clit with the head of his shaft. Julia wrapped her legs around Roman's hips, lifting her own. Still grasping his cock, she positioned him at her entrance, guiding him, pulling him in and thrusting up with her hips to meet him.

Roman moaned as he drove into her. This was where he belonged. Completely enfolded in Julia's body, in Julia's embrace. She held him to her as he traced her skin with his fingertips. Slowly Roman began moving. He slid between Julia's thighs with an even, smooth, exquisitely slow motion. Julia made soft moaning noises, encouraging him to quicken his pace, yet he maintained his deliberate actions. She began thrusting against him, her hips moving at twice the pace his moved, their movements like a complicated dance, their rhythm like music.

"Oh gods, Roman, that's really good. That's really... oh..." Julia squeaked, trying to stifle her ecstatic moan of triumph as she came in Roman's embrace.

With Julia's clenching orgasm, Roman no longer maintained his slow pace. He began frenetically thrusting into her warmth. Julia continued to quake and gasp as Roman pounded his lustful need into her. Roman's release escaped him with a growl. He held himself deep in Julia as he spilled into her. He collapsed into her arms.

Julia held on to her mate, stroking his brow and hair. She kissed him on the bridge of his nose. "You do that well, Mr. Aventine." She chuckled.

"Anything to please you, Ms. Palatine. Anything."

The spread of warmth that emanated from her heart momentarily caught her off guard. The mate aura wasn't wrong. This man, this one, he made falling in love not so scary. She knew she didn't have to stop being herself to be with him. He would do anything for her, and yet he wouldn't demand anything from her. She knew she would have to be careful and make sure she gave of herself equally.

Roman's head rested on her chest; his breath caressed her skin. "Julia." The sound rumbled into her skin.

"Thank you."

"I think I should thank you; that was unexpectedly intense."

Roman chuckled. "That was spectacular, but I meant for coming here with me. It's going to be a tough couple of days. I need you with me. I feel better already knowing you are here."

"I'm your mate; where else would I be?"

Roman chuckled. "Fighting me on this, finishing up the conference, back in San Francisco."

"No, I'm your mate. I realize that, and I'm all in. I'm with you now for better or for worse."

"You're all in? That's not exactly romantic, is it?"

"You're the romantic, not me; I'm pragmatic. I am emotionally invested and committed. I need you as much as you need me." She couldn't say it. Her tongue stopped just short of saying the words.

"I'll take emotionally invested and committed." Roman snuggled into her embrace.

"Roman, I…"

"Julia, we're just getting started in this. Emotionally invested and committed is good. It means you are willing to fight for us. I am willing to fight for us. My feelings for you are deep and frightening; it's good to know you plan on being around as I figure them all out."

"We'll figure them out together," she whispered.

He placed a kiss on the center of her breastbone. "Sleep. Tomorrow is going to be another hard one."

Julia sat at the end of the long table in the formal dining room. Where her family home had many different open spaces for formal and mostly informal gatherings, Roman's family home had defined formal rooms. None of which seemed to provide her with an out-of-the-way work area. No matter where she set up, she was going to be in Blackston Aventine's way.

Initially she began working at the family-sized table in the breakfast nook attached to the kitchen. The cook kindly informed her that Mr. Aventine Senior would be down for his breakfast. When Julia said that he wouldn't bother her by sharing a table over breakfast, she had been informed that her presence would be a bother to him.

After being booted out of several other locations in the house, Julia took refuge in the formal dining room. There was no possible way she could be in his way here. This room looked like it hadn't been actively used for years.

Roman was no help. He had left the house early to follow up on the arrangements for his mother. When Julia volunteered to accompany him, he kissed her on the cheek and informed her that he knew how much work she really did have to get done, and that he would be fine.

Now that she could admit she was falling in love with him, she wanted to be with him constantly. She needed to be there for him in case he hit a hard patch today. Roman and his mother had been close. Easily as close as she had been with hers, only he had had more time with his. The hurt welled up in her chest, making it hard to focus.

She didn't want to relive the pain, pain that this morning felt as fresh as the day she had gotten the call from Uncle Remi that her parents and Dante's father had been in a fatal car crash. Pain was a dark void that could not be filled. She needed to be with Roman as much for the support he offered to her, and for the support she might be able to offer to him.

Julia closed her eyes and breathed deeply, pushing the pain away, shrinking the void, controlling her focus. She didn't need to get much done, but there was work that needed to be completed today. Especially since yesterday had been spent holding Roman and traveling to New England from the conference in Nashville.

Julia opened her laptop and powered it on. The computer made a loud bonging start-up noise that echoed through the large space. Julia mentally reviewed her to-do list. She opened her e-mail program.

Any message not from Kathleen, Meyers, Dante, or Dr. Rosemund was immediately ignored. First and foremost she checked everything from Kathleen. IT confirmed e-mails were secure. A sweep of the offices found a single short-range frequency radio bug in her phone. A recording device was discovered in a nearby supply closet, with a USB drive that must have gotten switched out for collecting phone recordings. All telephonic hardware was in process of being replaced. The current janitorial service contract had been terminated, just in case, and Kathleen was personally researching a new cleaning service. Julia nodded with satisfaction at the actions being taken.

She typed out a quick apology to Dr. Rosemund, explaining that she and Roman left the conference early because of a family emergency. She wanted to assure him that their interest was sincere, and she hoped they would be able to schedule a meeting soon. She forwarded Kathleen's contact information and informed him that Kathleen would be making arrangements with him. Julia made sure to CC Kathleen in on that exchange.

She sighed with relief when she saw a message from Meyers in Canada indicating that he was in contact with Dante and transportation of Cindy Science was handled. Unfortunately as of yet there was no news on Dr. Kimbro. Julia hoped they would find her alive. She didn't care what they did with Cindy Science.

Last on Julia's work list for the day was to go through all of Kathleen's unflagged e-mails. She had Kathleen order an arrangement of flowers to be delivered to the funeral tomorrow.

Julia scanned through to see if there were any messages from her agent regarding a lab. Nothing. She started to make one last pass to make sure she hadn't missed anything from Dante when the door to the dining room opened.

A uniformed maid stepped in and then paused. "Excuse me, Miss Palatine. I did not mean to interrupt you."

"You aren't interrupting. Let me guess; Blackston actually eats his dinner in here every day and you need to set up?" Julia scoffed. It was ridiculous. The man didn't acknowledge her existence—hell, he barely acknowledged that Roman was in the house—yet here she was getting chased out of his way.

The maid nodded in affirmation.

"Well, do you mind if I continue to work while you..." Julia looked the woman in the eyes. Julia laughed. "I'm in his seat, aren't I? No, don't answer. I am." Even if she wasn't, she would be sitting in his seat. The help around here seemed to not want her around at all, constantly chasing her out of any room that Blackston might walk through. Now, if Roman had been with her, it would be a different story. They clearly adored the younger Mr. Aventine and did whatever he asked.

"Give me ten minutes to wrap this up, and I'll be out of your way. Will that be okay?" Julia asked.

The other woman nodded and disappeared behind the closed door.

Julia started spitting cuss words as she shut down her computer and began gathering her papers. "Not one fucking place I can get any work done without being in the way."

She collected her belongings and pushed her way back through the door. The other woman was hovering, waiting for her opportunity to come in and set up for Blackston's dinner.

"Is there any place in this house where I won't be in Blackston Aventine's way?"

Julia shook her head when the other woman shrugged, providing no answers. She climbed back upstairs and into Roman's room.

Julia kicked her shoes off and crawled into the middle of Roman's bed. She spread her papers out around her and began working. She preferred to spread out on a table and sit upright. But she had work to do, and this was the only room in the mansion she was fairly certain Blackston Aventine wouldn't find a way to have her evicted from.

She pulled out her phone and began typing.

Things going as well as can be expected.

Deaths and funerals are tough; take it easy on the man. Mel texted in reply.

I will, see you in a few days.

I'm glad you found each other, but you still owe me Fernando!

Julia was asleep across her paperwork when Roman returned. She slowly came awake to the sounds of him pulling papers off the bed. He removed the laptop from her sleepy grasp and set it aside.

"Today has been longer than the hours that encompassed it," he confessed as he eased onto the bed and wrapped around Julia.

"You get everything done you needed to?" She snuggled back into his embrace.

"I think so. It doesn't matter at this point. If it didn't get taken care of, it just won't be. The funeral is tomorrow, no matter if I missed ordering the right canapes for the reception or not." Roman's voice sounded tired.

Julia rolled over in his arms and looked into his eyes. "You are going to wrinkle your suit if you stay in bed."

"You're right." Roman let go of her and sat up. He removed the jacket and laid it across the back of his one side chair. He continued to remove the rest of his clothes.

"What are you doing?" Julia asked as he curled back around her.

"If I plan on staying in bed, best to not have any clothes on to get in the way." Roman began pulling at her blouse and unfastening buttons.

20

The weather was cold and dreary, as if it too were in mourning. Julia stood quietly to the side as Roman, an uncle, and several other men Julia hadn't met served as pallbearers. The service had been heartfelt, somber, and well attended. She watched as they carried the dark wood casket from the church to the back of the hearse.

The family and a few friends followed to a small graveside service, while most others headed back to the estate for a reception.

Preparations had already begun when she and Roman left that morning. The Aventines were very different from the Palatines. Any event, sad or happy, was always filled with food and noise, lots and lots of noise. Everyone here was so quiet. So stoic. Everyone followed the lead of their primary alpha, down to emotional responses.

Roman's father hadn't spoken to them much at all the day before. Julia still hadn't had an opportunity to offer her condolences. As far as she could tell, Blackston Aventine thought she was just another piece of furniture. Under other circumstances Julia might take offense and break out with some alpha-war moves. The man had just lost his wife, his mate. Julia was beginning to understand what that meant now that Roman was hers.

They rode to the cemetery in silence. Julia understood this was not the time or place to introduce herself or expect to be introduced. Emotions were too raw. This family's reaction of showing no emotion explained Roman's propensity toward sarcasm. Roman was full of life and not afraid to show his emotions. This environment must have been stifling for him.

At the cemetery an older woman claimed Roman's arm and led him toward the front of the gathering. Julia eased her way toward the back. She wanted to be able to watch Roman, make sure he was okay.

"Hi." A blond man about the same age as Roman leaned over, extending his hand. "I'm Dallas." Similar coloring indicated they were related, bone structure suggested closely related.

Julia shook his hand. "Julia."

"Sorry you got such a crappy day to meet the family. As a group there is a very large stick up their butts."

Julia smirked. "Are you allowed to talk to me?"

"I'm the black sheep of the family; I do what I want. You're with Roman. Does that mean what I think that means?"

Julia smiled, nodding. "Possibly. We're mates."

"Ah, so it's still new?"

"What do you mean?" she whispered back.

"Your choice of words: mates, not dating, not partners, not engaged. It also tells me you're one of us." He winked. "Has Blackston disapproved of you yet?"

"Absolutely. The first time we met, he refused to speak to

me. Currently he treats me like furniture. I'm not sure he even realizes I've been around for three days."

"That's good ole' Uncle Blackston. He's a prick. It's a miracle Roman took after his mother. A shame really. The world needs people like her, and yet she dies. Blackston wouldn't be missed, and here he still is."

"So, Dallas, if you never tell me how you really feel, we'll never get anywhere with therapy."

Julia watched the man bite his lips to keep from laughing.

They hovered in the general area as the service ended. Julia watched and waited as Roman was greeted and offered condolences. He stood between his father and an uncle from his father's side. Roman towered over the other two; he had a grace, a beauty that had to have come from his mother's side, while the pale coloring with piercing blue eyes clearly came from his father.

"This should be entertaining," Dallas said conspiratorially, nodding toward a thin blonde woman in a bright red dress stalking toward Roman. "The only time anyone dresses like that at a funeral is if they are trying to get all the attention."

"Oh hell no," Julia spat. "Excuse me; I have to go slap a bitch."

Julia slid in behind Britt as she approached the grieving line.

Britt stepped toward Roman. "Roman," she purred, reaching up to embrace him.

"Touch him and I will personally rip off your arms," Julia hissed in Britt's ear.

Britt stopped mid-movement and turned. She stepped back. "I... I thought you left with that other fella. The one from South Africa."

"I did not; now smile, offer your condolences, do not touch Roman, then move along."

"You are forgetting he's my husband."

"I haven't forgotten. But it seems you have forgotten the word 'ex,' as in ex-husband."

"Roman..." Britt whined his name.

"I see you couldn't even stand to let my dead mother upstage you. Whatever, Britt, I'm done." Roman stepped past her, took Julia's hand, and began walking toward the waiting cars.

"Roman," Britt whined again. "We owe it to your mother to get back together and have children. She would have wanted that."

A snarl escaped Roman's lips as he lunged forward. "Do not ever invoke my mother as an excuse, for anything, ever. She would not have wanted me to sire children on you. Being married to you was a mistake, a mistake I made a long time ago. I haven't thought about you for years, and I really do not appreciate you having been thrown back into my company, for any reason." He kept his eyes locked on Britt; they glowed with anger. "I told you I would have you removed if I ever saw you again. Someone take this trash out. Britt, make sure you stay out."

Britt began to protest as a bulky security guard approached her. She threw her hands up in the air in defeat. "Fine, be that way. I didn't like your stuck-up bitch of a mother anyway. I never would have bothered if you hadn't gotten mixed up with this bitch and that guy from South Africa."

This time Julia lashed out; Britt screamed, then landed with a jarring thump on her backside.

"I am not any bitch; I am the bitch that will end you if I ever see or hear of you again. And don't think for one minute I won't or that I can't. I will start by financially ruining you; I can do that. Then I'll make you think you're going crazy. Your friends will desert you; your family will wish they were never related to you. And then you will disappear. I will feed you to piranhas and vampires, and your life will become a living hell before it ends. I have friends with very special skill sets; I can make this happen. No evidence of your existence will ever remain. What friends you might have left will begin to think they made you up." Julia emphasized the sharp consonant sound of the P. "Have I made myself clear?"

Britt, still on her butt in the mud, nodded, her eyes wide with terror.

"Good. Never bother Roman or his family again. I don't care how much money anyone offers you to do so. It will never be enough to compensate for the hell I will personally rain down on you." Julia glared at the woman, her eyes glowing with intense rage.

Britt scrambled to her feet, staggering in her heels on the damp ground. She said nothing as she hastily made her retreat toward the line of parked cars.

Julia turned away from the retreating figure.

Roman chuckled. "Remind me to never piss you off."

Somewhere behind them Julia heard a "damn" of appreciation.

"Don't threaten me or mine. I didn't reach alpha status without reason." She smiled up at Roman.

Blackston Aventine looked up at the commotion as if the fog cleared from his vision for the first time in days. "Roman," his voice boomed out. His eyes narrowed as he recognized Julia.

"What is Ms. Palatine doing here? This is a private family matter."

"She's with me, Father." Roman put an arm around her shoulders and approached his father. "She's been with me for the past few days."

Blackston shook his head, obviously not remembering. "Why?"

"She's my mate, Father," Roman explained simply.

"What a stupid thing to do, mate yourself to the Palatines. That Brittney would have been a more suitable mother for Aventine children. I like blondes. But you couldn't keep her."

Roman looked at his father; had he not just witnessed that exchange? His brow furrowed as if he had the same thought that raced through Julia's head. Was it possible Roman's father had missed it; he had been functioning like a zombie ever since they arrived.

"No, Britt is not suitable, Father. Julia is..."

"A Palatine!" Blackston bellowed.

"Yes, and we have put all that animosity behind us to work together for a better future for our families," Roman explained.

"That was you mother's idea." He turned to look back at the grave site. "I'll honor her, let it be her legacy. I never fully agreed with her."

"I know that, Father, but I do. Most of us do. The Palatines are good people. They are ready to be over our feud as much as we are."

"Did you have to go and be mated to one?"

"Do you have to be so prejudiced against her because of some ancient grudge match? Mother was right; it's all nonsense and we will be stronger together. Alone, separate, that's when we fail. Is that what you want? To destroy this family, let it collapse in on its own weakness?"

"Palatine grandchildren will destroy this family. They'll be weak. Leave her." His father sneered.

"I'm mated to a Palatine alpha, we will be married, and our children will be the most powerful alphas our kind have ever seen."

"She's no alpha. Female alphas would be an abomination if they existed. I won't condone your marriage. No, and that's the end of this discussion." Blackston Aventine turned and walked away with a parting glare.

Roman grabbed his father's upper arm, spinning him around. "Do not think you have won this, old man. You destroyed this family when you cheated on Mother. Do you honestly think that attempting to sire an entire generation of Aventines was going to be healthy? She knew. Did you realize that? She knew, and she never said anything. She told me the last time I saw her alive. That's why I was an only child; she couldn't bear to be with you even though you were her mate. She knew every single one, and she told me she wanted to hate them because of you. But she never did, and she never let you know."

"Roman, you will stop this line of discussion right now. Just because your mother has passed does not mean you get to air your grievances."

"Grievances? Grievances? This is hardly a grievance. This is coming clean with indiscretions of your past. This is me finally claiming the family you denied me." Roman turned, scanning the remaining mourners. He waved, beckoning over who he was looking for. "Dallas, you remember that DNA test I requested."

The other man nodded.

"Did Aunt Beverly ever tell you who your father was?"

"No, always a different story each time I asked too."

"Roman, stop this now," Blackston growled.

Roman pointed to his father. "That sorry bastard is your father. You're my brother."

Dallas looked dumbfounded at the news.

Roman nodded. "Yeah, you're my half brother, and because our mothers were sisters, we're almost DNA matched as full biological brothers. How's that for a kicker?"

"My brother? I have a brother?" Dallas chuckled, then turned his attention to Blackston. He pointed into the older man's face. "This asshole is my father. That's quite the bomb you just dropped on me there, Roman. I'm not sure who to deck, you for springing this on me or him for letting Mom struggle and leaving us in near poverty." Dallas turned his gaze to Julia. "Okay, not Roman. She scares me." He pulled back and punched Blackston across the jaw.

Blackston stumbled back. Regaining his composure, he rubbed where Dallas made contact. "This will not go unnoticed, Dallas. I never claimed you for a reason. Roman, you'll be disowned over this."

"You'll have a hard time drawing up those legal papers, Father. You signed over way more than a controlling interest in the company when you retired. You'll find that you're only the alpha of this family in your own head. I own the business, and I've been making the majority of family management decisions for a few years now."

"But the accord with the Palatines..." Blackston sputtered.

"You had to do that on your own; think of it as a lesson learned."

"Your mother—"

"My mother is the reason we didn't do this sooner. My mother is the reason you still have the title of alpha, even if it is in name only. My mother deserves better from you in her death than she ever got from you in life." Roman turned, put his arm around Julia, and walked away from his father.

"You can't marry her," Blackston called out after Roman.

"Why not? Are you her father too?" Roman called back.

∽

Roman pulled Julia into his arms once inside the back of the limo. She sighed as his warmth surrounded her. They were mated, she conceded. It wasn't a defeat; she realized she'd won, just as Roman had. They won each other. It was a heady thought. "What if I don't want to get married?"

"You don't want to marry me?" Roman cocked a single eyebrow as he looked into Julia's glowing golden eyes. She was testing him, attacking with words, looking to see if he would fight back or let her skewer him. Instead he figuratively gave her his neck, submitting to her lead.

"Then we are together as partners, significant others, living together in sin, as your Catholic grandmother would say."

"You expect me to live with you?" Julia asked.

"I expect to live with you," Roman clarified. "We don't have to be married to have children."

"What if I can't have children?"

"Then we have puppies or we adopt or we have plants. Julia, you are my endgame, and being with you is what I want."

"What if," she continued, not certain of her own feelings regarding children, having never actually thought about having them before, "I don't want children?"

"Still not a deal breaker. Whatever you choose to nurture: pets, plants, the business, it will thrive. And I will be there by your side. But I do want children. If you tell me no, then I'm good with that. I know you'll understand if I become more involved with your nieces and nephews or join Big Brothers or become a karate teacher or something. Just as I support your choice, I know you will support mine."

"You love me then?" She was unsure, they were mated, but wasn't that really just a biological need to perpetuate the race? Yet Roman said all the right things; he hadn't pushed an agenda on her.

Gently Roman caressed the side of her face. "With all my heart, Julia, with all my being."

"Then say it."

Roman chuckled. "As you command."

Julia began to protest; that wasn't her intent. She didn't want him only saying words because she wanted to hear them; she wanted him to feel them. Roman silenced her with a finger to her lips. "And with great pleasure. I want you, I love you, I long for you, and I will always be true to you. I love you, Julia Palatine."

Julia felt tears sting her eyes. She had underestimated the impact hearing those words would have on her.

"I love you too," she whispered as Roman leaned forward to capture her lips with a kiss.

EPILOGUE

Dante stomped his feet. His breath turned to steam. Damn, it was cold.

He glanced back at the woman in the station wagon. She beat ineffectually on the door. "Let me out," she whined.

Dante was sick of Cindy's whining.

His coat was not warm enough for this climate. He thought of different ways he could help the salesman who sold it to him experience this level of bone-deep chill. He was tempted to shift so that he could have some fur protecting his body heat.

It was almost two hours past time to give her another dose of medicine. Dante thought maybe it was time to let her fully wake up, especially since he was passing her off to her alpha. Let him take care of her. For once.

From the sounds of things, the Meyers's alpha had disregarded and underestimated Dante's reluctant guest. Cindy pretty much wreaked havoc on his cousin Julia's plans for finding a science-minded wolf to help understand the ramifications of wolf-shifter DNA showing up as an ethnicity in ancestral DNA tests. Cindy had managed to render a local

Meyers wolf incapacitated, steal her plane ticket, and arrive in her stead at a genomics conference in Nashville.

Cindy was working on the misconception that killing an alpha would transfer all their powers to her, and thought she would be able to accomplish this at the conference. Had she received a proper education from the existing hierarchy of her family, she would have known better and possibly not caused harm to Dr. Kimbro.

Cindy started yelling and rocking the car back and forth trying to get out. Dante chuckled; child safety locks were a beautiful thing. He pushed hard against the car, causing it to lurch. Cindy stopped her thrashing.

A dirt-covered SUV rolled to a stop in front of Dante. The window lowered.

"Palatine?"

Dante nodded. "Meyers?"

The SUV pulled over, and a broad older man got out of the car. "Thanks for delivering the package."

"I should thank you for picking her up. She is a pain in the ass."

The station wagon started rocking again, and Cindy screamed curses.

Dante hit the window with his elbow, effectively shutting Cindy up.

"How did you get her all the way up here without causing an issue at the border?" Meyers asked.

"Benadryl. Told the border guard my girlfriend was asleep in the back. She was so groggy it didn't occur to her to not answer the guard's questions: name, birthdate, where we were headed."

"What did she tell them?"

"Home. You have something to keep her restrained? She flails about a lot otherwise."

"Yeah, we're good." Meyers turned and leaned into the back seat of the SUV. When he straightened, Dante was looking at the barrel of a pistol.

"Well crap, I thought you guys didn't do those up here." Dante sighed and stood up from his relaxed posture against the station wagon. "Let me guess; you're not Meyers."

"Good guess, asshole." Not-Meyers waved the pistol at Dante. "Release the girl."

Dante slowly turned and opened the car door. He reached in. Instead of releasing Cindy, he instantly shifted into wolf form and plunged through the back, breaking out the rear window of the station wagon, running as fast as he could for the woods off the side of the road. A gunshot rang out behind him, but he kept running.

Dante circled around in the underbrush. Not-Meyers leaned into the car. Dante ran. In seconds he was out from under the trees and on the other man's back, his teeth buried into the thick sweater at the man's neck. *Stupid appropriate cold-weather wear.*

Not-Meyers threw Dante from his back and turned with alpha-like speed, shifting into a light brown timber wolf. From the noise and the rocking of the station wagon, Cindy was still restrained and struggling against her bonds. Dante ignored her and faced off against the newly shifted wolf.

Not-Meyers apparently had access to Meyers's information. How else would he have known to meet Dante and Cindy here? *Did Cindy have more support in her efforts of undermining the local alpha? Who was this guy?*

The two wolves continued to snarl and circle. Finally Not-Meyers lunged. Dante countered with a snarling bite for the throat. Claws scratched, teeth gnashed, fur flew as the wolves rolled over each other, broke away, then attacked again.

Three large black SUVs stopped with squealing tires, blocking the first SUV in and surrounding the fighting animals. Several men spilled from the vehicles.

"Stop it," a loud, commanding voice barked, followed by the ratchet sound of a cocked shotgun. "Jesus, Graham, I told you what was going on with your daughter, not so you could be an idiot, but so that you knew she was one." The big man with the shotgun stomped over to the Not-Meyers wolf and kicked him back away from Dante.

"You must be Dante Palatine." He nodded to Dante. "Someone find him some clothes."

Dante stayed in a crouched defensive position. Jeans and jacket dropped in front of him.

"Turn, man. I'm Jeff Meyers. We need to talk."

Dante slid into the passenger seat of the Escalade, grateful the heater was on full blast.

"My people have a lot of cleanup thanks to those two. I thought I could trust Graham; he's my wife's brother. Went Smith on us after his wife died, and unfortunately for the girl, she was neglected and ended up with a lot of misconceptions regarding her own kind and who to trust. She made a real mess of things for you folks down in Nashville, didn't she?"

"She certainly tried. She's smarter than you think, but not as smart as she thinks she is."

"Ain't that the way?" Jeff Meyers chuckled. "How did you get her across the border? After we couldn't arrange for the Cessna, I wasn't sure you weren't going to be stuck with her for longer."

"Creative applications of allergy medicine. Look, she has some seriously bad information on how pack structure works. I don't know, and I don't want to know your plans for dealing with her. But if rehabilitation is on the list, she needs wolf-shifter 101 on an epic scale. Most ten-year-olds know more than she does," Dante said.

Jeff Meyers nodded thoughtfully. "This has been an eye-opener. We are a fairly closed-off group, never thought we needed to think of what kind of influence vamps would have on our family. They got some prime manipulative fodder with Cindy. I can only blame myself."

"The vampires are stirring up something on the West Coast," Dante started. "From something Cindy mentioned, it sounds like its having a ripple effect across the continent. And they are dragging wolves in, but no one knows exactly why. They tried to rekindle a family feud between the Palatines and the Aventines. You might want to consider reaching out to your nearest neighbor, and make sure you're all on the same page when it comes to how to handle any influx of bad from the vamps and their day-walkers."

Meyers nodded.

"How is Dr. Kimbro?" Dante asked. "Last I heard, you had found her, unidentified, in a coma in a local hospital."

"She's on the way to a full recovery. She had some memory issues, but with each change she recovers more memory and more capability. She was never a strong wolf, so the change was always a slow process for her, and now apparently it is exhausting for her as well. She's only shifting every few days or so. You know, we can handle cuts and shots and even broken bones, but traumatic brain injury in one of our kind isn't something I think any of us have any familiarity with. Her skull was broken up pretty good; if she were a typical human, she would be damaged for the rest of her life. That's if she recovered." He huffed. "Remedial wolf-shifter 101 is the least of Cindy's worries. Now that she's delivered, what's next for you?"

"Someplace warmer. But first I have to return to the store

and the jerk who sold me this coat, telling me it would be plenty warm for Canada."

"And do what?"

"Get a full refund. He lied. I'm freezing."

Jeff Meyers laughed.

~

Dante finds more than warmth on his next assignment.
Read about it in Dangerous.
Keep reading for a sneak preview.

DANGEROUS, LEGATUM BOOK 3

Family goof-off and all-around playboy Dante has been tasked with finding the missing branches of the family tree. It's a big tree, but luckily he's a trained investigator. What he finds instead is Geena. Only she doesn't understand how important she is to him and she's slipped through his fingers. Now he wants to drop all his responsibilities and track her down.

Geena's traveling companions are the trifecta of feminine beauty. They are thin, rich, and stylish, so she's shocked when the hot guy starts hitting on her. What she doesn't know yet is that Dante isn't just a guy. And to him, she's not just another in a long string of women in his loose past. Dante has seen the mate glow and he knows what it means.

How can he convince Geena that this time he's serious? And what about all those pesky family members he has to find? The ones who might blow the family lore wide open if he doesn't get to them first...

EXCERPT FROM DANGEROUS

The bike was a citrusy orange color with licks of lime green flames and paler pinstriped scroll details. The chrome work looked new. Geena wasn't usually a motorcycle enthusiast, she didn't need to be one to admire excellent artistry when she saw it. This looked like it had come from one of those TV shows where they make customized choppers, maybe even more beautiful. No wonder he was obsessed with it.

She hoped the man was half as attractive as the bike. *Please, oh please, oh please be as gorgeous when you stand up.* She caught a glimpse of curling dark hair, his head was tilted forward and away from her. When he straightened up, he unfolded up taller and taller. He stood well over six feet with dark, curly, thick hair that brushed his collar.

When he turned around, Geena stopped breathing. She continued to lean against the RV, as any stability she did have vanished as she admired the man. His jaw was square and sculpted, his nose long and straight with the slightest arch, his cheek bones high and sharp. He had thick black eyebrows that topped large, deep-set hazel eyes in a slightly olive complexion. He smiled. It caused the slightest creasing at the corners of his eyes. His teeth were perfectly straight, and his skin set off their Hollywood dentistry white. Geena was too dazzled to think that maybe he was too unrealistically perfect, but Brooke was not impressed.

"She said she's not interested, why don't you just drop it," Brooke snapped.

"No offense," he said, "I really was asking if either of you wanted to take a ride."

Geena found her voice. "Does that offer include me?" She paused to catch her self-confidence, "'Cause I'd love to be taken for a ride." She would take any ride this man offered. If she had to describe her ideal dream lover's looks, this is the picture she would expect to see.

The man angled toward her, seeing her for the first time. He paused, and slowly looked at her. Geena felt his gaze rake up and down her form as if he made physical contact. If it was possible, the broad grin he sported grew even larger. "That offer most definitely includes you, pretty girl."

Geena watched as he licked his teeth, running the pink tip of his tongue along the edge of perfect white teeth. The sex appeal in that one swipe of tongue made her mouth go dry. He gave her a predatory gaze the likes of which she never received before. The gaze identified her as a woman he was interested in doing manly things with. She desperately hoped she was reading him right or she was about to make a fool of herself. She had to remember how to flirt and not just throw herself on him.

"It's a pretty bike," she said approaching him. She tried not to sway her hips as she walked toward him, but something in his gaze made her want to swish everything she had in his direction.

"Don't be naive Geena, he's not talking about a ride on

his bike. He's being a perv." Brooke had clearly taken offense at this guy.

"Ya know Brooke, sometimes an offer for a ride on a motorcycle, is just that, an offer for a ride on a motorcycle. He's got the pretty bike out, he obviously plans on using it. I'm sure this is just what it appears, an offer for a ride on the motorcycle." She turned back to the man "Right?"

He sighed, "Yes, this is what it appears to be at face value, a ride on the bike this lovely evening."

"There isn't room for your butt on that bike Geena, get real." There is was, Brooke had lasted almost two days before letting the weight comments slip. Brooke always seemed to want to deflate her joy. Geena wasn't going to let her take this moment from her. She gritted her teeth and grinned as if she hadn't heard a word.

"Oh there is plenty of room for her," the man replied. Geena decided ignoring Brooke worked. And to think, she thought Brooke had gotten over her earlier foul mood. This went beyond having a bad day at work. Usually, Brooke went after the tall, good-looking ones, for some reason this evening she was on the verbal attack. Hannah was just being Hannah. She barely talked to men now that she was engaged. Geena couldn't help but think, fine they were not interested, then more for her.

"You don't even know him."

Geena turned a glare at Brooke, after turning back to the gorgeous man she stuck her hand out in greeting. "I'm Geena Davies."

He folded her hand into his larger one. She felt small and dainty around him. Geena never felt dainty, she liked this feeling. "Like the actress?"

"Daveez, not Daviss." She emphasized the eeez and the iss. "I get that a lot. I think she was kind of a big named actress when I was born, not really sure. My parents don't pay much attention to movies and things. They probably heard her name and thought the combination sounded good."

"Fair enough. Dante Palatine." He held her hand longer than what was politely necessary.

"Dante? Well, aren't you Italian?"

"Not as much as my name would suggest. I use spaghetti sauce from a jar." He winked at her.

Geena's insides did a flip. "Somewhere you have an Italian grandmother spinning in her grave."

"I'm sure I do, spinning at high velocity." He laughed. It was a deep warm sound.

Geena decided she could listen to him laugh forever.

Sign up for Lulu's newsletter to keep up to date with new releases and happenings. And get a free sexy short story.

https://lulumsylvian.com/newsletter/

ALSO BY LULU M SYLVIAN

Check out these other series

Legatum

Paranormal romantic suspense

The World of Wet Waterfalls

Paranormal reverse harem romance

Rockers

Contemporary and paranormal rockstar romance

Holiday Strippers

Contemporary, paranormal, ridiculous, romance

ABOUT THE AUTHOR

 Bio-engineered to be the only redhead in a generation of blonds, Lulu feels that "aliens" may actually be the best answer for a life-time of being asked, "Where did you get that red hair from?"

She did not come into writing from years of scribbling words on paper. Her background is rooted in visual arts and making pictures. Encouraged to make those pictures out of words Lulu began writing just to see what would happen. What happened was two full-length manuscripts in three months.

Lulu cannot ride a horse, a motorcycle, spin a hula hoop, or play roller derby. Yes, she has attempted all of those, even if it has been decades since she's been on a horse or a motorcycle. She embraces the crazy that comes with that one little genetic mutation, and attempts to live up to the reputation that proceeds her. Lulu would like to apologize for her contribution to the hole on the ozone layer from her use of hairspray in the 1980s.

For more information, visit:
www.LuluMSylvian.com